Bantan and the Mermaids

by

MAURICE B. GARDNER

Illustrated by David Prosser

Published by

THEO. GAUS' SONS, INC.
Brooklyn, N. Y. 11201

BANTAN AND THE
MERMAIDS
Copyright © 1970, by
MAURICE B. GARDNER

Library of Congress Catalog Card No. 79-122445

PRINTED IN THE UNITED STATES OF AMERICA BY
Theo. Gaus' Sons, Inc., BROOKLYN, N. Y.

Preface

IN THE OCEANS of our planet, it is claimed there is a fish that resembles each and every animal that inhabits the continents.

This world of ours has revealed the existence of a prehistoric era—as disclosed by the countless fossilized bones that had been remarkably well preserved—and indicated by their very size that their owners had ruled the world before the advent of man.

Even in the present age aborigines exist upon the continent of Australia, which, according to geologists, is the oldest land mass on our planet. They are hardly changed today in their method of living in the constant challenge of survival.

For centuries sea-faring men have spoken of the existence of mermaids—though, strangely, no mention was ever made of mermen. It is quite possible that the mermen might have been seen, but were considered a fish of some sort.

Then, again, the fact that months would pass in the old sea-faring days and the men aboard ships, not having had the opportunity of seeing women, would conjure the fantasy in their minds that mermaids could—and did —exist.

Many artists have depicted upon canvas their appearance as conjured in their imagination. Of all the oddities in the world of creation, considering the numerous so-called freaks of nature that have been recorded to date, the question may well be asked: Why couldn't it be possible that mermaids might exist?

And so it was, with this in mind, I undertook to write this Bantan novel and aptly titled it, *Bantan and the Mermaids*.

It reads well, and seemingly is logical. But, is it plausible?

While I have no definite proof that such creatures could—and do—exist, I firmly believe there is such a possibility. At least, the reading of the story should be entertaining—as I intended that it should be.

THE AUTHOR

CONTENTS

BANTAN AND THE MERMAIDS

CHAPTER I

Manta Ray

SEVERAL HOURS had passed and the cliff-encircled, primeval island was being left far behind as Bantan and Tama, with Mauria and Nulu in the canoe, continued their rhythmic paddling with the provisioned, hollowed log in tow.

Long since had Zarna and her warrior women deserted the small beach because of the discomfort from the bright, hot sun's rays to which they were unaccustomed. At the mouth of the passageway, the leader had paused with shaded eyes and watched the two water craft become smaller as the distance was increased. Then at last with a mournful shake of her head, Zarna turned and followed in the wake of her companions. In the blue sky hardly a cloud was in evidence. Some time before the sun had passed his zenith, since the afternoon now was well along. The two bronzed paddlers were guiding the canoe toward the east, and their eyes constantly studied the horizon. Sea gulls glided high above them, their sharp eyes scanning the water beneath for sight of a choice tid-bit.

The luminous eyes of Nulu, the white-skinned girl from the primeval island's interior, were invariably riveted upon the mightily muscled, bronzed back and well shaped head of Bantan. Time and again she would sigh as she tried to contemplate the great happiness that would be hers when at last, reaching their objective, they would become mated. Her lips were still warm from con-

1

tact with his, and, at the very thought, she tingled deliciously with the knowledge that such similar delightful contacts would be made time and again in the future.

Near her, Mauria, the Mandoes Island native girl, who had shared many adventures with the bronzed giant previous to Nulu's advent into his life, would time and again look upon Bantan with moisture in her dark eyes. She realized only too well when he and Nulu became mated, then her hope of ever winning him for herself would terminate.

Occasionally she would look back at Tama in the rear of the canoe, and when their eyes met, the lighter-skinned native would smile, his deep love for her clearly revealed. But with a choking sensation in her bosom, the native girl knew in her heart how unjust it was that Tama could only be a substitute for the precious love that she treasured for Bantan. Although she had confessed her secret to Nulu, she felt her secret would not be revealed.

Having paddled steadily now for several hours, for the first time the bronzed giant became acutely aware of his hunger. He realized his companions doubtless must be as famished as he was, for it had been some time since all had eaten. He discontinued paddling and turned to face the others.

"It has been some time since we have eaten," he remarked. "Let's eat some fruit and nuts."

Unanimous approval to his suggestion was voiced in answer. Tama drew upon the trailing rope until the provisioned, hollowed log was alongside the canoe. Each reached for fruit and nuts. While they ate, Bantan looked toward the cliff-encircled island now far to their rear.

"We were fortunate we lost no time leaving," he remarked. "Had Wilma and her warrior women appeared sooner I doubt if we would have managed to escape."

Tama shook his head dispassionately.

"Had Zarna recaptured us," he said, "I don't care to think what our punishment would have been."

Nulu shuddered visibly, as did Maura. Then a smile touched the latter's lips.

"But we *have* eluded them," she remarked. "*That* is what counts."

Bantan and Tama smiled and nodded.

"How you longed to be away from that island of constant dangers, Mauria," the bronzed giant reminded her. Then he shrugged noncommittally as he added: "As I have told you—whether we succeed in reaching Marja is a grave problem."

"Why worry about that now when we have a hollowed log filled with fruit and nuts to last us many suns?" Mauria added with optimism. "Perhaps we may come to some more hospitable island than the last and we will be very happy there."

A slight grimness touched Bantan's lips.

"And there is the possibility," he remarked, "that we may reach one that is less desirable."

Mauria pursed her lips somewhat, but there was a twinkle in her dark eyes as she spoke.

"Don't always look upon the dark side of life, Bantan," she gently chided him.

A soft chuckle escaped Tama's lips because of Mauria's ebullience. Nulu, however, registered no emotion.

Bantan shrugged. It was upon the tip of his tongue to remind the comely native girl that there was always danger from the ocean depths to be considered, but upon second thought dismissed such a possibility from his mind. He merely smiled as he looked at Tama in the rear of the canoe.

"Ready to resume paddling?" he asked.

The lighter-skinned young giant nodded as he gently pushed the hollowed log to its former position, announcing when the trailing rope had become fairly taut. In unison the two young men plied their paddles and their course was resumed.

As the hours of the late afternoon passed, in due time the sun sank beneath the western waterline as a ball of fire being swallowed. Presently as the dusk of oncoming evening overcame the gently heaving surface of the mighty ocean, the brightest stars made their appearance in the darkening heaven.

Bantan carefully studied the twinkling stars of first and second magnitude, as did Tama. He, too, had been familiar with the tropic constellations prior to his advent to the cliff-encircled, primeval island, as all Polynesians know their astronomy from childhood.

The bronzed giant's memory was keenly revived as to what certain constellations had hovered over Marja Island, and this was helpful in maintaining the course that he set. He knew that Mandoes was far to the west of that island; but what troubled him most was to try and calculate how far he and Mauria had paddled and drifted away from a true course when they had been lost in a mist for an entire week. Whether the primeval island had been east, north, west, or south of Mandoes was what puzzled him. He could only shrug and just hope present calculations would not be too far from a true course to his objective. More than that he could not do. Since Tama was not familiar with the location of Marja, he would not be much help as a navigator.

"We'll continue paddling awhile yet, Tama," Bantan said, when darkness had completely enveloped them. "I need not remind you that the more we paddle each sun into darkness the sooner we should reach some other island—even if it is not the one I hope to reach."

His companion agreed.

"If I can help, Bantan," Nulu murmured, "let me

know. I don't know anything about paddling a canoe, but I could learn."

A gentle smile touched the bronzed giant's lips.

"You can do nothing to help now, Nulu," he answered. "Perhaps on another sun when Tama and I become too wearied you and Mauria may spell us. I know not how many suns it will require to reach our goal. Sleep now in peace. Good night."

Nulu and Mauria curled themselves upon the soft grasses in the bottom of the canoe and sought sleep. After a little while the former listened to her companion's breathing. It appeared quite regular. She carefully arose to her knees and leaned toward the paddler near the front of the canoe. She rested a soft hand upon one of his shoulders.

"Would you kiss me once, Bantan, so that I might sleep with happy dreams?" she whispered.

The young giant missed a few strokes with his paddle as he leaned toward her and his lips pressed her seeking ones. Nulu sighed deeply as their faces drew apart.

"Thank you," she murmured. "Now I know I'll sleep happily with dreams of our future together."

Though Mauria had appeared to be asleep, she was not. With intently listening ears she understood what had taken place between Bantan and Nulu. Tears rose in her eyes and with a mighty effort she managed to choke back the sob that threatened to escape her tight-pressed lips. Though Nulu was presently lulled to sleep with the gentle lapping of wavelets against the side of the canoe, the Mandoes Island girl remained awake for a long while before sleep finally overtook her.

Considerable time passed while the bronzed giant and Tama continued to paddle with brief rests until at last the former decided they had accomplished sufficient progress for that day. Each curled in the bottom of the canoe upon grasses and within moments were fast asleep.

The sun was several hours high when Bantan awoke. A little lame but otherwise in good spirits, he arose to a seated position and looked about him. He saw that Tama and Mauria were still asleep, but Nulu, nearest him, was watching him with eyes of adoration. A happy smile beamed upon her features as their eyes met.

"My dreams last night were very happy, Bantan," she softly said. "All night long it seemed that you and I were upon a lovely island and we were very happy."

With the utterance of her words the smiling girl pursed her lips and leaned toward him. The bronzed giant's lips pressed upon hers as her arms locked about his neck. She sighed as they drew apart.

"I am so happy," she murmured. "And when you kiss me I am breathless with joy."

The bronzed giant's right hand stroked the girl's cheek lightly and he smiled gently. As he chanced to look beyond Nulu, he saw the anguished features of the native girl watching him, and he was not unaware of the moisture in her dark eyes. A soberness now overcame him.

"I hope you slept well, Mauria," he said.

The Mandoes Island girl managed a weak smile and nodded.

Tama now stirred and, rubbing his eyes momentarily, arose to a seated position. Looking toward Bantan he smiled and nodded, then asked Mauria if she had slept well. The native girl nodded, but the lighter-skinned native had reason to wonder at her somewhat dark-rimmed eyes.

"I don't believe we drifted much off course during the night, Tama," Bantan announced. "After we eat we'll resume paddling. Later in the day, perhaps Mauria and Nulu might take a turn with the paddles."

As he spoke, the bronzed giant arose to an erect position and studied the horizon. Nothing could be seen— the cliff-enclosed primeval island with its heavy cloud blanket above had passed completely from sight over the horizon, owing to the efforts of the two men upon the previous day well into the night. No sight of bird life, however, was to be glimpsed.

All cupped handsful of water and bathed. Tama drew upon the trailing rope until the hollowed log loaded with fruit and nuts was brought alongside. From it the four partook of what they wished. Afterwards, the two men took up their paddles and plied them rhythmically.

"By watching us paddle, Nulu," Bantan suggested to the white-skinned girl, "you may obtain an idea how a paddle is used."

Nulu smiled and nodded eagerly.

"I want to be as helpful as possible," she answered.

While the bronzed giant and Tama plied their paddles on their course in the face of the bright sunlight, their eyes were alertful. It was difficult at first to look directly ahead owing to the sun's position in the heaven facing them, but to each side, shading their eyes when necessary, the two paddlers missed no detail of what might be glimpsed. The sky was cloudless. No breeze stirred, thus the ocean surface was relatively calm.

The eyes of Mauria and Nulu were also scanning the horizon for sight of anything unusual. Though deep in her heart the Mandoes Island girl secretly envied the white-skinned girl, magnanimous of her, she could not bring herself to dislike her. It was no fault of Nulu's that she had been born of white lineage, and that she, Mauria, was of native blood. But, what wouldn't she have given if only she could exchange places with her companion for the affection of the bronzed giant!

Later in the morning, Bantan and Tama turned their

paddles over to Nulu and Mauria at the former's suggestion.

"I've watched you carefully, Bantan," the blonde-haired girl said with a smile as they exchanged places, "so I should not make too many mistakes."

The bronzed giant was amazed at the girl's aptitude mastering the art of paddling. It was true, she splashed the blade at times, and when drawing it from the slightly undulating water, upon occasions it dragged somewhat, but in general she performed remarkably well for a beginner. She would glance fleetingly over a shoulder upon occasions.

"Am I doing all right, Bantan?" she would ask with a smile.

He complimented her for her ability, and naturally Nulu revealed the pride that she felt by the erectness of her smooth shoulders and the confident tilt of her head.

Mauria was familiar with a paddle, but she, too, marvelled that Nulu did so well for the first time. She had to grudgingly admit the blonde-haired girl was capable of learning by merely watching what many moons ago she had accomplished only after several lessons.

In the meantime, Bantan carefully studied the waterline with shaded, keen eyes, hoping to catch a glimpse of some object breaking the even line that he looked at. Even Tama with shaded eyes also looked all about, but he saw nothing of interest, as did his companion. No bird life had been seen since earlier in the morning, and for that reason both men realized they were a considerable distance from any sort of island. A slight breeze now stirred in their favor, and the heat of the sun was less endurable.

The bronzed giant and Tama relieved the two girls of their paddles when some half hour had passed. Realizing their hands were soft, friction from the handles might have a tendency to blister the tender skin, and that painful experience they wished to spare them.

"You have done well, Nulu," Bantan complimented the girl as he exchanged places with her.

The blonde-haired girl smiled tremulously.

"I told you I wanted to help as much as I could," she reminded him.

"And you have done very well," he said.

Looking toward Tama who had exchanged places with Mauria, he nodded as the lighter-skinned young giant also nodded in understanding. Together, when the slack in the tow rope had been taken up, they plied their paddles, and the canoe with the provisioned, hollowed log in tow, moved more swiftly upon the sun-kissed water of a mighty ocean.

Mauria congratulated Nulu for her fine performance, and the blonde-haired girl expressed her thanks.

"I want to be able to do everything well—for Bantan's sake," she confided in a low whisper.

A slight twinge of dismay gripped the Mandoes Island girl, but she flashed an encouraging smile.

"Yes, of course, Nulu," she whispered. "A girl wants always to do her best for the man she loves."

The white-skinned girl heaved a deep sigh as she looked toward the bronzed giant. Then she turned to Mauria.

"I owe him my life—not once, but several times," she whispered. "And the fact he is taking me away from a cruel land where I knew no happiness makes me realize I can't thank him enough."

The native girl could merely nod her head in understanding. But inwardly how she wished that she were in Nulu's stead and would be rewarded with the love of the bronzed giant.

Two more days passed with almost continuous paddling from early morning until well into the night, and the occupants of the lead canoe calculated they had covered considerable distance since leaving the cliff-enclosed, primeval island. Checking the current, it was noticeable that during the nights while all slept it still was in their favor.

For brief periods during the morning and afternoon Bantan and Tama permitted Nulu and Mauria to take turns with the paddles while they rested their tiring muscles, and in this way their progress was much better than were it otherwise as they sought their ultimate goal which must lie somewhere beyond the horizon. Each evening when the bronzed giant checked the constellations in the heaven, he was positive he was following the best possible course.

Later on this day the bronzed giant and Tama again exchanged places with the two girls, and once again they scanned the waterline to their left, ahead, and to their right for a possible sight of land, but were unrewarded in their effort.

Several hundred yards to the left ahead of them, Bantan's keen eyes detected a slight disturbance upon the surface of the gently heaving water. He immediately called Tama's attention to what he had sighted, and while the lighter-skinned native's eyes followed his companion's pointing hand, he saw what he had discovered.

"It looks like a porpoise or a turtle, Tama," Bantan remarked.

As both intently watched, the disturbance was to be seen no more, and the water surface appeared relatively calm.

"It couldn't have been a turtle," the bronzed giant added reflectingly. "It would have no reason to disappear. Perhaps it was a porpoise after all."

"Whatever it was, Bantan," Tama declared, "I doubt if we have reason to worry."

With a shrug the bronzed giant dismissed the incident from mind. Before he and Tama exchanged places with Mauria and Nulu, they partook of fruit and nuts to keep their strength at normal, then with words of commendation to both girls, the two men took up the paddles and resumed their course.

Mauria and Nulu partook of nourishment as well.

Onward, still toward the east, with the sun now nearing the western horizon, the canoe was paddled while the hollowed log, provisioned with fruit and nuts followed, the towline being kept reasonably taut.

A hundred yards to their left the slightly undulating surface was again momentarily broken. Mauria chanced to note the disturbance and turned to Tama, telling him what she had seen; but when the paddler looked in the direction the native girl indicated, no disturbance was now to be seen. He laughed, revealing his perfect set of white teeth.

"Perhaps it was the same porpoise Bantan sighted," he assured the girl he loved dearly. "We have nothing to worry about, I'm sure."

Mauria smiled even though a slight chill pulsed through her.

"I'll hope that's all it was, Tama," she replied, as she resumed eating a banana, but her eyes looked expectantly to her left repeatedly.

Nulu smiled assuringly as Mauria's eyes caught hers and she shrugged her shapely shoulders nonchalantly.

Near the prow of the canoe Bantan had overheard Mauria, and he looked to his left repeatedly, but the surface of the undulating water was not disturbed the slightest by the presence of some possible denizen of the deep. No tell-tale fin of a shark marred the surface, and he was assured there was no need of worry even were a shark to make an appearance, for of all underwater life he despised and hated none more than a shark ever since his boyhood friend, Ramo, had been attacked and devoured by a vicious one many moons ago. Hating sharks as he did, Bantan entertained no fears thereafter, and at various times upon a matter of general principles he would attack and slay one, and feel that he had again avenged his boyhood companion's death.

The bronzed giant's sharp eyes were never still while he paddled. They looked to his right, and then as far ahead as his vision would permit before then trailing to his left. Occasionally he would look momentarily over a shoulder at his companions with the assurance that all was well. Sometimes he would catch Nulu's eyes, and the warmness in hers was all too evident that she was proud, confident, and so very much in love with him that a deep sigh tremulously escaped her lips as a sweet smile touched her features to the accompaniment of her accelerating heart.

In the west the lower edge of the sun, resembling a ball of fire, had now touched the waterline. The shadows of the canoe's occupants were grotesque and far reaching.

With no visible indication of weariness, Bantan and Tama continued to wield their paddles in rhythmic strokes that resulted in the leading canoe with the one in tow sharply cutting the slightly undulating tips of small waves without any cessation in the speed maintained. Ripples broke away from the leading canoe's prow upon each side in a steady pattern.

With a sudden start, scanning the distant horizon as he did, the bronzed giant was positive his keen eyes detected distant land. Almost simultaneously his acute perspicative faculties were aware of the unnatural heaving of the water upon his left which affected the canoe.

Quickly he shifted his attention, and the sharpness of his eyes perceived the grayish diamond-shape of an ugly-looking underwater denizen known as a manta ray. Its flippers extended all of twenty feet to each side and it must weigh fully a ton.

The hideous features were seemingly looking directly up at the watcher who had never seen one of these monstrous creatures, but not for a moment was he frightened for himself. It was of the others in the canoe that he worried at that perilous moment.

"Danger!" was the only word he could utter in warning.

CHAPTER II

An Unknown Island

AT THE NEXT MOMENT the canoe lurched violently as a heavy object beneath the surface bumped against its bottom. It was half lifted then turned completely over, spilling its occupants pell mell. The towline attached to the trailing hollowed log was snapped upon the instant as the large creature beneath the surface upset it as well, spilling its contents into the water.

Bantan's alerted faculties had caused him to fill his lungs after shouting a warning to his companions a moment previous to the contact of the grayish, diamond-shaped monster against the canoe's bottom. He was flung into the churning water head foremost, and luckily, after turning a complete somersault, landed completely free of the canoe.

With eyes opened, the bronzed giant's powerful arms and kicking legs forced him upward through the churning water to the surface. He shook the moisture from his hair and looked with anxious eyes about the nearby vicinity. He saw first the capsized canoe about ten feet from him. And then he recognized the hollowed log also floating upside down, dismayingly knowing its contents had been spilled into the water. The manta ray was nowhere to be seen. Having caused this catastrophe, it had apparently submerged again and continued on its aimless way.

Bantan swam toward the capsized canoe while looking about the surface for his companions. He was somewhat

THE CANOE LURCHED VIOLENTLY

concerned at not readily seeing them. The rays of the half-concealed sun bothered considerably as he looked in that direction.

"Nulu! Mauria! Tama!" he shouted as he gripped the prow of the overturned canoe.

"Bantan!" The voice that answered was Mauria's.

Looking in the direction from which his name had been uttered, he saw the Mandoes Island girl swimming toward him. There was a smile upon her features. Her brown arms glistened in the diminishing sunlight, and her black hair shimmered over her shoulders. He waved to her, then looked anxiously about.

"Nulu! Tama!" the bronzed giant shouted. "Where are you?"

His sharp eyes continued to scan the surface for sight of them as he swam around the canoe until he had reached its middle.

"Nulu! Tama!" he again called out.

Within another minute Mauria had reached Bantan. Her features were now worried as her eyes met his.

"I haven't seen either of them," she gasped, treading water alongside him.

He shook his head sadly.

"I'm going to right the canoe," he said to the girl.

With his words he gripped the gunwale and started rocking the canoe as he treaded water. Several times he did this until the vacuum of air trapped within was broken. And then with a final, mighty tug, he turned the canoe rightside up with a minimum amount of water in its bottom. He turned to the girl.

"I'll steady the canoe from the other side while you draw yourself into it," he said.

Quickly he disappeared beneath the water craft to reappear upon the other side in another moment. With strong hands he gripped the gunwale.

"Now, Mauria," he bade her.

Somewhat laboriously, the native girl drew herself upward, resting first upon her forearms. Drawing a deep breath and smiling assuringly, she managed to hook a foot over the gunwale. Thereafter, it was only a matter of moments before she was ensconced within the canoe.

"I'm all right," she announced as she arose to her knees.

"Look for the others, Mauria," Bantan said.

As he spoke, his eyes were roaming about the immediate vicinity, and luckily he spied a paddle. Quickly he swam toward it and returned to the canoe with it, handing it to the native girl. Meanwhile, she had been scanning the surface in apparent hopelessness for sign of Tama or Nulu. She shook her head sadly and tears blurred her vision.

"I don't see any sign of either of them," she said chokingly.

"Balance the canoe," the bronzed giant directed, "while I draw myself into it."

Mauria did as she was bade, and within moments he agilely drew himself into the canoe. Standing erect, he looked searchingly for swimming forms, indicating Nulu and Tama were in need of succor. In the passing moments, accompanied by a sorrowful shake of his head, Bantan was dismayed as the grim truth was realized. Nulu and Tama had been rescued from a cruel, primeval land of constant dangers only to have come to their end thusly. It was difficult to believe that Fate had dealt this cruel blow when all had been so serene during the past few days.

"Nulu! Tama!" he called again with faltering voice, seemingly realizing how futile it was to call to them.

As his keen eyes searched the water about the canoe in which he and Mauria were, he observed a second paddle with his bow and some arrows floating nearby. With a shake of his head he paddled in that direction, telling the girl to pick them up. With nimble fingers she did so.

Bantan then maneuvered the canoe near the overturned, hollowed log. Some fruit and nuts were floating about. With Mauria's assistance they gathered what was possible. Time and again the bronzed giant would survey the darkening water in the nearby vicinity with a sorrowful expression upon his face. Meanwhile, the native girl dried the bottom of the canoe with a bunch of grass which she wrung over the edge.

By this time the quick setting of darkness was to be noticed. Not speaking much for the most part, Mauria now broke the oppressive silence that hovered over them. She drew close to Bantan and placed a gentle hand upon his shoulder as he sat with lowered head and hands tightly clasped upon his knees.

"I can't find the words to tell you how very sorry I am at what's happened," she said in a trembling voice. "If I could have had my wish, I would have had Nulu live instead of me. I know how much you loved her. Please believe me."

The bronzed giant uttered a deep sigh, and though his hands remained tightly clasped, he forced a smile to his lips as he looked at the Mandoes Island girl. He shook his head sadly as he spoke.

"How can anyone explain the tragic events life deals to us?" Again he shook his head. "Though I loved Wanya, because she was as a sister to me, I could not consider her as a mate. After Leona Brown realized my heart belonged to Kalma and she sent me to her, Kalma, believing me dead, took her own life rather than submit to the bestial demands of the Jap captain. I have forgiven her for that. There was Nao, the Amo Island girl. I loved her dearly and would have mated with her had not an enemy

spear ended her life. It was after that that I vowed not
to love another native girl, for disaster always was their
fate. And then there was Luane; but a jealous father intervened. There was Mena from the primeval island, and
she went unknowingly to her death escaping from a hairy
beast man. And last, there was Nulu, also from the same
island and so much like Mena in all ways. Sometimes I
wonder why I must be the victim of such tragedies in
life. What have I done to deserve such punishment?"
And with his concluding words Bantan buried his face
in his hands and again uttered a deep sigh.

The maternal instinct within Mauria was not to be
denied. She gently stroked his damp hair into place.

"Many things happen to us in life that we do not wish,"
she murmured compassionately. "But there must be a
reason. Some day I'm sure you'll understand."

Another deep sigh found its way to Bantan's lips. He
again shook his head. Presently he uncovered his face,
and as he spoke his voice was calm and composed.

"Yes, Mauria, some day I may understand." One
hand reached up and covered hers that again rested upon
his shoulder. "You, too, have reason for sorrow. I ad-
mired Tama very much and I know he would have been
a good mate for you."

A slight tremor pulsed through the native girl.

"Yes, I know," she murmured with a slight choke in
her voice.

He now squared his shoulders and his hand uncovered
hers.

"Just before the canoe was upset," he said, "I was
almost sure I had sighted what looked to be an island
directly toward the east. Stars are now making their appearance. With them to guide me, I should be able to
make considerable progress so that we may hope to
reach the island some time during the next sun."

"I'll help paddle," Mauria volunteered. "Want me to go forward?"

The bronzed giant merely nodded.

The native girl knelt near the bow and took up the paddle. Looking back in the almost impenetrable darkness that had now enveloped them, she spoke.

"Say when you are ready, Bantan."

"All right," he answered.

In unison their paddles stroked the gently undulating surface, and the canoe moved swiftly over the water. While they paddled in silence the thoughts of each had reason indeed to function as they did.

Though Mauria was saddened because of the swift passing of Tama, who had loved her very much, she was forced to admit to herself that she had not loved him in return as fully because of Bantan being the true object of her affection. Hopelessly this was on her part, for she had been told by the bronzed giant to expect no reward in return. But now that Nulu, the object of his love, presumably had gone to her death, within the native girl's heart there was still hope that he might yet learn to care for her. One could not foretell what circumstances the unknown future might present.

Meanwhile, as he paddled, Bantan's thoughts were sorrowed and confused by the sudden turn of events. It was almost unbelievable that Nulu and Tama were no longer among the living. Everything had been so perfect before the manta ray had appeared. He was positive he had sighted land in the distance, and even before he could announce the glad tidings, the appearance of the underwater denizen had altered everything. Once again he and the Mandoes Island girl were together. How strange that this should be. What was the reason that Fate had spared her instead of Nulu? With a shake of his head he realized how impossible it was to foretell the future with any degree of accuracy. Vaguely he wondered if the Omnipotent One Father Lasance had told him about could be a just God.

His eyes became accustomed to the almost pitch darkness, and he could perceive the outline of the native girl in the bow as she wielded her paddle with no complaint. He was comforted that they had gotten along so well in the past and he was hopeful they would do so in the days to come. He compared Mauria with Wanya, his foster sister, and with a nod convinced himself that she was very much like his foster sister—always trying to please him and never objecting to anything that he planned. He decided he would treat her as considerately as he would Wanya.

When some time had passed and the canoe had covered a number of miles, Bantan became aware that Mauria was tiring, for her strokes were faltering. The paddle would strike the side of the canoe and he could hear the splash of the blade as it was withdrawn more slowly after each stroke. There was no question the girl was very wearied, but she would not admit it. He, too, was tiring as well.

"Mauria, we have paddled enough for now," he said to her. "I know you must be very tired."

"But I can paddle longer," she mildly protested.

"No, we have paddled enough," he insisted. "Let us sleep now. When we wake in the morning I'm sure the island I think I sighted will be much nearer and we can easily reach it before another night comes."

The girl placed her paddle in the bottom of the canoe and uttered a sigh.

"Poor Nulu and Tama!" she murmured, as she curled upon her right side and pillowed her head upon her hair. "It is hard to believe they are not with us."

He sighed audibly.

"Yes, I know," he murmured. "Try and sleep now, Mauria. We know not what the next sun may bring, and we want to be prepared for whatever it might be."

The girl bade him good night, to which he replied. Within moments, so utterly wearied each were, they were fast asleep. The night was not cool, for which they were grateful.

Bantan slept soundly even though his dreams were somewhat disturbed because of Nulu's sudden death, also that of Tama. He was refreshed as he opened his eyes shortly after the sun had cleared the horizon. Looking toward Mauria, curled in the bow of the canoe, he saw that she was still sleeping. She was upon her right side, her head pillowed upon her lustrous hair. Her knees were drawn close to her bosom.

Reaching over the gunwale, the bronzed giant cupped a handful of water and washed his face. Then he carefully arose to his feet. Shading his eyes from the blinding sunlight, he looked toward the east. Below the sun's rim, he could easily distinguish the island that he had been sure he had sighted on the late afternoon of the previous day.

Once more seating himself, he reached for some fruit and was partaking of it when he noticed the native girl stirring. In a few moments she was fully awake. As her eyes opened and she saw Bantan, she smiled and arose to a seated position, rubbing her eyes.

"The island!" she exclaimed.

He smiled and nodded.

"It is not too far away, Mauria," he answered. "We should reach it easily by noon day."

"Is it Marja?" she then asked.

He shook his head slowly.

"Nor like Mandoes," he added.

The native girl turned and shaded her eyes against the

sun's bright rays and she, too, could sight the unknown island. Turning about, she nodded.

"Anyway, we'll have a chance to rest and feel earth beneath our feet before we continue on our way," she said with a wistful smile.

He nodded.

Mauria reached over the gunwale and cupped a handful of water and applied it to her face. With a smile she reached for some fruit and nuts and ate her morning meal. She shook her head sorrowfully and noticed Bantan watching her.

"I was thinking how fortunate it would have been had Nulu and Tama been with us," she murmured. "Everything had been going so well until—"

Again he nodded, offering no speech, but she could read the ineffable sadness in his dark eyes.

When they had eaten their fill, they nodded in understanding. Taking up their paddles they resumed their course toward the unknown island. As the time passed and the sun continued to rise higher in the heaven, with less difficulty they could look ahead. Even from the distance Bantan estimated the unknown island was not more than two miles in diameter, but he was positive they would have no worry about fruit and nuts, for it appeared to teem with trees of all kinds and growing foliage. Even from their present distance they could recognize the coconut trees that bordered the shore. They could also observe the strip of shining sand that indicated a beach surrounded the island.

The paddlers rested once during the forenoon, and while doing so commented upon the island they were nearing.

"I wonder if it is inhabited?" the girl asked.

"That is difficult to say," he answered. "It appears too small for a native tribe of any size to inhabit it; but we cannot be sure until we have landed and look around."

"At least, I'll hope none of the monsters that we knew upon the one we left will be there," she added with a shudder.

He smiled and nodded.

Once again taking up their paddles, they resumed their course. Looking about the gently heaving surface, Bantan could see no form of danger threatening from underwater denizens—no tell-tale evidence of sharks prowling about. For that reason he and Mauria did not exert themselves. Already the freshness of growing verdure and the aroma of exotic flowers reached their nostrils, and they breathed deeply and exhaled with reluctance.

In due time they were approaching the outer fringes of a gentle surf. There was no need of instructing the native girl how to handle her paddle, for she appeared confident and proficient. Very little white-foamed water washed over the canoe's sides as it glided through the surf, and presently the prow grated upon the soft sand. At the next moment, laying down their paddles, both the man and the girl stepped out of the canoe. With a nod, they gripped the gunwale and drew the canoe up the sandy stretch of beach to the edge of the foliage some twenty feet distant. As they straightened and faced each other a smile touched their lips.

"Mmmmmm, it is good to feel the sand beneath my feet again," Mauria exclaimed. She breathed deeply of the scented air.

Bantan nodded as he looked toward the foliage upon his left and then right.

"Want to explore about a bit?" he asked.

"If you wish," she answered. "I'll follow wherever you go."

Several sea gulls were flying overhead screechingly as they veered this way and that, finally disappearing from sight over the tree tops. The high tide had deposited flotsam as it customarily did, but there was nothing of interest to the newcomers.

Bantan's right hand touched the handle of his dagger. The foliage confronting them did not appear too impenetrable, and the man led the way with the native girl close upon his heels. Some hermit crabs scurried up the boles of trees at their approach and from a vantage point surveyed the aliens with beady eyes. Small, beautifully colored birds flitted about, apparently unconcerned with the newcomers entering their eden.

The bronzed giant's eyes always studied the undergrowth for possible signs of the passage of other feet; but nowhere was there any indication that others had been here. There were places where the tangled foliage was too impenetrable and they skirted these, finding easier trails. In one place they came to a mucky pool, and remembering the quicksand within the primeval island, they wisely avoided it.

When some little time had passed they were aware of the gradual incline of the terrain. The foliage also was becoming more sparse until they reached a cliff overlooking shimmering water. It was all of fifty feet high. At its edge Bantan and Mauria seated themselves and breathed more easily.

"It is very beautiful here," the girl said with sparkling eyes as she looked out upon the shimmering water. A gentle breeze stirred her lovely dark hair about her brown shoulders.

Bantan admitted it was as he leaned slightly forward. He looked over the cliff's edge into the cove below. The waves gently slapped against the base of the cliff, and he could detect the sandy bottom through the translucent water. He noticed several circular openings half exposed some three to five feet in diameter near the cliff's base. As he looked at them, in his mind there was the thought to explore them at a later time, if only through mere curiosity.

"This reminds me of the cliff on Beneiro Island," he murmured. "Many times in the past I would lie there facing the water, hoping to sight a shark that I might continue time and again to avenge the death of Ramo, my boyhood companion. And I did so. Wanya was often with me afterwards, and one day she fell into the water. A shark was nearby and I plunged into the water to save her from the fate Ramo had suffered. She took poor Ramo's place in my life after he had been devoured." He nodded in retrospection. "Wanya and I got along very well afterward. She seemed always to read my thoughts. My foster father and mother adways hoped we would become mated, for they knew how much Wanya cared for me. But having known her so many moons as my sister, for some reason I could not remove that thought from my mind. Only once did I dream that we were to be mated; but upon awaking, I felt ashamed, and vowed to never even give a further thought of such a possibility."

While Bantan had been speaking, Mauria looked at his averted features with warmness in her dark eyes. A wistful expression was upon her features.

"How fortunate Wanya was to have known you so long," she murmured.

The bronzed giant then lapsed into a silence, his dark eyes watching the shimmering ocean surface beyond the cove's inlet. The Mandoes Island girl contented herself by merely feasting her eyes upon his noble features, realizing as she did that being silent when he wished to be would greatly be in her favor.

But at last Bantan stirred and arose to his feet with a deep sigh. He turned to Mauria who also arose at his side.

"Would you care to dive from the cliff and we can swim out of the cove to the sandy beach beyond?" he asked. "It would be easier than pushing our way through the foliage to where our canoe lies."

The native girl looked down at the water below. It was higher than she had ever dived before. But with a deep breath she smiled confidently as she faced the bronzed giant.

"Would Wanya have done so?" she asked with twinkling eyes.

"She would do anything I did," he answered with a nod.

Approaching the edge of the cliff, the girl repressed the slight shudder that gripped her spine, then with a smile looked back at Bantan.

"I'll go first," she said.

He nodded agreeably with a smile.

At the next moment Mauria turned and without hesitation leaped outward. Her body formed a perfect arc as she seemingly sailed downward and plunged into the water with a minimum of disturbance to its placid surface.

CHAPTER III

Sirena, the Mermaid Queen

THE BRONZED GIANT marvelled at Mauria's neatly executed dive. He stood poised upon the cliff's edge, watching with unfeigned admiration as the girl plunged beneath the surface. The moment her momentum was checked sufficiently, she curved her hands upward with all intent and purpose of surfacing, and there to await Bantan joining her.

But—what was that?

From the second opening to his right near the base of the cliff, peculiar forms that resembled both fish and human, swam speedily in the direction of the native girl. The creatures must be women because of the long hair streaming behind their heads and trailed far below their shoulders. This presently was an undeniable fact as their bare, well formed breasts were revealed when one or another twisted in the water so that the front, upper portion of their anatomy was to be glimpsed.

Bantan blinked his eyes and stared down at the swimming creatures in amazement. Their bodies from the waist down were covered with a coating of scales that shimmered dully from the light penetrating the translucent depths, and as far as he could observe their only clothing was a mesh covering which tightly encircled their mid-section. But what astonished the watcher most of all was that these creatures did not resemble the women he had known heretofore. Where their hips should have been, instead, the lower portion of their body was fashioned much as a fish. Where their feet should have been there was a sturdy fin. The only other adornment they wore was a necklace, fashioned doubtlessly from the teeth of some vicious fish—quite probably a shark.

While the bronzed giant looked down into the water with such astonishment, he appeared seemingly frozen in a state of inactivity, for what he witnessed was incredible. There were three of the swimming creatures and that the native girl was the object of their mission there was no question. Their fins were waving vigorously and their arms moved rapidly in sweeping strokes as they swam with amazing speed. Quickly they overtook Mauria.

At the moment of being apprehended, the native girl struggled valiantly, but in vain, in her horrible predicament, for she was outnumbered beyond hope of escaping them. The fish-like women had a method in their concerted attack, for two of them drew alongside their victim and seized her flailing arms. The third encircled the thrashing brown legs and drew them together. Then they slipped downward along them until they locked about the girl's ankles. The three creatures apparently were ready now to bear their captive back from whence they had come, for they exchanged nods. The fins where their feet should have been waved to and fro vigorously and they quickly headed toward a circular opening to the base of the cliff. The free arms of two of them at the girl's side helped to draw them through the water with increasing speed.

Even from the distance that spanned and the translucent water intervening, Bantan's amazed, sharp eyes detected the expression of hopelessness upon Mauria's features as, helplessly, she was borne off by her captors. The moment all four disappeared within the second circular opening to the right at the base of the cliff, the bronzed giant shook his head violently, still unable to believe what he had seen. But when he could no longer see the fish-like women and their captive, he stared down at the water as though in a trance, trying earnestly to formulate a plausible understanding at what manner of creatures the fish-like women were who had taken the native girl captive.

Now he nodded his head decisively. He knew he must rescue Mauria from the clutches of her captors, no matter at what cost—even his own life, if necessary. Vicarious by nature, he was not one to renege on a friend in dire need. In his memory he marked the particular circular opening into which the girl had been taken. But just how he was going to rescue her was what puzzled him, for it was not his intention to make rash decisions that might preclude such a possibility. He reasoned the matter intelligently.

It was apparent the fish-like women had been near the openings on guard, watching for some unwary victim, for the native girl had only struck the water a few moments previously when they had come swarming from the openings to take her captive. Bantan realized he had reason to wonder indeed what methods he might employ toward the girl's rescue. He studied each side of the cliff to the base where the water splashed against it. He could discern the high-water line about a foot above the present level. Where the lower one was he could not determine.

The bronzed giant decided it made no difference from which side of the cliff he descended. He chose the left side and quickly covered the distance on the summit, then carefully descended the rocky slope until he had reached the bottom where gentle waves slapped upon the rocky surface at his feet. He kept from sight of the openings from any chance watchers stationed within.

Now, carefully, he inched his way along the edge until he might reach the closest proximity to the base of the cliff. There was a sluiceway of sufficient depth for the purpose Bantan had in mind. Reaching it, he first ascertained his dagger was sheathed at his right hip, then he lay down into the sluiceway, facing the cliff. Filling his lungs, he slipped into the water. With eyes opened, his strong arms drew him beneath the surface, and he kept his attention focused upon the second opening at the base of the cliff through which Mauria had been borne by her captors.

In another minute he was confronting the opening he sought. Straining his eyes, he could observe nothing but blackness within. No sight of the fish-like women was to be seen. Quickly he went to the opening on his right. Nothing was there. He speedily reversed himself and swam toward the third opening from his right, pausing momentarily to look again at the second but still observed nothing. Then from the third opening, where the result was negative, he approached the fourth. Still nothing was to be seen within.

By this time his lungs were clamoring for renewed air, so just within this opening he allowed his feet to touch the sandy bottom and his head emerged from the water. When he stood erect the water was below his shoulders. He inhaled deeply and stared within the darkened tunnel with piercing eyes and listening with alert ears.

He could hear nothing but the gentle slapping of water against the sides of the opening through which he had come. His right hand closed about the handle of his dagger and he withdrew it. Then without further pause, he waded slowly within the tunnel, his feet groping their way. He reached his left hand upward and slightly ahead toward the roof and he could barely touch it with his finger tips.

As he advanced into the darkening tunnel, Bantan became aware the water continued to recede as he moved at a slight incline. Where at first the water was just below his shoulders, after a few minutes it was on a level with his hips. The fingers of his left hand would occasionally touch the ceiling, though upon most occasions couldn't.

Still he advanced through the shallowing water with feet still groping. His eyes strained against the darkness. Becoming accustomed to it by now, a short distance ahead he could perceive a blank wall which reflected only a small portion of the dull light that was emitted through the small space below the top of the opening and the water.

Within another few minutes the bronzed giant was stepping upon dry sand. A few yards ahead he paused at the foot of the blank wall. Looking to his right and then his left, he saw no openings that might lead elsewhere. He was at the dead end of the tunnel. With a shrug of his broad shoulders, he turned and retraced his way toward the opening. Since this one led nowhere he would try his luck with the next. Meanwhile, he tried to think what poor Mauria thought of his prolonged absence and must wonder why he had made no attempt to rescue her from her plight.

Bantan moved faster upon his return to the opening. Since he had not encountered any rocks on the floor— and that was why he had groped his way—he could now accelerate his speed. Presently he had reached the opening. Peering around the edge toward the next in line, he observed none of the fish women. He waded to the next opening several yards from the one he had explored and looked within.

Seeing no one, in another moment he had entered, his dagger still clutched in his right hand. This opening appeared slightly larger than the first, but the water was the same depth. Once again with eyes strained and ears alert, he groped his way along the tunnel, his left hand reaching upward and ahead so that he might not strike his head against a chance low-hanging rock from the ceiling.

At first nothing out of the ordinary was experienced as the bronzed giant continued his way into the tunnel. As in the first one, the water receded as he advanced at a slight incline. But his alert ears became aware of muffled sounds to his right beyond the wall far ahead. Listening intently for a moment as he paused, the sounds were quite distinguishable and appeared to be of a babbling nature.

With greater interest now Bantan resumed his way with increasing speed, but still being careful that he encountered no rocks on the tunnel floor and as well his left hand upraised before him for the possibility of a low-hanging rock from the ceiling. His eyes detected a dull glow issuing from the right wall near its end and his curiosity was more so aroused. As he continued, his alert ears determined the babbling sound from the next tunnel was more clearer from the aperture in the wall through which the dull glow was emitted.

With nearer approach, the babbling sounds appeared more distinct, and now the bronzed giant was positive they were the voices of women because of their high-pitched tones. As he presently stepped out of the water and drew closer to the opening, which was some six feet from the tunnel floor, he stood upon his toes and cautiously looked through. What he saw resulted in astonishment appearing in his eyes.

Phosphorescence from the walls and the smooth ceiling emitted a soft glow, and Bantan's amazed eyes looked upon a seeming amphitheatre in appearance, except there were no seats. In the center was a pool of unrippled water some fifty feet in diameter. These matters were extraneous to the watchful eyes in the aperture, for what arrested his attention foremost was the fact he saw Mauria being held upon her back by two of the fish-like women who had made her capture possible.

The third creature was more regal in appearance with a mass of reddish hair caught with a bone brooch at the nape of her neck to prevent it from tumbling over her shoulders in front. A crown of intricately fashioned fish bones encircled her forehead just above the hairline. A more extravagant mesh covered her mid-section. The toothed necklace about her neck was larger, trailing down between her large, bare breasts. In all probability she was the leader or queen of the fish-like women.

She was crouched at the native girl's side and her hands were exploring the dark-skinned anatomy from the waist down. With curiosity she felt of Mauria's hips and then drew her hands down the sides of her thighs, upon out and inside, beginning where they joined the lower part of the body. And while she was thus engaged, Mauria was watching with wide eyes, but no fear was to be detected in their dark depths.

The examining hands continued to the captive's knees and these she felt with seeming awe, even going so far as to lift one of the girl's feet and then lower it and observe how the knee bent. Then her hands went down to the girl's feet and with some awkwardness removed the sandal covering one foot. At sight of the toes that were revealed she uttered an exclamation of surprise, as did her companions.

With increasing interest her fingers gripped each toe in turn, lifting it and drew it from side to side. At last, her examination completed to her satisfaction, she leaned back and surveyed the native girl with studying eyes. And then for the first time she spoke to her.

"Who are you and from whence have you come?" she asked in a tongue that was similar to the one Mauria was familiar with.

The native girl nodded in understanding.

"May I be seated first?" she asked. And when the leader did not seem to understand, Mauria added: "There is no need to hold my arms. I shall not attempt to escape. I would be more comfortable if I might be seated."

The leader nodded to the two fish-like women holding the captive's arms at her sides. When they were released, the girl arose to a seated position. She smiled with gratefulness.

"Tell me your name and from whence you came," the leader then said.

"My name is Mauria and I came from Mandoes Island," was the answer. Then looking at the leader, her eyes curiously trailing from her mid-section to the finned end, she added: "I have never seen a woman like you and your companions. What is your name?"

"I am Sirena," was the reply. "I am the queen of our tribe. The last of our males died some time ago. They, too, were as we. What do you call those things attached to your body?" As she spoke, Sirena indicated Mauria's legs and feet.

The native girl told her what they were, and that they were used for walking or running. She added, if the queen so wished, she would show her.

A solemn nod was the answer.

Mauria slipped her sandal on and arose to her feet and started walking about while the two fish-like women kept close to her, slithering upon the sandy floor, and occasionally using their hands when necessary.

Sirena appeared impressed as her eyes studied the walking girl's legs. She even noticed how the knees slightly bent and the ankles moved with each step. She raised her hands.

"That is enough, Mauria," she said. "Be seated again. I would talk more with you."

The native girl squatted upon her haunches and the queen appeared more interested in the captive girl's position which so differed from the last.

"Where you came from—all males and women are as you?" she asked.

Mauria nodded.

"We are called natives," she added in the manner of explanation. "What are you called?"

"We are known as mermaids," was the answer. "That is because we have been born as we are." The queen shook her head sadly, adding: "Now that there are no more mermen alive on our island, in due time when we die there will be no one to carry on our heritage unless—"

The native girl merely stared at Sirena.

"Unless?" she asked, importuning the queen to finish her statement.

Sirena moistened her lips with the tip of her tongue and her eyes looked up at the soft-lighted ceiling in despair.

"Unless a male comes to our island before we are too old," she explained. "There are only twenty of us now when there used to be many times that number. Upon the farther shore there dwell three very old native males. They are too old to be of any help to increase our numbers. Some time ago we affected a trade agreement with them. They furnish us with fruit and nuts and we exchange fish in return. I've learned they are the only survivors of what once was a prosperous village. The last of their females died about the same time our mermen did, so in time they, too, will become extinct."

Mauria's forehead wrinkled a trifle as she regarded the queen.

"Doesn't anyone else ever come to this island?" she asked.

Sirena shook her head sadly.

"This island must not be known to anyone," she answered.

The native girl could hardly believe that at some time in the past passing natives had not stopped here if only to rest before continuing their sea trip.

"No one has ever come here before?" she interrogated.

The queen appeared in deep thought.

"Long ago I have been told," she said, wracking her mentality, "several males were washed ashore. Though everything possible was done to make them well again, they died. Another time, when I was very young, a big bird that made loud noises as it flew fell out of the sky into the water. Our people were very much afraid though they had no reason, for the big bird sank into the water and was seen no more. Two males were washed ashore. They were clothed in strange garments, but they were dead. Since that time you are the only stranger who has come to our island."

Mauria nodded as she cogitated on what the queen had told her. She wondered vaguely what Sirena would say if she were to know Bantan had come to this island with her. Thinking of him, she wondered, naturally, why he hadn't dived into the water after her when she failed to rise to the surface. The thought stayed her as she subsequently realized he must have witnessed her plight, and even now was making plans to rescue her. She looked at the queen who appeared to be meditating.

CHAPTER IV

Mauria—An Uneasy Guest

"AM I TO BE CONSIDERED a prisoner, Sirena?" Mauria asked in an humble tone, breaking the short silence that prevailed.

The queen shook her head a trifle as though aroused from her meditations. Looking at the native girl for a long moment, a slight smile at last touched her lips.

"Let us say that you are to be considered a guest," she answered. "I find you interesting. I would like to know more from whence you came and the people of your island."

Mauria heaved a slight sigh of relief.

"How did you come to this island?" Sirena then asked.

"I came in what is known as a canoe," was the reply. "A paddle is used to make it move." She pretended she had a paddle in hand and moved her arms. "The sun rose and set three times since I left that island of danger with three others. Two were males and the other was a white-skinned girl. A big fish upset the canoe and I was the only one to survive."

The queen appeared perturbed.

"A white-skinned girl?" she murmured questioningly. "And the two males—were they white-skinned as well?"

"They were dark-skinned as I am," the native girl answered.

Sirena nodded in understanding, but the mention of the white-skinned girl still puzzled her.

"But the white-skinned girl," she said, shaking her

head. "Where did she come from that she differed from you and the two males?"

Mauria nodded almost eagerly.

"It is a long story, Sirena," she explained. "Do you wish me to start at the beginning?"

The queen inclined her head.

"I would like to hear about it," she answered with undeniable interest radiating in her hazel eyes.

Mauria began to tell the story of her life upon Mandoes Island until the time Bantan had made his advent upon the scene. From then on she sketched briefly their adventures after escaping Dr. Zarwood's wrath until they reached the cliff-enclosed, primeval island where they had come upon Tama, first, and then Mena and Nulu. While she spoke, the native girl would intermittently look at the queen and saw that she was intensely interested. When she had concluded her narrative, Mauria nodded, ending:

"And that was how I came here."

Sirena smiled.

"One of the males was your mate?" she asked.

The native girl shook her head sadly.

"I loved both of them," she answered. "But Tama, to whom I was promised, was not the one I really loved. It was Bantan. Because he had lived in the tropics nearly all his life, he became dark-skinned by the sun, but he was really white. Because he was of white birth he had told me he could not mate with a native girl. He was promised to the white-skinned girl."

The queen shook her head sympathetically and a rueful smile touched her lips.

"And now both of them are lost to you, Mauria," she murmured.

The Mandoes Island girl smiled weakly and nodded, not trusting her voice.

"I am very sorry for you," Sirena added. At the next moment her slumberous eyes brightened. "This Bantan you spoke of—the white man by birth who had lived nearly all of his life in the tropics—was he a big, strong, handsome male?"

A flush suffused Mauria's cheeks and she nodded in memory of the bronzed giant. A warmth appeared in her eyes.

"He was all of that, Sirena," she admitted.

The queen shook her head despairingly.

"It is unthinkable that such a perfect male must meet his death," she asseverated. "I wonder," she mused at the next moment with a dainty shrug of her smooth shoulders, "if such a male would have been attracted to a mermaid like me? I am not a native, though what my origin really is, I don't know. Do you think, Mauria, he would have been attracted by my beauty?"

The native girl shrugged.

"That I don't know, Sirena," she answered.

The queen heaved a deep sigh and for a few moments was lost in her reveries. When next she spoke the subject was of an entirely different matter.

"I am hungry," she said. Looking to each of the two fish-like women who had silently remained at Mauria's side, she addressed them. "Pegra and Beta, prepare food for our guest and myself."

The two mermaids nodded in acquiescence and in their sinuous manner slithered from the amphitheatre toward an opening in the farther wall.

The queen looked at her guest with a smile.

"Tell me more of Bantan until our meal is ready," she urged.

If there was a subject that Mauria enjoyed discussing, it was of the bronzed giant. And while she talked of him her heart beat a trifle faster and the love-light she treasured for him was clearly reflected in her soft dark eyes.

And while the native girl was thus loquacious on incidents wherein she and her "dream man" had taken part, Sirena, the mermaid queen, seemed hardly to exist. But that same personage was stirred to the uttermost depths of her womanhood at hearing of the exploits of the bronzed giant. Her heart beat a trifle faster and a warmness suffused her entire being as she visualized in her mind the epitome of perfect maleness that Bantan must have represented. What wouldn't she have given to have known such a male!

With the recollection that she was not as the women he had known, no sacrifice would have been too great that he accept her as an equal and would have considered loving and mating with her. A deep sigh found its way to her lips and an ineffable sadness overcame her to know that he was no longer among the living. The one hope she had expressed that he might have survived was indeed a forlorn one.

It was then that Pegra returned to the amphitheatre and announced to her queen that the meal was prepared and awaited consumption. Sirena shook her head slightly to dispel her reveries, and with a smile turned to Mauria and beckoned for her to join her in the dining room.

The native girl arose to her feet and started walking at the side of the queen who slithered over the smooth, sandy floor. At the opening of the short passageway Pegra had withdrawn. Within a few moments the phosphorescent-lighted corridor through which they went ended, and Sirena and Mauria entered a fair-sized room lighted from all sides and the ceiling with the glowing substance in the rock.

In the center of the room there was a low, smooth, stone table, and already Pegra and Beta were waiting for the queen and their guest to take their place. A rock seat completely surrounded the table, it, too, being low to conform with the table. The food had been placed in clam dishes and its aroma was pleasing to the nostrils of the native girl.

With a smile, Sirena seated herself at the end of the table, while Mauria was requested to sit next to her. Since the girl could not place her knees beneath the table, she turned slightly sideways, facing the queen. The main course of the meal was a fish chowder that was seasoned perfectly, and the guest found it a delightful change from her past diet since she and Bantan had escaped from the castle upon Mandoes Island. While she partook of the chowder, she wished that the bronzed giant might be at her side to partake of it as well, for she knew he would have enjoyed it very much.

While they ate, Sirena spoke pleasantly and Mauria was an attentive listener. Sometimes the queen spoke to Pegra and Beta. For some reason that she could not account, the native girl entertained the feeling that the two mermaids were a trifle envious of her being accorded the privileges of a guest rather than a captive.

When the meal was completed, at the queen's request all remained at the table, and they resumed their conversation uninterruptedly. Again Sirena importuned Mauria to speak more of Bantan, and to describe him in minute detail as well. And when the description of the bronzed giant was given, the queen vividly pictured the perfect male she had never seen, and she knew were she ever to see him in person she would recognize him upon the instant.

After some time had passed, Sirena announced that she would retire.

"Come, Mauria," she said to her guest, "I will show you to the sleeping chamber."

With her words the queen slithered from her seat and the native girl followed at her side. Pegra and Beta attended to clearing the table of dishes.

Through a short tunnel the two passed to enter a fair-sized room also lighted by phosphorescent walls and ceiling. A number of sleeping pallets were to be observed. Several mermaids were already asleep.

An opening was to be observed which led to still another room.

Sirena pointed toward it.

"That is my retiring chamber," she said. "You may select any of the unoccupied pallets."

Mauria nodded and thanked her host.

"I hope you sleep well," the queen then said with a smile; and with her words she slithered toward the opening to her retiring chamber.

The native girl looked at the sleeping mermaids—there were three of them—but they hadn't stirred. Glancing about, she noted a pallet in the farthest corner of the room was unoccupied. She went to it and lay down. Although she was wearied, she remained awake a short while with the handsome features of Bantan in her mind. She hoped that he was not too uncomfortable, and deep in her heart she wished that he would miss her somewhat.

✓   ✓   ✓

A silent witness to the proceedings within the amphitheatre, Bantan sighed with relief for Mauria's sake that she was to be considered a guest of the mermaid queen instead of a prisoner. Since Sirena had invited the girl to eat with her, he now realized that he, too, was hungry. Having no reason to fear for the girl's safety, he drew away from the aperture and returned to the opening in the tunnel. With the recollection that another mermaid was at large, he paused and looked toward the next opening for possible sight of a guard stationed there.

After a few minutes of careful watching, the bronzed giant decided it would be safe to swim away to the other side where he would be free from surveillance. And so he did, and in due time had regained the summit of the cliff. He was aware the sun was not far from setting, so without further loss of time he returned through the foliage to the shore where his canoe lay upon the outskirts of the foliage. He gathered fruit and nuts on the way. He ate his evening meal and afterwards gathered soft grasses before utter darkness descended upon the island.

Seating himself in the canoe he watched the stars in constellations make their appearance in the darkening canopy above. Thinking of Nulu, especially, and Tama in a lesser degree, he sighed deeply. Once again he wondered at the caprice of Fate that they should have lost their lives when all had been going so well since their hurried departure from the cliff-enclosed, primeval island. A sad smile touched his lips as he remembered the girl's radiance each time he had kissed her.

Wearied from the day's events, Bantan at last stretched upon the soft grasses lining the canoe's bottom. Before sleep overtook him he thought of Mauria. He earnestly hoped she wouldn't think ill of him for not attempting her immediate rescue and consoled himself that she was not to be harmed at the present after what he had witnessed. Thinking thusly, he fell asleep.

The sun was an hour high when the bronzed giant waked in the morning after a refreshing night's sleep. As he arose from the canoe, stretching his arms aloft, he suddenly realized how easy it was to detect the canoe's presence were anyone to chance by on the sandy beach or even beyond the gentle surf. Quickly scanning the view from left to right and seeing no one on either land or water, he stepped from the canoe and without loss of time proceeded to conceal it within the foliage. Knowing it was the only means of leaving this island when opportunity favored, he must take excellent care of it.

It was well that Bantan acted as he did. As he was about to emerge from the foliage and looked toward the gentle surf to his left, his sharp eyes caught sight of flashing arms as two swimmers side by side were speedily cleaving the calmer water beyond the surf. They had just recently come within view, and the young giant wondered if they had sighted him while he had been concealing the canoe.

At once he guessed they were mermaids, for long hair trailed over their shoulders. With ears alert as well, it was obvious the swimmers exchanged little conversation. The watcher noted that they intermittently looked shoreward as though hoping to see something of interest.

The bronzed giant remained in concealment until they had passed beyond his range of view. Then he ventured into the gentle surf and indulged in a brief swim before returning to the canoe and partake of some fruit and nuts he had left over from the day before. With Mauria in mind, he set out for the cliff upon the opposite side of the island, and in due time reached his objective.

To Bantan's ears came the sound of laughter and splashing water in the cove. He approached the edge of the cliff carefully until the cause of the happy utterances was revealed to him. Four mermaids were swimming about, and the watcher could discern Sirena's reddish hair playing about her shoulders. He also saw Mauria among them, and she, too, appeared to be enjoying herself to the utmost. As he looked at the native girl and the mermaids, it was easy to determine the latter were much more adept in the water than Mauria, excellent swimmer though she was. The mermaids appeared to glide and twist and turn with no apparent effort and it was obvious their fins aided greatly in this.

As the bronzed giant watched the antics of the swimmers, he noted that Mauria often cast quick glances in the direction of the cliff's summit, doubtless hoping to see him. Time and again he was about to wave to her for assurance that he was watching her, but he observed that the mermaid queen kept close to the native girl and appeared to be aware of her marked attention. As a result, Sirena, too, would questioningly glance at the summit of the cliff as though hoping to observe the reason for Mauria's interest there. In her mind perhaps she entertained some doubt that her guest had come alone to this island. Now swimming close to the native girl, the queen spoke to her.

"You seem interested in the summit of the cliff," she remarked. "Do you expect to see someone there—perhaps waiting for you?"

Mauria laughed somewhat nervously.

"Why do you ask that, Sirena?" she asked.

"You have been looking up there a number of times since we have started swimming," was the reply.

"I—I had a strange feeling that we were being watched," the native girl remarked. "But it can't be possible, since I came alone to the island. Would there be any natives, other than the three old men you mentioned, living on other parts of the island?"

The mermaid queen laughed gaily, but her suspicions were not entirely allayed.

"If there were anyone else," she said, "I would surely know about it—or should anyone come during the night. Each morning two of my servants swim entirely around the island for the purpose of ascertaining no one has come. The old males upon the other side of the island do not come this early."

Mauria tried to laugh assuringly.

"Then I must be mistaken about thinking I saw some-one," she said with a shake of her head.

Thereafter, she curbed any further promptings to look toward the cliff's summit where she was positive she had caught a fleeting glimpse of Bantan. She could not be sure the mermaid queen was entirely satisfied by her explanation, but would hope that the bronzed giant might be able to remain in concealment without discovery. A chill raced the length of her spine as she tried not to think what punishment would be hers were he found and captured. And as for his fate—she could only shudder.

When some little while had passed, Sirena waved and called to her servants, also Mauria, that they had swum enough for the time being. The queen spoke softly to one of the mermaids nearest her, and as they returned to the opening in the cliff, the native girl was aware one of the mermaids followed close behind her. Presently they had reached the amphitheatre.

Mauria slipped on her sandals. Meanwhile, Sirena dismissed the three mermaids, and guest and host were left alone. Remaining seated, the native girl looked at Sirena who was reclining upon her side, facing her guest. It was difficult to define the peculiar expression in her eyes. She smiled presently and the girl was relieved.

The queen recollected the brief report the two mermaids had made to her concerning the morning's inspection of the island shore.

"Mauria, you told me that you came alone to this island in a canoe," she said to her guest. "What did you do with the canoe?"

The native girl did not know for what reason Sirena desired knowledge of the canoe, but she immediately guessed Bantan must have concealed it in the foliage, for had the two patrolling mermaids seen it, they would surely have mentioned this to their queen.

"Knowing it might be seen were I to leave it upon the edge of the beach," she answered, "I concealed it in the foliage."

The mermaid queen nodded.

"That was the natural thing to do," she agreed, studying Mauria for a long moment. And then, breaking the short silence, she added: "Tell me more about the island from which you came. Also tell me more about this Dr. Zarwood who is known as The Great One. He must be a brilliant man from what you have previously mentioned."

The native girl smiled and did as she was bade, and Sirena became an intelligent listener. She interrupted only when some detail was not entirely clear to her; afterward she would smilingly nod and importune the girl to continue with her narrative.

Mauria had been aware of the absence of the three mermaids who had been swimming with them, and because of their absence she was becoming uneasy. She entertained the feeling they were searching for the bronzed giant—and in this surmisal she was not incorrect.

CHAPTER V

Silent Watchers

WHEN BANTAN SAW SIRENA beckon to the swimmers to return to the opening in the cliff, he regretted he had not been able to signal to Mauria. He was positive that she must have seen him; but, too, he had noted the queen's attention being centered in his direction, and he had reason to believe she was suspicious that all was not as it should be.

The bronzed giant remained near the edge of the cliff, alerted for the possible reappearance of the mermaids. Within a few minutes he saw three of them come into view from the opening into which they had disappeared with Mauria. They were swimming beneath the surface. So clear the water was, the watcher could easily discern their glistening bodies with the aid of the sunlight that penetrated the translucent depths.

About thirty yards from the opening they surfaced. Two of them turned to the left while the third to the right. Their intentions now became clear to the young giant. They swam to the rocks to each side and went ashore in their slithering manner.

Bantan remained just long enough to be aware of what they intended, and he was not long wondering. Using their hands, they were hurriedly mounting the inclining rocky surface toward the cliff's summit. Without delay, the watcher quit the immediate vicinity, and presently reached the concealment of a luxuriant clump of ferns which were all of six feet in height. From his vantage place he had an excellent opportunity of seeing the mermaids when they would appear without being seen.

Within another minute he saw one come into view on the right side of the cliff, and within moments the other two appeared upon the opposite side. They nodded to each other and, slithering about the short grass, appeared to study it.

Whether Bantan's sandaled footprints could be detected is problematical. But as he watched the mermaids while they moved about he marvelled at the manner they did so. Intermittently one or another would pause in her searching and, half arising, would look about the immediate vicinity with studying eyes. But at last the mermaids gave up their seemingly futile search. Approaching the edge of the cliff they poised momentarily and in turn dived into the water below.

When the last had disappeared from view, the bronzed giant hurried from his place of concealment and, peering cautiously over the edge, was just in time to see the last of them disappear within the opening beneath from which they had previously appeared. He nodded and assumed they were to report to their queen what they had discovered. Lying upon the edge of the cliff, he continued to watch the openings beneath as though momentarily expecting a reappearance of mermaids.

⚡   ⚡   ⚡

Mauria was relieved when the three mermaids returned to the amphitheatre where she had been narrating events upon Mandoes Island to the queen. Sirena raised a hand and bade the native girl desist speaking for the time being. When they had drawn close, the one named Pegra looked first at the guest, then spoke to the queen.

"Upon the cliff's summit we are agreed that there are footprints in the short grass," she announced. "They were made either by Mauria, or someone else. We saw no one, however."

Sirena looked intently at her guest. Although a slight smile touched her lips, her hazel eyes did not betray her, noting as she did there was the appearance of concern in Mauria's eyes.

"I wanted to make sure that no one was on the summit of the cliff, as you suspected," she said in a mollifying tone. "The footprints in the short grass must have been yours made on the previous sun."

The native girl smiled in apparent relief.

"Yes, of course," she agreed. "I walked about considerably before I dived into the water."

Pegra looked briefly at the queen, then at Mauria, but her expression was blank. Then Sirena smiled to the three mermaids and dismissed them with the wave of a hand. As they turned and departed, the queen smiled to the native girl.

"Tell me more about Mandoes Island and The Great One," she urged. "I find it very interesting to learn of other people and how they live. And don't forget to tell me more about Bantan. He must have been very interesting to know—while he lived."

Mauria smiled weakly and nodded in acquiescence as she resumed her narration to the interest of Queen Sirena. For a few minutes she spoke more of Dr. Zarwood and his experiments, but she became aware her host appeared uninterested in that subject.

"Perhaps speaking of Bantan would be more interesting to you?" she suggested.

At once the queen's dull eyes brightened.

"Bantan!" she murmured. "Just the sound of that name makes my heart beat faster." And then she shook her head sadly. "It is unfortunate and unthinkable that he lost his life," she deplored. After a brief pause she added hopefully: "Would it be impossible that he could have survived? After all, he must have been a strong swimmer and, unknown to you, might have managed to swim to this island. Tell me once again in more detail just what happened after the monstrous fish upset the canoe."

Mauria repressed the chill that sought to fasten upon her spine. That Sirena was suspicious there was no doubt, and she realized she must in some way convince the queen that Bantan was non-existent.

"It was nearly dark when the monstrous fish upset our canoe," she explained. "When I came to the surface my first thought was of the others. Although I could see no one swimming about I shouted in vain. While I was convinced presently that I alone had survived, my next thought was to right the overturned canoe which floated nearby. I swam to it and managed to do so. In the fast-setting darkness I saw one of the paddles floating near at hand. With my hands I paddled the canoe toward it and retrieved it from the water. Afterwards, I continued to call out to my friends until long after darkness had enveloped the water, but no one answered me. By that time I naturally assumed they must have been knocked unconscious and did not rise to the surface. With tears in my eyes I looked up at the stars, remembering the course we had been following with them as our guide, and I paddled for a long while until I was so wearied that I could hardly hold the paddle in my hands. Then I slept the rest of the night. In the morning I sighted this island and continued paddling, not knowing who lived here and whether they would be friend or enemy."

With her peroration, Mauria looked appealingly at the queen, and she rubbed her eyes with her knuckles.

"It makes me sad to even think of the horror of that night," she concluded.

Sirena nodded thoughtfully and a faint smile touched her lips.

"I'm sorry that I asked you to repeat what happened," she said in a soft voice, shaking her head sadly. But a sudden light appeared in her eyes at the next moment. "But, it is possible that Bantan was only stunned and later revived. It is even possible that he might swim to this island. Who knows?"

The native girl shook her head despairingly.

"I would not even dare to hope that he lives," she murmured.

"Perhaps that would be hoping for too much, Mauria," the queen agreed.

A short silence prevailed. The native girl longed for the sunshine outside. She was feeling somewhat depressed by the artificially lighted amphitheatre.

"Sirena, although I am considered your guest," she said, "may I have your permission to go outside in the sunshine? You may have several handmaidens accompany me, if you wish. I assure you I have no desire to escape, but away from the sunshine makes me feel depressed."

The queen pursed her lips and masqueraded any suspicion that was aroused within her.

"Of course, Mauria," she said with a nod. "I'll have two of my handmaidens accompany you. They do not get out into the sunshine as much as they should."

When she had spoken, Sirena clapped her hands smartly. Within a few moments Pegra slithered within view.

"What are your wishes, O queen?" she asked, lowering her head in obeisance.

"Pegra, summon two of the handmaidens to accompany our guest out in the sunshine," she said.

"As you wish, O queen," the mermaid murmured, and with a perfunctory bow departed.

With the passing of a couple of minutes, while Sirena and Mauria talked pleasantly, two mermaids slithered into the amphitheatre. Both were dark-haired and had the appearance of being strong if one were to judge their powerful arms and broad shoulders. They looked expectantly at the queen for her instructions.

"You will accompany our guest out in the sunshine," Sirena said to them. "She has promised to make no attempt to escape."

"Yes, O queen," the two mermaids uttered simultaneously.

They nodded to Mauria who arose to her feet and smiled her gratefulness to the queen. The three left the amphitheatre without delay.

As though awaiting their departure, Pegra then appeared and approached Sirena who beckoned her to speak.

The mermaid told of the two different sets of imprints in the short grass upon the cliff's summit, one being larger than the other.

"The larger ones must be a male's, my queen," Pegra added convincingly.

Sirena nodded and her hazel eyes became filled with bitterness in the knowledge Mauria had in all probability lied to her about being alone when she came to the island.

"Go with Beta to where the canoe must be hidden," she bade. "Bring back what you find within it."

Pegra nodded and bowed.

"We will do as you command, O Queen," she answered.

Within a few minutes two mermaids were slithering along a tunnel that branched from the first and presently emerged at its opening to the left of the cliff. Quickly they entered the water and were soon in the calm surface beyond the surf, and speedily swam in the direction of their objective.

✓   ✓   ✓

Bantan patiently watched and waited for mermaids to reappear in the cove. It was not long before two of them did so and swam leisurely upon the surface. He was surprised as he saw a peculiar weapon now sheathed at their waist on the right side, the end of which trailed to the fins at the extremity of their body. It was some four feet in length with three sharp prongs on one end. The mermaids did not devote any attention to the summit of the cliff, but even so the watcher continually moved so as to remain out of sight and yet manage to keep them within view. What they were doing, armed as they were, puzzled him, but presently he was to understand.

The tell-tale evidence that a shark had entered the cove was then apparent. One of the mermaids espied the triangular fin cutting the surface and she called her companion's attention to her discovery. The mermaid swiftly cleaved the water with her glistening arms to join the other. Both now withdrew the trident sheathed at their waist, and with the handle tightly clutched, they circled about the shark and prodded it so that it continued toward the cliff. Whatever efforts the shark made to avoid its present course, to no avail were its attempts, for the two mermaids relentlessly prodded with their weapons until the undersea monster had no choice but continue ahead of them.

It started to enter the opening that had been used most frequently, but a third mermaid, similarly armed and on guard there, discouraged the shark with the result it chose the next opening. The two mermaids in pursuit followed side by side and then disappeared from view.

Bantan marvelled at the bravery of the two mermaids. On second thought, he realized they must have been taught to trap sharks for reasons of their own, and he had to admit they were amazingly clever. He remained there, awaiting the reappearance of the two mermaids.

When some ten minutes had passed, he saw them reappear. The tridents of the two swimmers transfixed the now dead shark's head and tail, and thus they were towing and pushing the sea monster, leaving a trail of blood behind them. They passed into the next opening and were seen no more.

The bronzed giant was in a quandary what to do next. He wanted very much to rescue Mauria, but since she was not being punished and her status appeared that of a guest, he decided to further explore the small island to satisfy his curiosity that other than the mermaids it was uninhabited. And so he left the vicinity of the cliff and made his way beyond, coming at last to the beach and, keeping close to the foliage, with eyes ever roving and ears alert, he started to circumambulate the island shore.

He had just left the cliff's summit when Mauria and two mermaids appeared in view.

Knowing from past experience that island villages were invariably located near the edge of the foliage bordering the beach, Bantan hastened on his way. His nostrils sniffed the still air, for other than the sweetness of growing verdure, he would at once be alerted to the more acrid odor that a village would apprise him.

Occasionally he would pause to look backward at the curving shoreline. The last time he did so, he could no longer observe the cliff surrounding the cove. Ahead, as far as his vision would permit of the curving shoreline, only flotsam that the high tides bring littered the sandy beach strewn with occasional rocks. Sea gulls were to be seen at intervals as they glided in the warm air above the shore and some were out beyond the surf.

To Bantan's nostrils now came the acrid odor of a village nearby. He paused to sniff the vagrant breeze more carefully. Looking ahead, he was surprised that he saw no canoes drawn high up on the beach from the possible reach of a high tide. He thought it unusual that inhabitants of a village possessed no canoes. He proceeded on his way with more caution.

Some five minutes later he could see the first of the cone-shaped huts within the foliage, and he was disappointed at their shabby appearance. Some of the roofs had caved in, and the thatched walls of others revealed gaping holes as though some savage beast had forced an entry.

There were a dozen huts in all, and as near as the bronzed giant could determine not one of them had escaped the ravages of the elements. He entered a few of them through mere curiosity and the same desolate picture was presented inside each of them. From all appearances they had been unoccupied for some time.

Shaking his head in disgust, Bantan felt the dilapidated village would have been better reduced to ashes, and he was tempted to kindle a fire to this effect. However, he dispelled the thought, feeling as he did that Nature would soon complete the demolition of the unsightly huts that were scarcely habitable as they now stood. In a vague way he did wonder of the natives who had once constructed and occupied this apparently deserted village, and what had happened to them.

And so, feeling the village had not been recently inhabited, the bronzed giant did not bother to examine the ground that was more or less overgrown with vegetation.

For that reason he failed to observe the naked footprints that might have been detected had he resorted to more care. With a sigh of relief he presently passed beyond the outskirts and continued his way along the edge of the beach near the foliage's edge.

Unknown to Bantan while he had stood in the center of the dilapidated village, several pairs of aged eyes had watched him curiously from behind the concealment of a clump of ferns upon the outskirts bordering the island jungle. The owners of the watchful eyes remained motionless until the giant bronzed stranger finally passed through the village to the beach beyond. Only then did three extremely old men make an appearance.

They were clad only in a dirty loin cloth and their features were almost black. Sparse white hair covered their heads. When they walked, each was stooped with the weight of years they had lived. None possessed any teeth and their cheeks were sunken. They were thin, almost to a degree of emaciation. The apparent leader turned to his companions.

"A stranger has come to our island," he said. "It is our duty to report his presence to Sirena. She should reward us well. Let us lose no time going to her."

"Wait, Trebor," one of the others remonstrated in a high-pitched voice. "Don't you think we should trail the stranger to find out where he will go?"

Trebor merely squinted his bleary eyes and appeared to think. Then, after a few moments' hesitation, he shook his head.

"No, Troma," he said. "Sirena's handmaidens will be able to find the stranger no matter where he is." He turned to the other old man. "Isn't my plan best, Brona?" he asked.

The old man thus addressed merely nodded.

"You know best, Trebor," he said.

The leader then turned to Troma with a display of impatience.

"You always question me," he snapped. "Come, let us hurry to Sirena and be rewarded."

With his words Trebor turned to the narrow path that led through the island's interior and which had been travelled upon numerous occasions in the past so that Nature had failed to recover it with foliage. The other two old men followed in his footsteps.

In their simple minds the thought of added rations of fish was all that mattered—since food was all that they had to live for. They were too old to handle a canoe, had they one, and they were too feeble to fish, and fish they craved. Trebor was sure the mermaid queen would be exceedingly generous with the exchange of fish for the information he would bring her.

1 1 1

Meanwhile, Bantan resumed his way with no slightest inkling that he had been spied upon and his presence would be made known to the mermaid queen within a short while. Without any further matters of interest coming to his attention, he soon reached the place where his canoe was concealed. A glimpse into the clump of ferns assured him it had been undisturbed during his short absence.

The bronzed giant gathered some fruit and nuts from nearby and deposited them in the canoe. He then indulged in a brief swim before returning ashore and partaking of his noon day repast. While thus engaged, in his mind he tried to formulate a means of rescuing Mauria from the mermaids and thereafter they might resume their way to the ultimate goal of Marja Island. With a nod, he had to admit he missed Mauria's companionship; and knowing her as he did, he was sure she must miss him as well.

Bantan even considered risking a rash attack upon the mermaids in rescuing the native girl, but recollecting the weapons they had used to good advantage upon the shark made him realize they could be formidable foes should there be such occasion. And so he passed some while originating plans and discarding them almost immediately as impractical.

At last with a shake of his head the bronzed giant arose from the canoe, having decided to return to the cliff's summit and hope some unexpected development might rise that would give him the opportunity of rescuing Mauria. He parted the ferns as a matter of curiosity to look out at the expanse of water beyond the beach, and what he saw in the calmer water just beyond the gentle surf was reason for his wonder to be increased.

There were two mermaids looking in his direction, and they were talking in low voices. Then with a nod, they headed shoreward, allowing the gentle surf to carry them upon its bosom to the beach. When they had been deposited as far as the waves would carry them, Bantan saw that each was armed with a trident sheathed at their right side. One of the mermaids was dark-haired while the other was a blonde. In their sinuous manner, they slithered up the beach, their eyes scanning the sand.

The dark-haired mermaid was Pegra and her companion was Beta. The former called the attention of the other, and the watcher was certain they had discovered his footprints to the water's edge when he had indulged in a brief swim.

The two mermaids noted the direction from which the tell-tale footprints had come. They again conversed in low tones. In apparent agreement, they withdrew the tridents sheathed at their right sides, and with the weapon tightly clutched in their right hand, they continued up the beach in their slithering manner. Pegra was slightly in the lead. She was a trifle larger than Beta, and for that reason she was somewhat of a leader.

Although Bantan's right hand clutched the handle of his dagger, the act was more habit than design. At the approach of the two mermaids, he slowly backed away from the immediate vicinity, making as little noise as possible. Within a couple of minutes he reached the sanctuary of another smaller clump of ferns and concealed himself. From this new hiding place he could easily obtain a view of the cached canoe.

Almost immediately he saw the two mermaids appear and their eyes revealed their surprise as they looked within the canoe. They conversed in low tones. Pegra reached within the water craft and withdrew one of the paddles. She handed it to Beta, then reached in for the other. Handing this also to her companion, she again reached within the canoe and this time brought forth the bow and the several arrows that were there. The two mermaids examined them with surprise. They again conversed in low tones which the sharp ears of the eavesdropper could not overhear. Then without further loss of time the two mermaids departed, taking the two paddles and the bow and several arrows with them.

By the time Bantan reached the cached canoe and parted the surrounding ferns, the two mermaids had reached the water's edge. They had resheathed their tridents. One held a paddle and the bow while the other possessed the arrows. With them clutched in their left hand they lost no time entering the gentle surf. Handicapped as each was, they experienced only slight difficulty swimming through the surf. In the calmer water beyond they headed ostensibly for the cove about half way around the island from their present position.

Bantan was loath to see the two paddles, also his bow and arrows being confiscated thusly. He debated the wisdom of challenging the two mermaids to regain possession of them. He realized were he to do so, he might have to slay them, and he disliked to slay a woman. He knew he could replace the paddles, bow and arrows in a short time if needs be when the time came. For the present, he turned and made his way through the island's interior to the cliff's summit.

CHAPTER VI

Mauria—A Prisoner

MAURIA AND THE TWO MERMAIDS accompanying her swam through the tunnel into the calm water of the cove. Looking to her left, the native girl indicated she would swim there. Her two guardians nodded, keeping close to her. Reaching the rocky ledge, the dark-skinned girl drew herself out of the water as the two mermaids also did, one upon each side of her.

Basking in the warm sunshine, Mauria wrung her wet hair and allowed it to trail over her shoulders. The two mermaids had ensconced themselves upon the dry rock and did likewise. For a few minutes while thus occupied the three were silent. Meanwhile, the native girl looked curiously at each of her companions in turn. Both were comely in appearance.

"What are your names?" she asked of them. "I am called Mauria."

The one upon her left smiled eagerly in apparent friendliness.

"I am Majane," she volunteered, then looked over to her companion.

The native girl then looked at the mermaid upon her right.

"And by what name are you called?" she asked.

No smile touched the lips of the mermaid. Though her features appeared a trifle sullen, her dark eyes were not unfriendly.

"I am called Ano," she answered.

Mauria smiled and drew a deep breath, holding it for a full minute.

"I like being out in the sun," she murmured as she uttered a deep sigh. "Do you both come out often?"

Ano looked at Majane expectantly. The latter smiled as she answered.

"Each morning Ano and I swim around the island. We are always hopeful we may find that male strangers have come during the night." She sighed as she added: "We are doomed to extinction unless males come to our island."

Mauria nodded with a sad smile.

"Yes, I know," she said. "Your queen told me about that. What happened to the males on this island that none are now living?"

Majane looked toward Ano.

"She is older than I," she explained to the native girl. "She can tell about that better."

Mauria looked at the mermaid upon her right. Her dark eyes appeared sorrowed in reflection of her thoughts. As she noted the native girl's attention, she shook her head sadly.

"I am not sure," she said. "It happened so suddenly that all of the females in the grotto were shocked, including myself. I had recently become a woman at that time, and there was a young male with whom I was deeply in love as he was with me. Once every thirteen moons all of the males left the island to make a pilgrimage to our sea god—Neptuna. They would be gone seven suns. It was a secret where they went and none were allowed to reveal even to their mates under pain of torture and death. All of the males had been gone for two suns when a terrible storm overcame this region. All of us waited in vain while we beseeched our sea god to send our males back to us. But none returned, nor was a single dead body found upon the island's shore. Since then our females have not known a male's love. Many committed suicide, being unable to live without a male. Those of us who survive have managed to do so. There is no more to tell."

Mauria sensed the silent grief that wracked Ano, and she was compassionate.

"I am sorry," she murmured, and with her words she rested a gentle hand upon the mermaid's shoulder.

Ano looked up at the native girl with suffering eyes, but a sad smile touched her lips.

Mauria then turned to Majane.

"You were too young to know and understand the meaning of love," she divined.

The mermaid nodded.

The native girl smiled in understanding.

"As a female I know what you mean," she said with a nod. "Upon the island where I lived many males were interested in me," she added a moment later. "I could have had my choice of any of the unmated ones. But in my mind I had created a 'dream man' who was all that a young female wanted to father her children." Mauria sighed deeply in fond remembrance of Bantan. "That day came when I first saw him and I felt my dreams had come true. I did not wait for him to tell me how desirable I was to him. I told him how desirable he was to me. But he had other matters on his mind at that time to bother with love.

"I did not give up hope, however, and later I again saw him. By this time he had fallen in love with a female of his own race. He was of white birth, though he had lived nearly his entire life in the tropics, and was as brown of skin as I was. That white female he loved died through her own father's evil doing. At a later time Bantan returned to the island and, in sparing his life from the female's father, he took me with him. Oh, how I loved just to be with him, and what I wouldn't have given that he would love me as I loved him! But," with a sorrowful shrug, "I saw him fall in love with another white-skinned female; and when she met her death, another, who looked very much like her, was next to be loved by Bantan. She, too, met her death—as—as did my 'dream male,' so I am no better off than you, Ano and Majane. I can well understand how both of you must feel not to know the love of a male."

While Mauria had been speaking, the dark eyes of the two mermaids glowed with intense interest, and their bosoms rose and fell to their emotions. But when the end of her narration had been reached, their hopeless apathy was openly revealed.

"Bantan—dead!" Ano and Majane uttered simultaneously in piteous tones.

The native girl appeared very sad. She rubbed the corners of her eyes with her knuckles. Looking at each mermaid, she merely nodded.

Ano and Majane shook their heads sadly and sighed deeply.

For some little while silence prevailed. Mauria looked out upon the calm surface beyond the gentle surf. A few sea gulls were gliding through the still air some distance above the water. Occasionally the native girl cast a fleeting glance at the cliff's summit, but she saw no sign of the bronzed giant she hoped might be there.

Now, as her eyes looked to her left again, her attention was alerted, for in the distance her sharp eyes caught the flash of wet, bare arms beyond the surf. Studying them carefully, she noted that there were two swimmers, also, that they were using only their right arms for propulsion through the water. Even so, they were making excellent progress under the circumstances.

Mauria looked quickly to Ano and Majane to see if they were aware of the two swimmers, but neither were.

Once again she cast a fleeting glance at the cliff's summit but no sight of Bantan was to be seen.

"I'm becoming hungry," she announced as she looked up at the sun, then glanced at each of the two mermaids. "Are you becoming hungry as well?"

Ano and Majane smiled and nodded. The native girl arose, giving a quick glance in the direction of the two swimmers.

"Shall we return?" she asked of her guardians.

Both mermaids were agreeable to Mauria's suggestion, and without further loss of time dived into the water and swam toward the opening through which they had come. Reaching the amphitheatre, they found Sirena preening her lustrous red hair. She greeted her guest and the two mermaids with a smile.

"Mauria said she was becoming hungry," Majane explained.

"I, too, am becoming hungry," the queen said, "so we can go into the dining room."

While they were partaking of their noonday meal, Mauria was apprehensive at thought of the two swimmers she had observed. As well, upon several occasions she had noticed Sirena staring at her in an odd manner; and whether it were suspicion she harbored in her mind, the native girl could not determine. She endeavored to appear guiltless, but could not deny the chill that sought to fasten upon her spine.

The last course of the meal was just consumed when Pegra and Beta slithered into the dining room. As Mauria looked in their direction and saw what each clutched in their hands she experienced a slight qualm of weakness overcome her momentarily.

The queen's surprise appeared quite genuine. With an exclamation of delight she left the table and slithered toward the two mermaids. She accepted one of the paddles

Pegra handed her and turned to the native girl questioningly.

"What have we here?" she asked as she examined the paddle from one end to the other.

Mauria arose from the table and approached Sirena.

"That is a paddle," she explained. "It is used to make a canoe move over the water."

The queen nodded in understanding.

"But there are two of them," she remarked, noting the one Beta held.

The native girl smiled as she answered.

"I retrieved both of them from the water. There is always the possibility that one might break. Bantan and Tama were both paddling the canoe when the monstrous fish upset it."

Sirena nodded, for what her guest had said was reasonable. She placed the paddle upon the floor at her side. She turned to Pegra again and accepted the bow which was being extended.

"And what is this called?" she asked, turning to Mauria. She held it awkwardly by the bowstring, and was curiously examining it.

"That belonged to Bantan," was the answer. "It is called a bow. Without the arrows it is useless."

"Arrows?" the queen questioned.

Mauria indicated the slender, feather-tipped rods Beta held in one hand.

The queen placed the bow alongside the paddle and reached for one of the arrows. She noted the pointed end and that the other had a small tuft of feathers attached to it. Sirena looked wonderingly at the slender rod and then at the bow. She looked questioningly up at her guest.

"Do you know how they are used?" she asked.

The native girl smiled and nodded.

"Would you like me to show you?" she inquired.

The queen nodded. She reached for the bow and handed it to Mauria and also extended to her the arrow.

The native girl placed the tufted end of the arrow upon the bowstring near its center, the upper end of the slender shaft alongside her left forefinger and thumb which were curled about the bow. Then her right forefinger and thumb drew the string back as far as she dared. A rapt silence filled the dining room as all eyes watched her. She looked at the queen.

"Do you wish me to release the arrow?" she asked.

Sirena nodded.

Mauria indicated the wall with a nod of her head. With a twang of the bowstring the arrow sped across the room to strike the bare wall where the force of the impact broke the slender shaft.

One of the mermaids slithered across the room and picked up the broken arrow and returned it to the queen for her inspection. Utter silence prevailed as the awed eyes of the mermaids watched.

Sirena looked at the arrow in curiosity and then lifted her eyes to the native girl.

"What did Bantan use bows and arrows for?" she asked.

"Against beasts that were savage upon the island from which we escaped," was Mauria's reply.

The queen nodded. She could easily understand how potent the weapon might be used against humans as well.

"You use the bow and arrow very well," she remarked. "Bantan must have taught you."

A nod was the answer.

Sirena reached for the bow which Mauria handed to her. The queen's warm eyes seemingly caressed the weapon.

"Bantan must have been a wonderful male!" she exclaimed. As she spoke she looked up at her guest for assurance.

"He was, Sirena," the native girl declared fervently. "Oh, yes, he was."

The queen shook her head sorrowfully.

"And to think he is dead!"

Mauria shook her head disconsolately. She looked from one mermaid to another, all merely staring at her blankly. But Sirena's hazel eyes were not blank, for a slight narrowing of her lids was to be observed. She was looking up at her guest intently until she caught her attention.

"Who was with you when you came to this island, Mauria?" she demanded. "Do not tell me again that you came alone. Larger imprints of sandals along with your smaller ones have been detected in the short grass upon the cliff's summit. Was your companion Bantan?"

The native girl's heart stopped beating for an instant as she listened to the queen's altered tone of voice in accusation. As she looked about her, she saw that four of the mermaids surrounded her. Pegra and Beta's right hand clutched the handle of the trident sheathed at their right side. Ano and Majane, although unarmed, crouched menacingly. Mauria's shoulders slumped, realizing there was nothing she could say to extricate herself from the precarious position she now was in.

"You have nothing to say?" the queen demanded. "I trusted you and was becoming fond of you. I could never be a friend to one who has lied to me."

Mauria closed her eyes and clasped her hands tightly together. From the depths of her heart the one question was imminent:

"Where was Bantan, and why hadn't he rescued her?"

She now opened her eyes and looked dispassionately at the queen, for she expected no mercy.

Sirena was smiling in self-satisfaction, but her hazel eyes were blazing with bitterness.

"I have nothing further to add," she said in a voice that was chilling. "Three old natives who live upon the opposite end of the island have reported to me having seen your companion as he passed through their village. They were well rewarded for the information they brought to me."

Mauria felt a numbness overcome her with the realization that Bantan had been seen. In hopeless apathy she merely looked at Sirena who was now gloating because of the native girl's palpable anguish.

"You are no longer to be considered a guest," the queen declared. "From now on you are to be considered a prisoner until I can decide the just fate you deserve for having lied to me."

The native girl realized it would avail her nothing to make an attempt to escape. She now knew when she had the bow and arrow in hand would have been the appropriate time to have done so; but then she had been considered a guest. Her head lowered in submission to the fate that had been decreed her.

"Pegra and Beta," the queen then commanded, "escort the prisoner to the dungeon of darkness to await her fate."

The two mermaids withdrew their tridents and approached Mauria. Before they led the prisoner away, Sirena's eyes narrowed moreso.

"And, Mauria," she jeered, "know while you are a prisoner, the island will be carefully searched for your companion—and have no fear—he will be found!"

A shudder wracked the native girl and she drew a long breath, hoping in her heart that Bantan would be able to evade any searchers.

And then Pegra, with Beta at her side, motioned in what direction to proceed while they slithered behind her.

"You will find being a prisoner, Mauria," Pegra said in a sibilant voice, "not so pleasant as a guest."

The native girl made no response.

"What do you suppose our queen will do with her?" Beta asked her companion.

The dark-haired mermaid shrugged.

"Who knows?" was her enigmatic answer.

Through a phosphorescent-lighted corridor the three proceeded on their way for a few minutes when another corridor was reached.

"Continue left," Pegra instructed the prisoner.

Mauria did so with the two mermaids close upon her heels. Within a short while they had come to the apparent end of the corridor. There was an opening some three feet in diameter at the base of the wall alongside which a huge stone rested. The prisoner halted and turned to her guards.

Pegra indicated the opening.

"Crawl in there," she said.

The native girl went down upon her hands and knees. Looking within, Stygian darkness greeted her questing eyes. The air she breathed was foul and musty. Knowing there was nothing to be gained by begging for mercy, Mauria crawled within the opening. The moment she had done so, the large stone upon the outside was rolled across the aperture, and then beyond a question of doubt the truth was impinged upon her mind of her utter hopelessness. She doubted that even Bantan would be able to find her were he to search for her.

Arising slowly to her feet in the pitch darkness, the native girl's first thought was to explore the dungeon. With one hand stretched before her, and the other trailing the rough wall, she started along its side, her footsteps being tentative for fear of striking some jagged rock or encountering a bottomless pit. She could hear nothing except the loud thumping of her heart against the wall of her bosom and her rasping breath as it passed through her flared nostrils.

The wall ended some eight feet from the barred opening, and then she groped slowly along the farther wall for about the same distance until she came to its end. Within a few moments she reached her starting place where the large stone barred the opening.

She slumped to the floor upon her knees. With desperation she placed her hands against the barring stone and pushed against it with all her strength; but for all the good it did she might have attempted to push against solid rock. Her efforts did not move the large stone an iota.

Mauria now seated herself, and as the futility of her efforts were more fully realized, she covered her face with her hands and the tears came—tears of utter hopelessness.

"Oh, Bantan!" she moaned. "Why didn't you rescue me before? Why—why—why? I've missed you so. If we were together even now I wouldn't be so afraid—but alone—"

CHAPTER VII

Unexpected Rescue

BY THE TIME Bantan reached the cliff's summit the three old men, who had seen and reported his presence to the mermaid queen, were now returning to their dilapidated village. Each fairly staggered under the weight of dried fish that had been their reward for the information they had rendered, and many were the rests required before they finally reached their destination.

And so it was, the bronzed giant reached his objective without such knowledge and, because of it, Mauria was now a prisoner in a dungeon of despair. He upbraided himself somewhat because he had silently witnessed two mermaids remove the two paddles from the canoe, also his bow and arrows. The fact that they knew where the canoe was concealed made him wonder if it would be safe to sleep there during the coming night. He realized he could always remove it to another hiding place, and this was decided upon.

Drawing close to the edge of the cliff, Bantan went down upon his hands and knees and peered about the cove, but he could see no mermaids swimming in the water beneath. For some little while he remained there watchfully, then at last backed from the edge. Arising to his feet, he vaguely wondered what lay upon the other side of the cove. The thought that a tunnel might exist was not an impossibility, and perhaps it would be a means of gaining admittance to the grotto's interior without being challenged by guards as he would unquestionably be were he to try and enter through the openings at the base of the cliff. It would do no harm to investigate, and this he did.

Cautiously looking about as though expectant of being apprehended, the bronzed giant's right hand was close to the handle of his dagger as he crossed the short grass to the left side of the cliff. Drawing near its edge, he looked down the rocky slope to the base which was several feet from the water's edge. To his surprise he saw the opening which evidently led to a tunnel. From the distance that spanned, in the short stretch of sand leading from the opening to the water's edge, his keen eyes noted markings that would indicate something had been dragged either to or from the opening at the base of the cliff.

Without hesitation Bantan went down the slope to one side of the opening. In the stretch of sand from it to the water's edge he saw more clearly the markings of creatures that had slithered from the water to disappear into the tunnel. His keen eyes easily determined they were made very recently—perhaps by the two mermaids who had confiscated the two paddles and his bow and arrows.

Having satisfied his curiosity, the bronzed giant approached the opening of the tunnel which was about five feet in height and a little more than half that distance in width. His delicate nostrils sniffed as he stooped and peered within the increasing darkness that enveloped the area a short distance from where he stood. Scanning the walls and ceiling, he saw that they were fairly smooth and a trifle damp. The floor was sandy at first as he continued into the tunnel in a stooped position, but it changed to rock, and he was grateful in the increasing darkness that no loose rocks strewed his pathway.

When a few minutes had passed, Bantan wondered at the soft glow that radiated from the bisecting wall some distance ahead. Remembering the large room he had looked at through an aperture in the dividing wall on the previous day, he had the impression a similar condition must exist there. His alertful ears heard no sound that might issue from human throats. As he continued on his way uninterruptedly he also wondered vaguely at the whereabouts of the mermaids.

The only reason he could assume for the opening in the tunnel being unguarded, as several of the others leading from the cove were, was that little danger could be anticipated from this avenue since no water flowed into it. This nullified the possibility of sharks, octopii, or moray eels might enter and lurk in the darkness for the opportunity of victimizing an unwary passerby.

In due time the bronzed giant reached the end of the tunnel where it was bisected by the passageway lighted by the phosphorescence in the rock. He could stand erect here, the ceiling being a foot above his head. He paused momentarily, looking to the left and then right, undecided which direction to proceed. He noted a sharp bend in the right side a short distance from where he stood, while the left continued almost straight for a hundred feet or more. At once he became alerted. From beyond that point his sharp ears heard echoing voices. Looking to his right, he appreciated the short distance to the sharp bend.

Without a moment's hesitation he sped along the smooth rock floor until he reached this vantage place. Peering around it in the direction from which he had raced, in another moment he saw the first of the mermaids appear in their slithering manner that amazed the watcher because of the ground they covered so rapidly. Counting them as they rounded the bend, he was aware there were ten. His sharp eyes detected the trident that each clasped in her right hand. There was no question in his mind that theirs was a hunting expedition, and he grimly was aware that in all probability he was the quarry that was sought.

Bantan looked to his rear and saw that the phosphores-cent-lighted passageway continued somewhat erratically to another sharp bend a short distance from where he stood. He weighed his chances of reaching it should the armed mermaids continue in his direction. He realized only too well he would not be able to return to the dark-ened tunnel leading outside without being detected. With a shrug he again peered around the sharp bend to deter-mine what course the mermaids would take. Very little conversation was now heard, and the passage of their bodies over the smooth floor made an eerie, swishing sound with an occasional metallic clank of a trident striking the rock over which they slithered or the wall to which one came too close.

The silent watcher held his breath as the leading mer-maid neared the entrance of the darkened tunnel, and as he saw her turn and slither into it, he exhaled with unutterable relief. The fact the expedition was headed outside convinced the young giant of their intentions. When a few minutes had passed, the last of the mermaids had disappeared from view and the passage of their bodies was reduced to a low, murmuring sound.

Listening intently from the direction the mermaids had first made their appearance, and hearing no sound that would indicate others were following in the wake of their predecessors, the bronzed giant quickly moved to the edge of the darkened tunnel in which they had gone. The light from the opening at the end enabled him to discern the slithering forms and hear the occasional metallic clank of a trident coming in contact with rock. Now he turned, satisfied that he had nothing to worry about them for the present at least.

Bantan curbed the desire to investigate the direction from which the mermaids had appeared in preference to explore further the passageway to learn more about it and where it terminated. Without further delay he turned and continued on his way, pausing frequently to cast a fleeting, backward glance to be assured no one followed in his wake.

Within a few minutes after passing the sharp bend, the bronzed giant saw that the tunnel terminated shortly ahead. A large round rock arrested his attention, and he wondered if it merely barred the continuation of the passageway. As he confronted it, his eyes quickly ascertained that it could be moved, and he did not minimize his strength as not being capable of doing so. He braced his shoulder against the large stone and pushed upon it. It moved without difficulty along the wall, revealing the aperture it had concealed.

In another moment he stooped and peered within the darkened opening. His delicate nostrils were at once apprised of a familiar scent that his common sense refused to accept as proof. But at the next moment he heard a sharply indrawn breath and then his amazed eyes saw tear-streaked features surrounded by dark, lustrous hair framed in the opening. At the same instant of recognition, his name was uttered in a tone of ineffable relief.

"Bantan!"

The bronzed giant moved back from the opening as Mauria crawled out upon her hands and knees. At the moment he straightened with a gentle smile, the native girl likewise arose to her feet. Before he could register any disapproval, she flung her arms about his neck and clung to him tightly, uttering soft moans of happiness.

"Oh, Bantan," she murmured, "how did you know I was a prisoner and was confined in a dungeon of despair?"

"I didn't know, Mauria," he answered truthfully. "I had the feeling that you were a guest of the mermaid queen. For that reason I had been exploring the island, thinking you were in no danger."

"Oh, I missed you so!" the girl murmured, pressing her cheek to his chest. "Didn't you miss me as well?"

His arms had gone about the native girl.

"Of course I missed you," he assured her, resting his cheek against her mass of soft hair. "I wouldn't be human if I hadn't. After all, we have been through a lot of adventures together."

"I'd be happy to go through them again, Bantan," she declared fervently, "knowing you and I would be together."

The bronzed giant could make no answer to this expressed devotion upon the girl's part, but one of his hands tightened a trifle about her shoulders.

"Tell me," he then said. "What happened that you became a prisoner after being a guest?"

The native girl unlocked her arms from about Bantan's neck, and his dropped from her shoulders. She looked fearfully to one side of his blocking body and her apprehensive eyes swept the length of the passageway.

"Is it safe that we remain here?" she asked as her eyes met his anxiously.

"We should be safe for awhile, Mauria," he assured her. "Just before I discovered you I saw ten of the mermaids armed with weapons pass through a tunnel to go outside."

"They are going to search for you, Bantan!" she exclaimed.

"I suspected as much," he said with a convinced nod.

"Sirena, the queen, told me that you had been seen by three old natives in their village upon the other side of the island," she added. "They hurried to her with the information. All the while I was a guest I had told the queen that I had come alone to this island." She smiled faintly as she concluded: "I didn't want her to know that you had come with me. I had told her that you drowned."

Bantan shrugged but a gentle smile touched his lips.

"And just a short while ago I saw two mermaids take the two paddles and my bow and arrows from the canoe," he admitted.

"Yes, the mermaids brought them to the queen," the girl rejoined. "She asked me what they were and how they were used. It was after I told her that she informed me what the three old natives had told her. Because I had lied to her about you, she then condemned me as a prisoner to languish in a dungeon of despair until she had decided what my fate would be."

The bronzed giant appeared to be thinking of a grave matter, for his lips tightened.

"Come, Mauria," he then said, "let's get out of here. Our first concern is our canoe. Without it we cannot leave this island. In all probability the mermaids will have guards posted about it until I return; and while I admit having no paddle is somewhat of a handicap, it wouldn't take me long to fashion another."

The native girl smiled warmly and reached for his left hand with her right, clasping it in hers.

"Let's go, Bantan," she urged. "The sooner I'm outside the happier I'll feel."

With his dagger drawn and clutched in his right hand, the bronzed giant led the way along the phosphorescent-lighted passageway to the darkened tunnel which led outside.

"This is where I saw the mermaids going a short while ago," he told the girl.

She shook her head, but a slight smile touched her lips and her luminous dark eyes spoke more eloquently than her subsequent words.

"As long as I am with you I fear nothing, Bantan," she murmured.

A slight smile touched his lips as he entered the darkening tunnel. Wordlessly the bronzed giant and the native girl hurried through it to appear presently at its opening. He paused and looked to his left along the strip of beach, then allowing his eyes to stray beyond the gentle surf, but no sight of the mermaids was to be glimpsed.

"We'll go the cliff's summit, Mauria," he said. "From there we'll continue through the island's interior in the direction where our canoe is cached."

A nod from the girl was her agreement that what he suggested met with her approval. As they went up the incline Bantan's eyes studied it for recent signs of the mermaids having passed this way, but there appeared to be none. Within a few minutes they reached the top of the embankment with eyes darting in all directions. Relief was apparent upon their features to observe that all was well. Without further loss of time, with Bantan in the lead and Mauria close behind him, they sought the pathway which they had first followed. At the earliest opportunity and a suitable sapling was found, he paused to cut it with his dagger and trimmed the small branches from it. Handing it to the girl, he smiled.

"Now, you, too, are armed, Mauria," he said.

She accepted the improvised spear with smiling thanks and they continued their way without further pause. They hurried at first, but in due time when they drew nearer to where the canoe was cached, the bronzed giant turned to the native girl and cautioned her to silence.

"We are near where the canoe is concealed," he whispered.

Standing motionless, each listened intently. From the direction where the canoe was hid, they heard voices, indicating some of the mermaids were stationed there.

Mauria nodded as she heard the different voices.

"There are at least three of them on guard," she murmured.

Bantan nodded as he looked up at the sun. Late afternoon was at hand and within a couple more hours darkness would settle.

"Before it becomes dark they may leave," he whispered.

The girl nodded hopefully.

The minutes passed and the voices of the mermaids were to be heard intermittently, but not distinctly. The bronzed giant was becoming a trifle impatient. He caught the native girl's attention and he nodded meaningly in the direction of the voices near the shore.

"Remain here," he whispered. "I'm going to satisfy my curiosity and listen to what they are talking about."

"Be careful, Bantan," she cautioned.

He nodded. As silent as a ghost he moved in the direction of the voices while Mauria, with left hand pressing the vicinity of her heart, watched him with apprehension that some slight sound might be made to attract the attention of their enemies, for the mermaids could not be considered anything but. Yard after yard Bantan neared his objective, and clearer became the voices so that he could understand what was being said. Through an open patch in the foliage he could see the three mermaids stationed at the edge of the beach. He noticed, too, that they had drawn the canoe from its place of concealment for some reason of their own. As near as he could determine, the canoe had not been damaged in any way.

One of the mermaids addressed their apparent leader with weariness to be detected in her tones as well as her features revealing this.

"How long must we remain here, Pegra?" she asked.

"Our queen would be displeased should we fail to capture and return with Bantan, Delo," was the answer.

"Maybe the others with Beta may capture and bring him to the queen," was Delo's hopeful rejoinder.

"If such is so," the third mermaid added, "I hope the queen will share him with us and not keep him entirely to herself. Oh, how I have longed for the day when I might be held in a male's arms and loved."

"Hush, Ela," Pegra admonished. "You have lived all these past moons without a male's love. Surely you can continue to do so. Isn't the love our queen gives us enough to satisfy you?"

"She is very good to all of us," Ela admitted. "But I long so much to have babies to care for. Our queen cannot give us babies by her love."

"You shouldn't think the way you do and speak of it, Ela," Pegra said in bitter tones. "What would our queen think were she to know how you feel and speak?"

"But I can't help it if such thoughts overpower me at times," the mermaid protested.

"At least you shouldn't speak of them," was the begrudging answer. "All of us have thoughts at times which would be displeasing to our queen—were she to know of them."

"Then I alone am not the only one who has such thoughts," Ela uttered with relief.

Pegra studied the hapless mermaid for a long moment, then in compassion slithered over to Ela's side and placed a gentle hand upon her head. The mermaid looked up with anguished eyes and held Pegra's attention for a long moment. What she read in those dark eyes was what she wanted to know. She reached for the leader's other hand and pressed its back to her lips and tears formed in her gray eyes. Then she pressed the palm of the hand to the left side of her heaving bosom and held it there.

"I understand, Pegra," she murmured chokingly. "I understand."

Pegra shook her head as she removed her hand from Ela's bosom and the other from her head. She turned about almost abruptly as though ashamed of her weakness.

"Come," she said peremptorily, "let us return with the hope Beta has been more successful trapping Bantan than we were."

Picking up her trident, she slithered along the beach toward the water's edge. With adoration in her doe-like gray eyes, Ela followed close behind while the third, Delo, brought up the rear. In a few moments all three were drawing themselves through the gentle surf to the calmer water beyond.

With the departure of the three mermaids, a slightly puzzled Bantan turned toward where the native girl was concealed a short distance from him.

"Come, Mauria," he softly called to her. "The mermaids are now swimming in the surf."

Quickly the girl joined the bronzed giant. At his side, parting the fern fronds, they watched the mermaids now swimming in the calmer water beyond.

Presently Mauria heaved a deep sigh. She rested a warm hand upon Bantan's shoulder. He looked at her in silent wonder.

A lovely smile enwreathed the comely native girl's lips and her dark eyes glowed happily.

"Let's hope we have seen the last of them," she murmured.

The bronzed giant removed his eyes from the girl's and looked again out at the surf.

"Believe me when I tell you again how I regret poor Nulu isn't in my place," Mauria said softly. "Loving you hopelessly as I do, and knowing how impossible my love is, I realize how much happier you would be were I Nulu."

A rueful expression overcame Bantan's features. He closed his eyes for a long moment and his lips tightened. Watching him, the native girl understood the tension that he was undergoing.

"Forgive me, Bantan," she murmured compassionately. "If I have said anything to cause you pain, I am truly sorry."

His eyes opened and the tightness of his lips was relieved as he looked down into the native girl's troubled dark eyes now filled with moisture. Then he smiled gently and his arm went about her shoulder.

"You have said nothing to cause me pain, Mauria," he assured her. He then shifted his eyes to the sun hovering above the western horizon. "We have just time to gather fruit and nuts for our evening meal. And perhaps I might find wood suitable to fashion a paddle. We must not remain here another day if possible."

"Whatever you suggest, Bantan," she said smilingly, "always finds me agreeable."

CHAPTER VIII

A Merciful Man

BANTAN AND MAURIA gathered fruit and nuts within a few minutes from nearby. No growing wood that was feasible to fashion a paddle was found, however. Returning to the canoe, they ate their evening meal while they talked in low voices.

"Since the mermaids know where our canoe is located," the bronzed giant was saying, "it must be moved to another place."

The native girl nodded.

"Had we our paddles," he added, "I would even consider leaving this island at once. Each day that we remain, now that we know who inhabits it, will be one of constant danger of being captured by the mermaids."

The girl shuddered.

"That I do not wish for you or me," she remarked.

"If only they hadn't taken our paddles," he murmured, shaking his head regretfully. "And I watched them doing so."

Mauria could only shrug her shapely shoulders.

When they had eaten, what fruit and nuts remained was placed within the canoe. The sun now was about a third concealed by the western waterline. Bantan gripped the bow and nodded to the native girl.

"We'll drag the canoe to the water," he said. "When it can be floated, I'll push it."

"I'll help," Mauria cheerfully volunteered.

Since the surf was gentle, little difficulty was experi-

86

enced pushing the canoe, and when the sun had completely slipped beneath the waterline, they were nearly a mile from their starting place. The bronzed giant then drew the canoe ashore and, with Mauria's help, dragged it to the edge of the foliage.

"There," he said with a sigh. "The three old natives occupy a poorly kept village not far from where we are; but I don't believe they will bother us. I doubt if they venture outside their huts with night so near."

The native girl seated herself alongside the canoe, resting her back against it and looked appealingly at Bantan. He was looking out at the broad expanse of ocean in the settling darkness, and then without a word seated himself at the girl's side. With a shy smile one of Mauria's hands sought his as it rested at his side nearest her.

"Do you know," she said, "that when I told Sirena about you her eyes glowed with interest. Since I told her you were dead, she even asked that if you had lived that you might have found favor in her, queen of the mermaids as she was and so different from the other women you had known. Would you?"

A soft laugh escaped his lips.

"She is beautiful," he acknowledged, "even though she is a mermaid. At one time the mermaids must have been of white origin. I wonder what was the reason that they are so different from other women—having no legs and feet?"

Mauria could only shake her head.

"I wouldn't know," she answered.

"If Dr. Zarwood only knew of their existence," he added, "I have reason to believe he would be very interested. Through the retrovider he created he might be able to learn of their origin."

The girl shuddered at the mention of The Great One's name.

"I hope we never see him again," she said.

"Poor Luane," he murmured presently. "Until her father injected the counteracting serum into her veins, she appeared no older than you, Mauria. And to think," he went on, "it was because I wanted him to inject the longevity serum into my veins to keep me forever young that has resulted in you and I being where we are now. Dr. Zarwood may be an evil man, but he is a very brilliant one as well."

Bantan looked down at Mauria as he finished speaking. In the settling darkness he could read the awe in her eyes.

"How would you like to remain forever young?" he asked.

She shrugged, and then a wistful smile touched her lips. Her hand released his and she linked her arm with his.

"Only if you were to remain forever young with me," she answered. And when he did not speak, she added: "I know I shouldn't say things like that to you, Bantan, and I am sorry." She removed her arm from his and appeared humbled.

The bronzed giant smiled tolerantly and assured the native girl she was forgiven. Then he arose and reached in the canoe for some grass upon which to lay, telling Mauria she could sleep in the canoe.

"I want to be up early in the morning before the mermaids make an appearance so we can hide the canoe in the foliage," he reminded her. "Then I'll have to find suitable wood to fashion a paddle. That is very important."

The night was mild and no discomfort was experienced by either. Bantan was awake with the coming of daylight. Looking within the canoe he saw that Mauria still slept. Without waking her, he indulged in a brief swim. When returning to the shore his roaming eyes were attracted by a piece of board a short distance to his right that had been washed ashore during the night. Going to it, he picked it up, aware that he could easily fashion a paddle from it. It had originally come from a packing case. It was about five feet in length, four inches in width and an inch in thickness, and there were no weakening knots to be noticed.

Returning with the board to the canoe, he smiled as he saw that the native girl had now awakened. Looking up at him, she smiled in greeting.

Bantan showed her the board he had found.

"I have what I need to fashion a paddle, Mauria," he announced.

The girl was very pleased.

"We shall be leaving the island very soon then," she added, arising.

"It won't take me long to fashion a paddle from it," he said, nodding. "While you have a swim, I'll hide the canoe in the foliage and prepare fruit and nuts left over from last night for our morning meal."

This the bronzed giant did, and when Mauria returned from the water he was completing preparations. While they ate, they conversed in low voices. Afterwards, he lost no time with his keen-edged dagger as he started to whittle upon the board which was of a durable pine. The girl, meanwhile, gathered more fruit and nuts so that as little delay as possible be necessary before they departed from the island. Each time that she returned with arms ladened, she smiled and noted the steady progress he was attaining in fashioning a paddle.

The blade was perfect in design in a short while, and then the bronzed giant's dagger was busy on the handle. This would require more time, since there was more wood to be whittled. So engrossed he was in his handiwork, he gave no thought of pausing and looking out in the direction of the calmer water beyond the gentle surf to see whether the mermaids had made their early morning inspection of the island shore.

Enthusiastic as Mauria was in gathering fruit and nuts so that they could leave as soon as the paddle was completed, she did not give thought of aught else either.

Thus, the marks that had been left by the canoe's keel when they had moved it the previous late afternoon and the imprints of their sandaled feet were stark evidence of their new location. Such evidence was what two pairs of sharp eyes sought as two mermaids with a trident sheathed at their right side swam just beyond the gentle surf.

When Ano and Majane passed the shore where the mark of the canoe dragged to the water's edge was accompanied by sandaled footprints, they immediately guessed that the stranger had moved the canoe to a new location. In due time their sharp eyes noticed the mark on the beach and also the intermingled footprints. Speaking in hushed whispers, they nodded and swam ashore. Withdrawing the trident from its sheath, the two mermaids slithered up the beach to the edge of the foliage where they listened with intent ears. They had noticed the different set of imprints, one being larger than the other, and they appeared bewildered as they discussed in whispers the fact there were two sets of footprints. Just within the foliage they could hear voices, and they were surprised to overhear Mauria's when she was supposed to be confined in a dungeon.

Ano, the apparent leader, because she was older, nodded to Majane and indicated her intentions, and that she remain where she was. With her trident clutched tightly in her right hand she slithered cautiously through the foliage until she could see the bronzed giant and the native girl in a small clearing. At sight of the crouched Bantan, the mermaid's eyes widened with surprise because of the handsome specimen of maleness that he represented. But immediately thinking of the duty she had to perform, her eyes hardened a trifle, for that duty was to capture the stranger and Mauria.

Bantan had nearly completed the handle of his paddle, and a smile touched his lips as he spoke to his companion who hovered near him with admiration apparent in her dark eyes.

"It will only require a short time now," he said to her, "and we'll be able to leave this island." Then, with a sudden recollection, he paused in his work and stared up at Mauria. "The mermaids who make a morning inspection of the island shore!" he exclaimed. "I had forgotten about them. Look and see if they are to be seen."

"I'll hope not, Bantan," the girl answered as she stepped around him and slightly away from the spot where the watchful eyes of Ano stared.

Mauria parted the fronds of a fern and her eyes swept the calm water beyond the gentle surf from right to left and she was relieved that no sight of the patrolling mermaids was to be seen. And then her eyes rested upon the strip of beach before her. A puzzled expression overcame her features as she studied the sand more carefully. Almost directly before her it was apparent that two wet bodies had very recently drawn themselves from the water's edge to the very edge of the foliage. At once thought of the patrolling mermaids came to her. Without realizing she had left her improvised spear in the canoe, she parted the ferns and stepped out upon the edge of the beach with searching eyes. Almost immediately she caught sight of Majane only a couple of yards distant with her trident poised to strike. The mermaid's eyes were serious and her intentions were all too clear.

"Oh!" the single pathetic word the native girl uttered.

At the same moment from within the foliage Mauria heard a sudden movement.

"You are my prisoner, Bantan," Ano said in a meaningful tone.

Having heard Mauria's exclamation of surprise, the bronzed giant suddenly stopped working on the handle of his paddle, and he looked up, slightly puzzled at a sound of rustling foliage. He at once saw the mermaid with trident in her right hand in readiness to cast at the slightest inkling of resistance on his part. When she spoke, he realized that she was in earnest.

He dropped the paddle, but still clutched the dagger in his right hand. His eyes narrowed a trifle.

"Drop it, Bantan," the mermaid commanded in a brittle voice as she indicated the dagger with her left hand.

Instantly Bantan weighed his chances of overpowering the mermaid. Meeting her intent eyes, he realized the weapon she held poised to cast would be much more effective than the one he clutched. While he disliked intensely to surrender meekly, it appeared he had no alternative at the present moment.

"Drop it!" Ano again commanded in brittle tones.

At the bronzed giant's hesitation, the mermaid drew a little closer and her dark eyes were stern and somewhat angered by his delay to obey her. "My queen would never forgive me were I to kill you, but that I will if you force me."

From the beach Mauria could be heard weeping.

Bantan drew himself to his full height and his dark eyes blazed angrily.

"If harm has come to Mauria—" he growled.

A bitter smile touched Ano's lips.

"No harm will come to her if she submits to capture," she answered.

Evidently the native girl was not to submit so easily.

BANTAN AND MAURIA OVERCOME MERMAIDS

Her weeping ceased suddenly and there was a quick movement of the skirting foliage. And then there was the sound of a body coming in hard contact with the sand accompanied by an agonized: "Oh!" There was more movement, then Mauria's joyful voice called out:

"I've overcome the mermaid, Bantan!"

Although Ano had listened intently she did not remove her eyes from the bronzed giant who seemingly towered above her. Now a grim smile touched his lips. For the first time the mermaid entertained the fear that her weapon would be inadequate to stop him were he determined to force the impending issue. Her right arm trembled slightly.

So quickly Bantan acted, lightning could scarcely be more swift. He sprang forward, and before Ano could act, ready though she was to hurl the weapon she held, his strong left hand fastened upon her arm, numbing it in a crushing grip. The trident dropped from nerveless fingers.

Quickly the mermaid turned to slither away to safety, but the bronzed giant's crushing grip on her arm prevented the move. With her left hand she sought to tear at his face, but moving his head to and fro quickly, he avoided her ripping fingernails. Instantly he managed to sheathe his dagger, then his right hand fastened upon her left arm, also crushing it in a merciless grip. Ano gasped in pain as he then dragged her through the foliage to the beach where he found a triumphant Mauria straddling the other mermaid with a smile of victory upon her features. She gripped Majane's wrists in her strong hands.

Bantan now released Ano's arms which were black and blue from the pressure of his powerful hands. A sullen expression had overcome the mermaid's features, but there was no fear in her dark eyes. If anything, disbelief was revealed that she was not to be severely punished and possibly killed for her audacity.

"I have never punished or killed a woman in my life," the bronzed giant said to Ano, and then shifted his eyes to Majane, in whose dark eyes an awed expression had appeared at sight of him. "There have been times when women deserved to be punished and killed at my hands, but I could not do so. Mauria and I came to your island with no intention of harming anyone. We merely wished to rest and gather fruit and nuts before continuing our way. Mauria has been a guest and then a prisoner of your queen. Both of you would have been well rewarded to have returned us to your queen as prisoners. I am not going to punish either of you, but I am to keep the weapons you had so that you might not harm either of us. Go back to your queen and tell her that though you failed, I have been merciful to women who would have taken us prisoners."

As he spoke, the bronzed giant indicated to the native girl to release the mermaid she had overpowered and held prisoner. Mauria arose to her feet and drew near him while Majane slithered to Ano's side. The two mermaids exchanged wondering glances, but said nothing. Each then looked up in disbelief at Bantan for freeing them.

The bronzed giant then pointed at the surf.

"Go," he said. "You have no reason to remain here any longer. Consider yourselves lucky that I have been merciful. I might have severely punished each of you."

Ano nodded to Majane, and without a word each slithered down the beach to the water's edge. Before plunging into the breaking waves, both turned with wondering eyes to look back at Bantan and the native girl who were still watching them from the edge of the foliage.

"How can such a handsome male be so merciful?" Majane asked of her companion with bewilderment apparent in her dark eyes. "If he had beaten us unmercifully I could not have hated him."

Ano shook her head angrily and with confusion.

"I know our queen is going to be very displeased with our failure to capture Bantan," she muttered with a shiver pulsing through her. "I feel death would be more welcome than to face her wrath."

Majane sighed deeply.

"Bantan is such a handsome male," she murmured. "Oh, to be favored with his love—"

"Hush," Ano chided her younger companion. "Our queen would be very displeased to know one of her subjects could love a strange male. I will forget that I heard you make such a remark. Come, let us return and announce our failure to capture Bantan and Mauria."

Majane again sighed as she gave a last forlorn look at the bronzed giant, then joined her companion as she slithered into the gentle surf. After gaining the calmer water, the younger mermaid again looked with eyes of longing at the beach where Bantan and the native girl still stood, watching them.

The bronzed giant now turned to Mauria with a sigh of relief.

"That's over with," he said. "We'll place their weapons in the canoe and drag it to the beach. I still have more work on the paddle, and when I've finished we'll be ready to leave."

The native girl smiled eagerly as she picked up the trident Majane had possessed. Within the foliage where Ano had been, she found the one that had been dropped when Bantan had overwhelmed her. The bronzed giant placed his paddle within the canoe as the girl did the tridents, then together they drew the canoe to the edge of the foliage upon the beach. With his keen-edged dagger, he wasted no time as he proceeded to smooth the handle.

"Keep an eye on the possible return of more mermaids, Mauria," he bade the girl. "We don't wish to be taken by a surprise attack again when we are so near leaving the island."

The native girl assured him she would keep a watchful eye. She still could see the two mermaids swimming beyond the surf some distance from where she was. Intermittently she noticed that one of them would look in their direction as though loath to leave. She mentioned this to Bantan.

"Not knowing of a male for many moons," she added, "I imagine the mermaids are starved for love and attention from one."

"That may well be," he added with a slight shake of his head; "but I want no part of a creature that is half woman and half fish—even though they appear to be of white origin."

Mauria smiled teasingly.

"If you had a choice of being marooned for life upon an island," she said; "would you choose a mermaid or me?"

He paused and looked up at the radiant girl. He shook his head, though a smile touched his lips.

"What a question to ask, Mauria," he remarked. "You should know you would be my preference."

"Even though I am a native girl?" she insisted smilingly.

Again he paused to look up at her. He nodded decidingly as his eyes met her questioning ones.

"If only I were of white birth, Bantan," she sighed. "What wouldn't I give to be worthy of you."

A smile touched the bronzed giant's lips as he again looked up at the girl.

"Perhaps Dr. Zarwood on Mandoes Island might be able to make you a white girl," he suggested. "Would you risk it—if it were possible?"

The native girl's features were puzzled, but for only a moment.

"I'd be willing to risk anything—for you, Bantan," she murmured with devotion openly revealed for him.

CHAPTER IX

A Broken Paddle

WATCHING THE TWO MERMAIDS swimming beyond the surf, Mauria now sighed with relief as they disappeared beyond the bend of the distant shoreline.

"I no longer can see them," she informed Bantan.

"Let us hope we never see any more of them again," he declared.

As he spoke, the bronzed giant was rubbing the palms of his hands over the handle of the paddle he had been carefully scraping with the keen edge of his dagger. There still were a few rough spots, and with the blade end clasped tightly between his knees, he proceeded to scrape them carefully so that when he used it there would be no danger of raising blisters. After a few minutes he again rubbed the palms of his hands over it, and now he smiled, feeling his handiwork was completed to his satisfaction. He then sheathed his dagger.

Mauria chanced to look down at him.

"It's finished," he stated. "Now we can drag the canoe to the water's edge and be on our way."

The native girl smiled with relief.

"I'm ready when you are, Bantan," she said.

Without further delay they dragged the canoe to the water's edge. Bantan indicated for Mauria to step within. When she had done so, he waited briefly for a favoring moment, then pushed the canoe into the surf, leaped within, and in another moment was plying the paddle carefully because of the added weight of the fruit and nuts, and not knowing for certain how sturdy his newly fashioned paddle would be. He felt it quiver to his powerful thrusts in passing through the surf, and he was relieved within a few minutes to have gained the calmer water beyond. He paddled in the opposite direction the mermaids had swum, for he realized there was danger of encountering more of them when the two who had been disarmed reached the grotto and informed the queen of their failure to capture him and the native girl.

Mauria was smiling with delight.

"It feels good to be free of danger again, Bantan," she said with a sigh.

He, too, smiled, but his dark eyes were not free of the possibility that danger might not yet threaten.

"I'll feel free only when we are a considerable distance from the island," he declared.

He had studied the sun's position in the heaven. To continue an easterly course, he would have to circumnavigate the southwestern shore in order to do so. He realized he would be within sight of the cove that the mermaids frequented and he hoped none of them would see the canoe and its two occupants. As they passed the southwestern end of the island, Bantan called Mauria's attention to the dilapidated huts which could be glimpsed just within the outskirting foliage.

"I never saw such poor huts in my life," he added. "I was even tempted to kindle a fire and destroy them completely."

"The three old natives who live there wouldn't have had any place to stay if you had, Bantan," the native girl reminded him. "A poor hut is better than none at all."

She continued to look in the direction of the village. Now she uttered a little gasp of surprise. From the foliage outlining it she saw three little old natives appear, walking in their stooped manner. One of them apparently had sighted the canoe some two hundred yards distant, and he called the attention of his companions, indicating it with a skinny hand that visibly trembled because of his infirmity.

"The stranger is leaving," he said. "The queen's handmaidens failed to capture him. We are not to blame."

His two companions shook their heads despairingly. They wondered if future rations of dried fish would be limited to them when they brought fruit and nuts in exchange.

Bantan looked toward the three old men when Mauria called his attention to their appearance upon the beach.

"It would have been a shame to fire their huts, spies that they were," he admitted. "They would have been unable to construct others, and I do not believe in wanton destruction of property, poor though it might be."

The native girl merely smiled and nodded. Her eyes swept the shoreline as far as possible. She could distinguish the cliff and the outer part of the cove as well. Carefully she studied the water adjacent to it. She was almost positive she could distinguish the glint of sunlight upon wet, bare arms, indicating swimmers were in the calm water beyond the gentle surf. The sunlight glistening upon the slightly undulating surface's wavelets intervening bothered somewhat, and as the moments became minutes there was movement to be detected. She turned to the bronzed giant, shaking her head in perplexity.

"I'm not sure," she said. "But looking toward the cove, there appears to be swimmers. What do you think?"

Bantan's lids narrowed to mere slits and he paused in his paddling to stare in the direction Mauria indicated. There was no doubt of the presence of swimmers and, unless he was mistaken, there were at least a dozen of them. When a full minute had passed, and he watched intently, meanwhile, he was positive they had sighted the canoe and its occupants. They were speedily swimming in their direction. He looked at the girl discouragingly and nodded.

"There's no doubt they have sighted us, Mauria," he said in low tones. "The two mermaids we sent back have reported us as being almost ready to leave the island. If this paddle can stand the strain, we'll be able to outdistance them even though they are swimming rapidly."

"We can hope anyway," she said with an encouraging smile. "It is regrettable that we haven't an extra paddle so that I might help."

His smile now was grim as he plied the paddle with increasingly powerful strokes. The canoe surged ahead, but with each stroke that he made he could feel the improvised paddle quiver somewhat to the strain it was being subjected to. All he could do was hope that it would pass the test. Had he the two paddles that had been confiscated by the mermaids he knew he would have no reason to worry, for they had been made from durable wood that could be relied upon. With considerable fruit and nuts in the canoe, adding to its weight, the water craft could not be propelled too easily.

Mauria kept a close watch upon the swimmers and she could determine that they were keeping a safe distance from them. She was optimistic of Bantan's ability and hoped the swimming mermaids would soon tire and give up the chase.

The bronzed giant did not share the girl's optimism because of the improvised paddle he wielded. Each time that he applied extra power behind thrusts he could feel a quiver pass through it and he practically held his breath, hopeful that it would not snap. He cast apprehensive glances in the direction of the mermaids who were swimming at right angles with the canoe. In due time at the speed they maintained, being excellent swimmers, they were bound to overtake the canoe. As he looked in their direction he could see that two of the swimmers were considerably in advance of their followers, and each time that he glanced he could easily determine they were increasing the distance.

"They are very good swimmers, Mauria," he murmured presently. "See how the two in front are increasing the distance from their followers."

The girl nodded after studying them. Then she looked at Bantan with questioning apprehension in her dark eyes.

"Do you think there is a chance of them overtaking us?" she asked.

He shook his head, and the beads of perspiration upon his forehead were shaken free.

"I'm not sure," he admitted. "The extra weight of the fruit and nuts has slowed our progress considerably. And this paddle is not to be trusted as the others were."

Mauria shook her head and vexation appeared upon her features.

"If only we had gotten away before the two mermaids came upon us," she murmured regretfully. "They wouldn't have been waiting and watching for us."

He smiled encouragingly as a sudden thought came to him.

"I'll bear to the right away from them," he said. "That will make it farther for them to swim and at the same time should tire them sooner than were I to maintain a direct course."

"You know best what to do, Bantan," she said, smiling with optimism.

"At the speed they are swimming it is the only thing I can do," he answered with a shrug.

And so with each stroke of the paddle Bantan gave it

that extra twist that resulted in the prow gradually turning to the right without abatement of speed. Casting inter-
mittent glances at the pursuing mermaids during the
passing minutes, he saw that so long as he maintained the
present, slightly deviating course, there would be no
danger of being overtaken. The two swimmers far in advance of their followers were steadily increasing the distance that spanned, but they were not gaining upon the
canoe they hoped to overtake. The bronzed giant was
confident now that it would only be a matter of time before the pursuing mermaids became too tired to continue
the chase.

The muscles of the paddler slid in well oiled grooves
as he continued to ply the paddle, while Mauria was now
smiling complacently as she continually looked back at
the pursuing mermaids.

And then almost without warning a sudden snapping
sound was to be heard, and Bantan looked dumbly at the
handle of the improvised paddle. It had broken off neatly
a few inches below his hands. With dismay he reached
quickly into the water for the broken end of the blade
that momentarily seemingly avoided his clutching hands,
but at last he managed to retrieve it.

"What I feared has happened, Mauria," he said with
a mournful shake of his head.

Moisture appeared in the native girl's dark eyes.

"What shall we do now?" she moaned.

He cast a quick glance back at the swimming mermaids.

"I have two choices," he said with a tightening of his
lips. "I can continue paddling with the broken end which
will reduce our speed considerably. The mermaids will
notice this and, gaining upon us, will be less inclined to
give up the chase. Or, we could return to the island. I
have no doubt I would be able to reach it by circling
about. We'd have to conceal the canoe in the foliage again

and hope we can avoid being captured until I can find the proper wood to fashion a sturdy paddle. What do you think, Mauria?"

The native girl shook her head dismayingly.

"The decision is yours, Bantan," she answered. "You know best what the chances are with the broken paddle. Whatever choice you make I'll be in accord that you did what was best."

He shrugged and drew a hand across his perspiring forehead.

"I'll continue on our course," he said then. "Keep a sharp watch on the two leading swimmers and let me know if we at least are holding our own."

"I'll do that, Bantan," the girl assured him.

For a hundred yards the bronzed giant wielded the shortened paddle almost savagely, and looking at Mauria his eyes importuned her to inform him if their lead was being maintained.

"They are not gaining upon us," she said hopefully. Noticing his freely perspiring forehead she shook her head almost distressfully. "But you are paddling much harder now than before," she added.

He nodded, wondering whether he could maintain the gruelling pace he had set before the pursuing mermaids would tire and finally give up the chase.

"I'll keep at it, Mauria," he said from between tight-pressed lips. "Let me know if they should begin to gain upon us." Casting a fleeting glance over a shoulder toward the island, he nodded as he added: "I still could reach the island ahead of them."

Once again he wielded the paddle with savage strokes, and though the canoe surged ahead, he knew its speed was considerably reduced because of the shortened paddle he used. Another hundred yards were covered before his eyes met the girl's.

Mauria shook her head sadly.

"I'm afraid the two leading swimmers are now gaining upon us," she murmured distressfully.

Bantan paused to look in the direction of the two mermaids considerably in advance of their followers. It was true, they had gained upon the slower-moving canoe since the last hundred yards had been covered. He could see no evidence of tiring muscles on the part of the two leading mermaids, for their sleek arms flashed as vigorously as in the beginning of the chase. He shook his head sadly as he looked at the silently watching native girl.

"It's no use," he said. "The mermaids appear tireless. Much as I want to try and outdistance them, I'm afraid ours is a losing race if I continue. If only a shark might be nearby and give them battle, we would have a better chance of getting away; but that would be hoping for too much."

Mauria remained silent, realizing as she did she could offer no encouragement in their present desperate straits. She shivered at the thought of returning to the island again, knowing how they would have to be constantly on the alert to avoid capture. Having already escaped once from them, she knew the precaution of their jailers upon another occasion would be redoubled.

With a regretful sigh the bronzed giant maneuvered the canoe about in a somewhat wide arc, hoping to disconcert the pursuing mermaids so that he might gain that much more distance upon them before they realized the intentions of their quarry.

With mighty strokes of his shortened paddle, he now directed the canoe in a straight line with the tip of the island. To make the task lighter, he nodded indicatingly to the girl to toss the fruit and nuts upon the opposite side from the pursuing mermaids. With alacrity, Mauria did this, and in the passing minutes the canoe's increasing buoyancy was appreciably noticeable, for riding higher on the surface, it skimmed with less resistance.

Pegra and Beta were the two mermaids far in advance of their followers. When Ano and Majane reported to Queen Sirena their failure to capture Bantan and Mauria as well, her instructions were given Pegra to take other mermaids and at once circumvent the getaway of the strangers. She advised what route to take, feeling that Bantan would not paddle beyond the cove in fear of being discovered. And Pegra, with Beta at her side, had already entered the water and were swimming to the right of the cove in the calmer water when the canoe had been sighted. Being excellent swimmers and noted for their endurance, they soon outdistanced their followers.

Upon the shore where their dilapidated village was partially concealed by fringing foliage, the three old natives stood in a stooped position watching the canoe now returning to the island. Their bleary old eyes had also sighted the mermaids in hot pursuit. Naturally, they hoped the strangers would be recaptured.

Perspiration was continually forming on Bantan's brow as he plied his shortened paddle with savage strokes in a supreme effort to outdistance the pursuing mermaids. For brief moments he would pause to flick away the profuse moisture on his forehead with the edge of a hand. Some, however, managed to run down into his eye sockets and the salty content made him blink repeatedly. Overhead, the sun's torrid rays continued to beat down upon him with seemingly increasing heat.

Mauria kept him informed of their progress as the minutes passed. She clasped her hands upon her knees and clenched them nervously time and again. Moisture filled her own eyes at sight of the grimly paddling Bantan and her heart was sorrowed beyond words to tell, knowing that they must return to the island of their enemies.

By the time the canoe was nearing the tip of the island just beyond the breaking surf, Pegra and Beta made a valiant effort to increase their speed; but by this time, excellent swimmers though they were, they were beginning to tire. At a distance to their rear, some in advance of others, Ano and Majane, having swum considerably earlier in the morning, trailed behind.

The three old natives upon the beach shouted imprecations and waved their skinny arms futilely at the occupants of the canoe as it passed around the island's tip. Then, when the canoe could not be seen, they turned their attention to the two swimming mermaids in advance of their companions and shouted encouragement for them to overtake the canoe.

In these final minutes Bantan's shortened paddle was wielded more powerfully than before and, through his supreme effort, managed to gain more distance upon his pursuers. He looked at Mauria with a grim smile.

"We'll beach the canoe and drag it to the concealment of the foliage before the mermaids round the island shore," he said. "If we ever hope to leave this island, nothing must happen to the canoe. A paddle can be fashioned more easily than building a new canoe."

Bantan cast a quick look to his rear and could see no sight of the pursuing mermaids as yet. Then with a smile he noted they were near where they had set out. He informed the native girl of this, and she recognized the mark of the canoe's keel upon the beach. She nodded eagerly as he now headed the prow through the gentle surf. As it grated upon the sand, the bronzed giant and the girl quickly leaped out. A quick glance was again given in the direction they had come, and fortunately, the two mermaids in the lead of their followers still were not to be seen.

"Quick—we'll drag the canoe along the same path," he said to Mauria.

Laying hand upon the bow while the girl pushed upon the aft end, within a minute they had dragged it to the concealment of the foliage. With gasping sighs, Bantan and Mauria parted the foliage and looked to their left. At that very moment the two leading mermaids now rounded the shoreline beyond the gentle surf and were looking in amazement for the quarry they pursued.

Standing side by side, their shoulders touching, the bronzed giant's arm went about the native girl's shoulders protectingly as they watched the two mermaids.

Mauria looked up at her companion with questioning eyes.

"Do you suppose they will suspect where we are, Bantan?" she asked.

He turned to her and his hand upon her shoulder tightened a trifle.

"We'll have to wait and see what they do," he answered. "If they come ashore here, we'll have to take the weapons from the canoe and retreat into the island's interior."

She smiled and nodded.

"And to think a broken paddle prevented us from escaping," she murmured.

CHAPTER X

Bantan's Plan

WATCHING THE TWO MERMAIDS as they drew nearer in the calm water beyond the surf, Bantan and Mauria were aware they were swimming less vigorously as though realizing they had temporarily lost their quarry. Upon their features disappointment could be clearly distinguished. The two watchers now saw the straggling mermaids appearing around the shoreline in the wake of their leaders. But their immediate attention was focused upon the two who were now nearing the place where they had come ashore.

"They are now hesitating, Mauria," the bronzed giant whispered to his companion. "We will hope they continue on their way."

The native girl nodded.

Pegra and Beta now treaded water as they looked shoreward, their sharp eyes missing no detail. They conversed in low tones for a few moments, and then the leader nodded with determination.

"Come," she said to her companion, "we'll go ashore here."

Watching them from the concealment of the foliage, Bantan now nodded to Mauria.

"We'll have to leave," he said.

The native girl nodded mutely.

Reaching within the canoe, the bronzed giant withdrew the two tridents that had been confiscated from Ano

110

and Majane. He gave one to the girl. Then with extreme care they retreated from the immediate vicinity.

As soon as Pegra and Beta reached the shore, each withdrew the trident sheathed at their right side. With it clutched in their right hand, they slithered up the beach. When reaching the edge of the foliage, they peered within. The canoe was there but, as was to be expected, the man and the native girl were not.

Pegra nodded to her companion.

"They have the advantage over us by having legs and feet to penetrate the island's interior," she said. "But they will not escape from the island a second time. That I promise on my life."

Beta nodded and grimness tightened her lips.

"How Mauria escaped is a mystery," she murmured.

"Bantan must have found her," the leader answered.

Looking about apprehensively, Pegra slithered to the side of the canoe. Looking within, she reached for the shortened paddle and the end that had broken off. She nodded in understanding that the improvised paddle had broken. Recollecting the two that had been brought to the queen and which she had examined, a cursory appraisal of this one easily revealed its inferior quality.

Beta drew close and wordlessly examined the pieces of pine board that had been fashioned into a paddle. She nodded mutely.

By this time the first of the straggling mermaids were coming ashore. In turn, they slithered up the beach to join their leader. At last all of the mermaids, twelve in number, were gathered around the canoe. Pegra spoke to them.

"Because of this broken paddle," she said, "the strangers who were fleeing were compelled to return to our island. Our queen is most anxious, as you all know, for their capture. We know they cannot escape so long as their canoe is here. This time four mermaids shall keep watch over it." She nodded to each as she spoke their names: "You, Ano, Majane, Zola, and Remo remain here until we others return to our queen with the report of our failure to capture the strangers. In due time each of you will be relieved. My parting words are that each of you be alertful, even ready to sacrifice your lives if necessary—but the strangers must not be allowed to leave the island."

The four mermaids promised their alertfulness and loyalty.

Without further delay, Pegra turned to her followers.

"Come, let us return to the grotto," she said.

Bantan and Mauria had retreated a short distance from the vicinity of the canoe. There they listened to the conversation between the mermaids. Having heard what Pegra had said, each looked at the other and nodded, their eyes revealing their dismay. The native girl reached out a hand and gently rested it upon the man's bronzed arm.

"Things look dark for us right now," she murmured with regret in her eyes. "But I'm sure we'll find a way to leave this island."

Bantan covered her hand with his and his smile was gentle.

"We'll hope so, Mauria," he answered in a soft voice.

Then she sighed deeply and a wistful smile touched her lips.

"Why couldn't this island have been uninhabited?" she murmured. "How wonderful it would have been."

The bronzed giant could only shake his head in regret.

"Life is not always what we wish it," he reminded her.

She looked at him earnestly for a long moment, the wistful smile still lingering upon her slightly parted lips.

"How well I know that, Bantan," she agreed.

He was no clairvoyant, but he readily understood what the native girl inferred. A slight smile touched his lips and he removed his eyes from her adoring ones. He could not deny the regret in his soul that Mauria was not of white origin, for were she, without a question of doubt he knew only too well he could have loved her utterly and desired to mate with her. Now, with a shrug and to change his trend of thought, he asked the girl if she were hungry. She nodded.

"It was wasteful that you asked me to throw out of the canoe the fruit and nuts," she said in a low voice. "But if I hadn't done so, we might not be free as we are now."

"Being free is more important," he added. "While we're searching for fruit and nuts, I'll also be looking for wood to fashion a more dependable paddle than the last."

A short while later Bantan and Mauria were seated in a little glen and were partaking of their noon-day repast. Thus far there had been no suitable growing wood found to fashion a durable paddle, but the young man was not altogether hopeless. He explained to the girl his intentions.

"After we have eaten," he said, "we'll search some more. Since we'll have to remain upon the island this coming night, later we'll find a suitable place to sleep."

The native girl nodded in accord with his wishes.

For several hours they carefully picked their way about the island's interior with the bronzed giant's eyes always looking hither and yon, but a couple of hours before sundown they conceded their quest had been in vain. They mutually decided for the evening to return to their first place of landing, feeling it would be comparatively safe there. They gathered fruit and nuts, and after eating, grass was gathered for their sleeping pallets.

Since an hour remained before darkness would envelop them, Bantan suggested they steal toward where the mer-

maids had been guarding the canoe. When they reached
the near vicinity they were aware that four of them were
still on guard. He turned to the girl at his side.

"They are making sure we won't steal the canoe," he
remarked.

Mauria only nodded and tightened her lips as she
shook her head somewhat distressfully.

They remained for a short while, listening to the desultory conversation between the mermaids, and it was
well understood how irked they were becoming from
their guard duty, though at intervals in turn each of the
original four had been relieved and at present new re-
cruits were present.

Bantan's sharp ears heard voices issuing from the direction of the beach. Peering through the screening foliage
he saw two mermaids now passing through the gentle
surf. When they reached the shore they slithered up the
beach. He recognized them as Pegra and Beta. They
lost no time approaching the four guards who were relieved to see them.

"Our queen has decided that we bear the canoe to the
grotto," she announced. "In that way no one will have
to remain on guard. She is positive the strangers will not
leave the island this night."

The four guards were relieved to hear what Pegra had
said. All placed their tridents within the canoe, then the
six mermaids lay hand upon it and, pushing and dragging
it, they reached the water's edge without too much
difficulty. With three upon each side, they floated it
through the gentle surf to presently gain the calmer water
beyond. Heading the canoe in the direction of the cove
beyond the bend in the shoreline, they swam leisurely at
its side.

From the concealment of the foliage, the sorrowful
eyes of Bantan and Mauria wordlessly watched them un-

til the canoe had disappeared from sight. The girl's warm hand gently rested upon the young man's arm, and as their eyes met each was aware of the other's hopelessness. He covered her hand with his and shook his head sadly.

"Come, Mauria," he said, "let's return to where we'll spend the night. I now wish," he added with regret, "that I had continued with the shortened paddle. We might have been fortunate to outdistance them. With our canoe in their custody, our hopes now are practically extinct."

Moisture welled in the native girl's dark eyes and she could think of nothing encouraging to say.

Wordless for the most part, they returned to where they were to remain for the night. The sun was just sinking below the waterline when they reached their objective.

"Want to sit on the shore at the edge of the foliage for awhile, Mauria?" Bantan asked. "It is too early to go to sleep."

The girl nodded and accompanied him to the edge of the beach where they seated themselves. In the setting twilight the girl looked up at the bronzed giant as though asking permission; then she drew closer to him and linked her arm with his, their shoulders pressed close. She rested her head in the hollow of his neck.

"I don't know what dangers another sun may bring, Bantan," she murmured. "But now we have nothing to worry about anyway."

Though his eyes were studying the calm water beyond the surf in the direction of the cove, the bronzed giant nodded in reply, feeling words were not necessary. When a few minutes had passed, Mauria spoke again.

"Do you think the girl from America will ever return to this region again?" she asked.

"I hardly think so," he answered with a deep sigh. "Many times I have wondered how I would have fared in America where I was born. Being but a small boy at the time I was shipwrecked, I cannot remember what it was like."

"If you had returned with her, Bantan," the girl said, "I would never have known you." She hugged his arm linked with hers a little tighter. "That I wouldn't have wanted, for knowing and being with you is wonderful."

Bantan chuckled softly.

"If you hadn't known me, Mauria," he said, "in all probability you would have mated with some warrior of the Mandoes village, and by this time be the mother of little ones."

The girl shook her head and her voice was serious.

"No, I think not," she answered. "Have you forgotten that I formed a 'dream man' in my mind? I was determined I would mate with no other, and only as a last resort, when he could not be mine, would I then turn to another."

Bantan looked at the native girl with sober features.

"Perhaps it would have been better had Tama survived instead of me," he said. "I know you would have been happy with him."

A quiver coursed through the girl and a choked sob almost escaped her tight-pressed lips.

"Please let's not talk anymore, Bantan," she said presently in a low voice. "Let's just look up at the stars as they appear over the horizon."

Several hours later they arose and sought their sleeping pallets. The bronzed giant reminded the girl they should be up at sunrise in the event the mermaids started searching for them early in the morning.

After a fairly sound night's sleep Bantan and Mauria arose as the sun cleared the horizon. They risked a brief swim before returning to the concealment of the foliage and procuring their morning meal. They had just completed eating it when the young giant arose and peered through the fringing foliage. He was not surprised to see a couple of mermaids swimming in their direction beyond the gentle surf, and their eyes were carefully scanning the beach. The girl drew alongside her companion and she, too, was able to see the two patrolling mermaids.

"Do you think they'll come ashore, Bantan?" she asked.

At that very moment the two mermaids paused and treaded water. Their eyes were studying the beach and they were aware of the wet imprints upon the sand. For a few moments they spoke to one another, and then with a nod, Ano, the leader, headed for ashore, with Majane, her companion, following her.

The bronzed giant turned to the native girl.

"We'll have to leave," he said. "But before we do, we'll strew the grasses of our sleeping pallets about."

This they did without loss of time. Bantan reached for the two tridents and handed one to Mauria. He nodded and indicated for her to follow him. Cautiously they stole away from the immediate vicinity and did not halt until they were some distance from the edge of the beach. There, pausing, they listened to any comment that might be forthcoming from the two mermaids. Presently they heard the one known as Ano speaking to her companion.

"They must have slept here during the night, Majane," she said. "You will notice the grass strewn about. Had we come a little earlier we might have surprised and captured them while they slept."

Bantan nodded to Mauria.

"It was well that we arose early," he said.

She smiled knowingly.

They continued to listen for further remarks, and when they presently heard a slight rustling of the foliage, the bronzed giant nodded to the girl to follow him, for if possible he did not wish the two mermaids to suspect they were in the immediate neighborhood. Almost with the silence of disembodied spirits, they moved toward the island's interior where they were sure the hunters would not follow. They came to a rest in a tiny clearing. Bantan appeared somewhat discouraged, thinking as he did of his canoe in all probability being concealed in the grotto beyond his reach and hope of reclaiming without attracting attention.

Mauria drew close to him and looked at him with anxiety in her dark eyes.

"What is troubling you?" she asked solicitously.

He looked at the girl and shrugged.

"The canoe," he said. "I don't believe we can remain in hiding long enough to fashion another. If there only was some way I could know where the mermaids hid it, and how I might recover it."

Mauria shook her head in dismay, unable to help him with his problem. But within a few moments a light appeared in Bantan's eyes, indicating he was not without a glimmer of hope.

"Listen," he said. "I think it is the only way. My plan will be dangerous for us, but listen and tell me what you think."

The native girl merely stared at him, her questioning eyes importuning him to speak further.

"While you were a guest of the queen," he said, "do you know whether guards were posted during the night?"

"There would have been no reason for guards," she answered. "I don't believe there were. But now, with us at large, it is quite probable that guards will be posted to keep watch over the canoe."

He nodded, the eagerness in his eyes dimming somewhat.

"Later this afternoon we'll try to camp near the cliff," he said. "Then late at night when all of the mermaids are supposed to be asleep, we could enter the tunnel that leads to the large room. If the canoe is anywhere, it must be there with the two paddles, my bow and arrows. I think it is worth the risk and is the quickest way to leave this island."

Mauria's lips tightened and there was indecision in her dark eyes. She continued to look at him hopelessly."

"But if you are caught—" She shook her head dismayingly. "It would be the end for both of us. The mermaid queen would never let you escape. And as for me—" She shrugged. "I could expect to be tortured to death. The mermaids have no use for me; but you, Bantan, they would want more than anything else. I don't think Zarna would have been as cruel as I feel Queen Sirena would. If you were captured, I would not want to live anyway."

Tears were in the native girl's eyes when she finished speaking.

Bantan clasped his hands and his lips drew in tight lines. His eyes did not meet Mauria's for long moments. But at last he faced her.

"Do you know of any other way we can recover the canoe?" he asked.

The girl rubbed her moist eyes with her knuckles, and then shook her head as she met his questioning eyes.

"Do whatever you think best, Bantan," she said in a low voice that quivered a trifle. "What you decide upon I'll follow and hope you are successful."

He reached for her hands with a gentle smile and clasped them in his.

"I think my plan is the only way, Mauria," he said convincingly.

They remained where they were, keeping their eyes and ears alert at all times, while the day wore on and the sun moved across the heaven. After they had eaten an early evening meal, Bantan nodded and indicated that the time had come to move in the direction of the cliff's summit. In silence the native girl followed close behind him.

The bronzed giant and Mauria reached their objective by the time the sun disappeared beneath the waterline. Before twilight overcame the world, he looked carefully about, and seeing no sign of any mermaids, he then crept to the edge of the cliff and peered down into the cove. There was no sign of life anywhere. He turned to his companion.

"The mermaids must be eating their evening meal," he remarked.

The girl nodded mutely.

"All we have to do now is wait," he added.

Twilight came quickly and presently they were enshrouded in complete darkness. The man and the girl maintained watchful eyes about them, and were soon accustomed to the darkness so that they could see fairly well.

The hours slipped by, and stars rose higher over the horizon until at last after a long silence Bantan turned to Mauria.

"I think the time has come," he murmured. "Follow me."

CHAPTER XI

Escape

WITH EXTREME CARE, Bantan leading and assisting Mauria down the acclivity, within a few minutes they were standing near the water's edge. Gentle waves lapped the smooth, rocky surface near their feet. They stood motionless, their eyes focused upon the darkened area at the base of the cliff above the water's edge where the openings were to be faintly discerned. The ears of both strained for any alien sounds. After what seemed long minutes, the bronzed giant whispered warningly to the native girl at his side.

"When swimming make as little noise as possible."

With his words Bantan slipped gently into the water and at the next moment Mauria followed him. They swam side by side with eyes fixed upon the aperture they were to enter. When a few minutes had passed they allowed their feet to touch the bottom. The water reached well above their waist.

In the lead with his dagger drawn and clutched in his right hand, the bronzed giant whispered to the girl that they would proceed within the opening. The soft glow from the end of the passageway where phosphorescence in the walls and ceiling artificially lighted the amphitheatre increased as they advanced. The water receded until presently they stepped upon the dry, rocky floor. The eyes of both were intently focused upon the large chamber ahead. As yet they saw no sign of living beings. The smooth surface of the pool reflected the soft glow of the ceiling.

Closer they drew to the end of the passageway, and Bantan's eyes were eager for sight of his stolen canoe. Pausing momentarily, he nodded to Mauria in the lightening dimness of the passageway and she nodded understandingly as he again proceeded ahead.

The bronzed giant's dark eyes missed no detail of what was to be seen, and his keen ears were alerted for the slightest sound that could be alien. Now at last he drew to the very end of the passageway and could view the entire amphitheatre. Upon the pool's end to his left he could now see his canoe where it had been brought. And, dishearteningly, he saw about fifty feet from him two mermaids seated side by side and armed with tridents were on guard.

They were in such a position that they were slightly sideways to the opening in the passageway from where Bantan and Mauria were watching. It was easy to determine that the two guards were very sleepy, for their heads were bowed forward and their eyes would remain closed for as long as a whole minute before opening. The fact that they did not engage in conversation was ample proof of their utter weariness. But at no time did their right hand clasping the handle of their trident relax its hold.

The two watchers at the mouth of the passageway studied them for long moments, then the bronzed giant turned to his silent companion and nodded indicatingly. As she stepped backward, he followed so that they were out of possible sight of the two mermaid guards. He appeared in deep thought to the extent a slight furrow appeared between his eyebrows. The native girl could only watch him mutely. As he looked down at the floor, a smooth stone the size of a hen's egg arrested his attention. Stooping, he picked it up with his left hand. As he straightened, he sheathed his dagger and transferred the stone to his right hand. He nodded to his silent companion then looked to his right. The opening of the passageway that led beyond the left side of the cove was within view —a distance of a hundred and fifty feet.

Bantan looked again in the direction of the two mermaid guards and saw that there was no change in their position. Then, looking at the mouth of the passageway, he brought his right hand backward with the smooth stone clutched in his palm and hurled it as hard as he could. The stone, true to his aim, landed just in front of the passageway and bounced within, striking one side of the wall and, because of its momentum, clattered toward the opposite wall farther down.

Instantly the attention of the two mermaid guards was alerted. Their keen ears immediately detected the direction of the disturbance. A quick exchange of conversation ensued, then gripping their tridents, in accord they slithered along the edge of the pool toward the passageway where the stone had been cast.

A grim smile touched Bantan's lips as he saw the two mermaids moving quickly across the smooth floor. He then looked at Mauria and nodded. New hope appeared in the native girl's eyes. With his lips close to one of the girl's ears he whispered what his intentions were and what he wanted her to do to help him. She nodded understandingly.

The bronzed giant then looked in the direction of the two mermaids. They were now about fifty feet from the mouth of the passageway but were moving slower as though anticipating possible danger. He noticed that not once had they paused to glance to their rear.

Bantan nodded to Mauria, and together they raced quietly toward the canoe, casting fleeting glances in the direction of the two mermaids, who still were unaware of their presence.

The bronzed giant reached the canoe first, and from within quickly brought forth the two paddles, his bow and arrows which in turn he handed to the girl at his side. Then he nodded for her to be on her way. She hesitated a fraction of a moment, wondering at his intention.

Bantan grasped the canoe with both hands upon each side of the gunwale at its center. With a sudden straining of coordinated muscles, he picked it up and swung it above his head, holding it there with mighty arms. To relieve the strain, he allowed his head cushioned with thick hair to bear a part of the weight. Quickly looking toward the two mermaids he saw they were now entering the mouth of the passageway with apparent apprehension. Without a moment's delay he followed in Mauria's wake as she hurried toward the passageway from which they had come.

The native girl reached their objective first, and just within the opening she paused momentarily. The bronzed giant was only a few yards behind her. As he appeared within the passageway he whispered for her to continue on her way, adding he would carry the canoe until the water was reached. Within a few minutes the girl announced that she had reached the edge of the gently lapping water. Breathing somewhat deeply, Bantan was relieved to set the canoe down. Turning to Mauria, he told her to place the paddles and his weapons within and to enter.

"I'll push it toward the entrance before I do so," he added.

In another moment the native girl was ensconced within the canoe, and the bronzed giant pushed it toward the opening.

"I wouldn't have thought it possible," the girl whispered.

A smile touched his lips.

"We were lucky," was all he said in answer.

He had hardly uttered the words when from the end of the passageway they had recently quit shrill screams of rage were to be heard, echoing the length of the corridor. Evidently the two mermaid guards had been aware of the absence of the canoe. At the opening of the passageway they were now screaming their threats of reprisal, and, as well, arousing the attention of their sleeping companions in a nearby chamber.

A grim smile touched Bantan's lips as he paused to look backward. He could discern the two forms now pursuing them. Mauria as well had been attracted by the screams of unmitigated rage and she sat spellbound with her hands pressed against the region of her wildly thumping heart.

"The mermaids have discovered the canoe missing!" she gasped.

"Nothing can worry us now," the bronzed giant answered in a low voice. "We have our canoe and the two paddles—that's all that really matters."

From the amphitheatre were to be heard less articulate voices as the awakened mermaids were emerging from their sleeping chamber. Even Queen Sirena had been aroused from her slumber and she appeared at the doorway of her private apartment. Quickly learning the reason for the disturbance she, too, joined her handmaidens in giving pursuit to their escaping quarry.

Pushing the canoe toward the aperture leading to the cove, the water was now midway to Bantan's thighs. He informed Mauria that he would draw himself into the canoe and instructed her what to do while he did so. In another moment he had attained his objective. Taking up a paddle, he plied it to good effect, and within another couple of minutes the canoe emerged from the opening and was in the cove.

"Want me to paddle as well?" Mauria asked then.

"It would help," he answered.

The native girl picked up the remaining paddle and carefully made her way toward the forward portion of the water craft. Kneeling, she plied the paddle expertly, and with her added assistance, the canoe glided more speedily over the slightly ruffled surface of the cove. As they approached its outer edge, Bantan indicated they would continue toward the right.

"We will have to stop later and gather what fruit we can," he said. "Even though we are in no immediate danger of being recaptured, we cannot paddle away from the island without any fruit and nuts. As we know from past experiences, a lack of food can be a hardship in our effort to reach our ultimate goal."

"Yes, I know," the native girl answered.

Presently they were paddling parallel to the shore a short distance beyond the breaking surf and the canoe responded favorably to their combined efforts. They were several hundred yards from the edge of the cove before the first of the pursuing mermaids appeared and their screaming voices could be distinctly heard. Owing to the darkness and the intervening distance Bantan's sharp eyes could not perceive their presence, but he could well imagine the chagrin that must stamp their features through the vicious tone of their shrill, raging voices. He was grateful no moon lighted the ocean surface, for the enraged mermaids would not be able to see them. In a soft whisper he cautioned Mauria to be careful, as he also would be, that her paddle did not come in contact with the side of the canoe, for their enemies would not then be apprised of the direction they were moving. As they proceeded on their way his keen eyes remained constantly alert.

Meanwhile, Queen Sirena reached the cove with her handmaidens, but she, too, was baffled at the direction their escaping quarry had taken, for strain her eyes as she did, and look to her left, directly ahead, and then to her right, the darkened water revealed no sign. Though she strained her ears in the hope she might hear sounds indicative to their presence, in this she was likewise disappointed.

However, she was not to give up so easily. She cautioned her handmaidens to silence and listen to her. When they had grouped about her, she gave them instructions. As a result, several mermaids took to the water and swam to the left of the cove, keeping beyond the breaking waves, others swam directly outward, while others swam to the right. All were armed with tridents and had been instructed, if possible, capture of their quarry was in order and they were to be returned alive. If resistance was too great on the part of the captives, then they were to be slain, but only as a last resort.

When Bantan and Mauria had paddled a reasonable distance, the former realized they were not too far from the almost deserted village that the three old surviving natives inhabited. He whispered to the girl that they would go ashore. When the prow touched the sandy beach the occupants laid down their paddles and stepped out.

"We'll draw the canoe to the edge of the foliage," the bronzed giant informed the native girl.

Laying hand upon the gunwale, Bantan in front and Mauria in the rear, within a few minutes they had reached the edge of the fringing foliage. Although their eyes were long accustomed to the darkness, they still could not see beyond the edge of the beach and, accordingly, in the event mermaids had been pursuing them, they would not be able to distinguish them anymore than they could be seen.

The bronzed giant realized only too well the difficulty they would have gathering fruit and nuts in the darkness and, too, there was the thought in mind of their awkwardness in so doing might result in unnecessary noise that might attract attention of any pursuing mermaids. Realizing as well that dawn could not be too far from the present, he decided it would be best that they rested until that time. In the early morning light they would be much more efficient gathering the fruit and nuts they would require. In a hushed whisper he spoke to his companion of this decision.

Mauria could clearly understand how much easier it would be to do as Bantan suggested. While she disliked to remain upon the island longer than necessary, she realized how utterly impossible it would be to gather fruit and nuts in the darkness.

"If you think it best, Bantan," she murmured, "I am in full accord."

"Then lie in the canoe and rest," he urged. "I'll remain on watch. It should be light in a little while, and I'll waken you."

Without a demur, the native girl did as he bade. She moved about a trifle as carefully as she might until she had attained a fairly comfortable position. Though she had no intention of falling asleep, the transition came sooner than she might have anticipated.

Meanwhile, Bantan crouched at the side of the canoe with ears keenly alerted and eyes that were a trifle wearied and strained as he looked toward the water. The gently breaking surf nullified extraneous sounds that otherwise might have been heard. His right hand clutched the handle of his dagger in readiness for any emergency. He was thankful the night was not uncomfortable. Facing the east, his eyes hopefully awaited the first streaks of dawn to herald the new day. His keen ears were aware of Mauria's gentle breathing and he was pleased to know that she was sleeping. Later in the day, after they had left the island and no danger of pursuit being apparent, he, too, would have an opportunity of a nap while the girl paddled.

And so time passed its weary way. Several times Bantan's eyelids would close momentarily, but almost immediately he would force them open. After a little while had passed and he continued to do this, he arose and went to the edge of the beach where the washing waves laved the sand. With a handful of water he bathed his tired eyes and felt much refreshed when he presently returned to the canoe.

It was not long thereafter that the bronzed giant detected the first streaks of dawn peering above the water line. With the passing minutes pink streaks, finger-like, were probing more rapidly into the darkened area above.

As the utter darkness began to pale, Bantan's eyes more carefully scanned the ocean surface beyond the breaking surf and he was happy to notice the absence of any mermaids. Now that he could begin to distinguish objects, he decided to gather fruit and nuts. A glance at Mauria assured him she was still sleeping peacefully.

In the immediate vicinity where they had beached the canoe, the bronzed giant was aware there appeared to be a generous assortment of fruit and nuts. He gathered several armfuls and returned to the canoe, depositing them at its side. Each time that he returned he made certain to scan the water with relief, and then he would ascertain that the native girl was still sleeping. When he returned with the fourth armful, feeling he had gathered sufficient, he reached within the canoe and placed a hand upon Mauria's naked shoulder and shook her gently.

Almost at once the native girl's eyes opened with a startled expression apparent in their dark depths. But the sight of Bantan's smiling features looking down at her immediately brought a sweet smile to her lips and her dark eyes became radiant.

"It is morning already!" she exclaimed.

"I've already gathered sufficient fruit and nuts," he added with a nod. "All we have to do is load them in the canoe. We must not forget a couple of mermaids are accustomed to swim about the island shore each morning —and if we do not wish to be observed by them, we should not lose any more time than necessary being on our way."

Mauria at once arose and stepped out of the canoe. Together, she and Bantan placed therein the fruit and nuts he had gathered. When this was done a smile was exchanged.

"And now we shall be on our way," he said. "We can eat after we are safely away from the island."

Gripping the canoe, Bantan in front pulling, and Mauria at the aft pushing, they noted the added weight made the water craft more difficult to ride down the sandy beach; but after some few minutes of perseverence in their efforts had terminated the canoe was being floated. The bronzed giant held it until the native girl had entered and took up her paddle in readiness. In another moment he, too, had entered and picked up the other. In unison they plied their paddles and without too much difficulty negotiated the gentle surf to presently gain the calmer water beyond.

It was then that they heard shrill voices from the shore they had recently quit. Turning, the bronzed giant saw the three old men who occupied the dilapidated village standing upon the beach. They were waving their skinny arms with bony hands clenched. What they were shouting he could not understand, but he felt certain it was not pleasant for their immediate welfare. Mauria turned about as well and saw the three grotesque figures. She shivered slightly, but as her eyes met her companion's, she smiled.

"They will report us to the mermaid queen," he said. "But little we care now. We'll soon be too far from shore to worry about pursuit, especially with our more dependable paddles in hand."

Turning about and facing the brilliant rays of the rising sun, Bantan and Mauria plied their paddles in unison and the canoe responded as well as could be expected. At intervals the bronzed giant would turn and look back fleetingly at the receding island in their wake. The three old natives were to be seen as they were moving toward the cove as fast as their bent old legs would carry them. Looking in that direction, at first he could see no sign of any mermaids. After several such glances, he did see a couple of them swimming beyond the gentle surf not far from the cove. It was evident they saw the three old natives.

Informing Mauria of this, the two desisted paddling for the time being, and watched proceedings. The two mermaids had now swum ashore and slithered up the beach to be met by the three old natives. It was apparent what was being said concerned the escaping fugitives, for all were looking in their direction in the face of the rising sun. It was doubtful that the canoe and its two occupants could be distinguished because of the brilliancy of the sun just clearing the horizon.

"Do you think they will pursue us, Bantan?" the native girl asked with a trace of concern in her dark eyes.

The bronzed giant merely grinned.

"If they do we have nothing to worry about now," he answered.

As he spoke he looked down at the bottom of the canoe, for he had become aware of a sudden dampness about his knees where he knelt. He saw water slowly gathering, and a closer examination revealed that one of the leaks he had caulked with pitch before leaving the beach of the cliff-encircled primeval island without a name was permitting water to seep through.

Mauria noticed the object of his sudden concern.

"I hope it won't be serious," she murmured.

He smiled assuringly.

"Later I'll try and repair it," he said. "But for now, let's paddle until we are a considerable distance from the island."

CHAPTER XII

Nula and Tama Again

AS THEY CONTINUED to ply their paddles, Bantan kept a wary eye on the water seepage about his knees. He did not forget to frequently glance back at the receding mermaid island, and with unfathomable relief was aware that no pursuit was being given them. By this time he was feeling hungry, and he surmised that Mauria as well must be nearly famished though she had not complained.

"We'll take time out to have our breakfast," he said to the native girl. "There seems to be no sign of pursuit being given us by the mermaids."

As Mauria desisted paddling and placed her paddle in the bottom of the canoe she turned to face her companion. At the same time she was relieved of the glare of the morning sun. She drew the back of a hand across a slightly beading forehead and smiled.

"I'm nearly famished," she declared. Then, noticing that he was looking down at the canoe's bottom where considerable seepage was to be seen, she added with sincerity: "I hope it won't be too serious."

"After we've eaten I'll repair it," he said in reply.

For their morning meal Bantan husked a coconut and bored into one of its eyes with his dagger point. They exchanged the shelled nut several times until its contents were drained. The shell was broken into several pieces with the butt of his dagger, then with the point he loosened the pieces of white meat adhering to the inner side and shared them with the native girl. Afterwards they ate a plantain and some figs.

When he had eaten to his fill, the bronzed giant cut slender strips from the coconut husk. With his dagger point he stuffed these into the small crack and tapped gently with the butt end until at last he was sure he had stopped the leak.

Mauria watched him in fascination, for Bantan seemed capable of accomplishing the impossible and he always did so with methodology. Looking up at her, he smiled.

"At least I've stopped the leak for the present," he said. "Should we come to another island I'll search for the pitch certain trees provide to do a more thorough job on it."

After he had spoken, he arose to a standing position and surveyed the waterline in all directions, shading his eyes when facing the sun as would be natural.

The mermaid island was all that could be sighted with clearness. A few sea gulls could be seen also in that direction. However, in the direction the canoe had been proceeding, the bronzed giant thought he detected a small floating object, but he could not be certain. His curiosity had been aroused, however, and for that reason he wanted to be sure of its identity before he decided to have a nap. By that time the dampness in the canoe's bottom should have evaporated. He told Mauria to keep watch directly ahead, as he also would, for the floating object that he mentioned to her.

Mile after mile was covered as the sun rose higher, and the floating object Bantan had sighted was now well in view. There was a seeming familiarity about it that had him guessing for a little while. And then with the suddenness of thought itself he recognized it for what it was.

"Mauria, it is the hollowed log!" he exclaimed. "It

has taken these past suns for it to float hither from where we left it."

"It does look like it," the native girl agreed, nodding her head.

From one end of it was to be seen a dangling rope which trailed in the water.

"It must be," Bantan added, convinced, indicating the trailing rope.

As he continued to stare at the floating object, memories of Nulu and Tama flashed across the screen of his recollection. And now with a slight furrow appearing between his eyebrows he appeared to be in deep thought. Unless he was mistaken, when they had left the hollowed log it had been overturned. Now it was right side up! While he realized a number of incidents could have caused a reversal of position, he dared not hope human agency had done so. But he must know for a certainty.

"Quick, Mauria," he said with insistence, "let us hurry. It may be possible—"

The several hundred yards intervening were speedily spanned, and as the canoe drew alongside the hollowed log, Bantan's eyes anxiously looked within. Joy and then concern appeared upon his features. In one end he saw the brown shoulders and arms of a native lying on his side back to and his arms covered his features. But there was a seeming familiarity about that body. And now as the hollowed log tilted slightly, the eyes of the bronzed giant looked toward the other end and his heart almost stopped beating as he saw the much lighter-skinned legs and body of a blonde-haired girl also lying back to with her slender arms covering her features.

Nulu and Tama! In some miraculous manner they had not perished as had been thought.

"Mauria, it is Nulu and Tama!" he exclaimed with great joy in his heart.

The native girl uttered a gasp of incredulity.

As he spoke, Bantan grasped the gunwale of the hollowed log and drew it close to the canoe. Mauria also clutched it with trembling hands as she looked within at the two prone bodies.

"Nulu and Tama!" the bronzed giant cried. "Are you all right?"

Because they appeared so still he hardly dared breathe. Reaching within, he gently touched one of the girl's warm arms that covered her features.

A plaintive moan issued from the blonde-haired girl's lips and she made a feeble effort to turn over upon her back.

"Nulu, what has happened?" Bantan added with deep concern. "Have you been injured? Look at me—please."

The blonde-haired girl uttered a low moan and again made a feeble attempt to turn over upon her back, but apparently lacked the strength to do so. Whether she recognized the voice of the speaker could not be determined.

The bronzed giant realized now that something was out of the ordinary. He reached within the hollowed log and, with one hand upon the girl's shoulder and the other about her waist, he gently eased her over upon her back so that he might look down upon her dear features. The girl uttered another plaintive moan as he moved her. Looking down upon her flushed features, he placed a hand upon her forehead and realized that she was burning with fever. She also appeared to have wasted away somewhat since he had seen her last.

"Nulu," he murmured. "can you hear me? Open your eyes if you can."

The white lids fluttered for several moments and finally opened. Her eyes moved back and forth, up and down, and though they finally met his worried ones, there was no sign of recognition in hers.

Meanwhile, Mauria had been trying to revive Tama, but he was not as responsive as Nulu had been. That he lived was evidenced by his slow breathing. Though the native girl called him repeatedly by name, he gave no indication that he heard her. She, too, placed a hand upon his forehead and found that he was burning with fever.

The bronzed giant looked toward Mauria in perplexity for a moment. Then with a sudden thought he pushed the hollowed log sufficiently apart from the canoe to insert his right arm in the space afforded until his hand was immersed in the water. With his moistened palm he placed it upon the girl's burning forehead. Looking toward the native girl he indicated that she do likewise with Tama.

Repeatedly both continued this ministration, and to their utter relief their patients apparently appreciated the coolness against their burning foreheads. A quick survey of both bodies revealed they appeared unmarked from bruises.

Bantan spoke to Mauria of his intentions, and the native girl nodded. Quickly then he picked up a coconut and husked it, and bored into one of the eyes with his dagger point. He nodded to his companion and handed her the coconut, telling what he intended, though it was hardly necessary. Reaching into the hollowed log, he lifted Nulu to a seated position, though her head was inclined to bow forward. He slipped an arm about her shoulders supportingly, then with the fingers of his left hand gently pried open her mouth. Then he nodded to the native girl. She held the shelled nut above the girl's opened mouth and allowed a few drops to trickle into it. Nulu momentarily coughed, but she managed to swallow the small quantity of milk.

"A little more," the bronzed giant murmured.

Mauria tilted the nut a trifle and more fluid entered the unconscious girl's mouth. As it trickled down her throat she again gagged for a moment, but she did not spew up any of it. The small amount of coconut milk that she had swallowed appeared to have revived her somewhat, for her white eyelids fluttered and she breathed more gently and evenly. No further plaintive moans issued from her throat.

A gentle smile touched Bantan's lips and his dark eyes appeared less worried. He looked at his companion and nodded.

"A little more, Mauria," he said, "and then we must do the same with Tama."

A third time they repeated their feeding, and this time more coconut milk was swallowed without any ill-effects. Again Nulu's eyes opened, and though there was no apparent awareness to be detected in them, there did appear an unconscious expression of gratitude. Before easing her back to her former position, the bronzed giant pressed his lips upon the unconscious girl's for a long moment. Then he and Mauria turned their attention to Tama.

Bantan turned the native over upon his back first, then placed a strong arm about his shoulders and lifted him to a seated position. His feeding was the same as Nulu's, and no difficulty whatsoever was experienced in swallowing the refreshing coconut milk. After a third administering, Tama drew a deep breath and his eyes opened. They appeared rational, though perplexed, but presently an awareness dawned within the dark depths as he recognized the features of Bantan and Mauria. In a whisper he uttered their names in gratitude. The effort was strength-consuming, but Tama managed to tempo-

rarily arouse himself from the lethargy that had claimed
him.

"Take it easy, Tama," Bantan murmured. "You will
be all right."

The native heaved a deep sigh and the trace of a smile
touched his fevered lips.

"It is good to know you and Mauria are alive," he
murmured hoarsely. Then, as though recollecting his companion, he spoke again with anxiety. "Nulu! Is she all
right?"

The bronzed giant assured him that Nulu would be
all right, and Tama smiled in utter relief to know this
as he closed his eyes, and again sighed.

Bantan eased him back to the bottom of the hollowed
log. With moist eyes, Mauria leaned over and pressed
her lips to Tama's.

"You must get well, Tama," she murmured. "You
must—for my sake."

The bronzed giant recollected the trailing rope. Upon
an examination it proved it could still be used for a towline, so he attached it to the aft of the canoe. He regretted they could not be upon some island where it
would be more convenient to care for their patients. He
dared not return to the mermaid island because of the danger to their well being and to the interests of Nulu and
Tama.

To solve the problem for the present he suggested to
Mauria that she enter the hollowed log with some fruit
and a coconut as well to administer to the needs of their
patients. Meanwhile, he would forego the nap he had
planned earlier in the morning and, though somewhat
wearied, would continue to paddle with the hope another
island might be sighted before the sun sank beneath the
waterline at the end of the day.

The native girl did as she was bade, and alone, Bantan

paddled the canoe with the hollowed log and its human cargo in tow. Naturally his progress was not what he would have hoped, but the fact Nulu and Tama were alive did not cause any regret upon the paddler's part. Even as yet he could hardly believe it credible that they had survived the upsetting of the canoe when the manta ray had passed beneath them. He hoped the early recovery of consciousness by either Nulu or Tama would render an account of their miraculous escape from death.

Intermittently as he plied his paddle, the bronzed giant would look backward to Mauria and inquire of the welfare of her patients. The native girl assured him they were no worse. Should they reveal a marked improvement she would happily announce such tidings. He did not forget to look down at the leak he had caulked earlier in the morning and was relieved to notice no further seepage of water.

With the sun rising higher in the heaven, Bantan was more able to sight the eastern horizon, and always his sharp eyes were scanning the seemingly interminable stretches of water before him. He was ever hopeful that another island would be sighted, and this time most earnestly wished for once such an island would be uninhabited, for it had appeared in the past all islands he had visited were inhabited by peoples who were enemies to all others, and woe befall the stranger, however peaceful his intent, that came to their alien shore!

Synchronously in his mind fleeting thoughts of those islands he had visited in the past crossed the screen of his recollection, and he would shake his head, thinking how very fortunate he had been in those experiences to have come through unscathed only to be confronted with newer adventures of incredible proportions.

At last, feeling the requirement of nourishment to keep his strength at its peak, he paused in his paddling to

partake of his noonday repast. He turned to Mauria and
asked if she wished to join him. At her nod, he drew the
trailing hollowed log alongside the canoe and the native
girl carefully stepped into it. Bantan looked at the unconscious forms and there appeared no appreciable change
in their condition. While he and the native girl partook
of their meal, she rendered a more detailed account of
their patients.

"Tama appears to be responding slightly more than
Nulu," she said. "When I bathe his forehead with a
moistened palm, he sighs deeply. Sometimes he opens his
eyes and just looks up at me in adoration. When I urge
him to drink coconut milk he offers no protest and has
no difficulty in swallowing. I am sure his fever is beginning to leave him."

The bronzed giant's lips were touched with a gentle,
hopeful smile.

"And is Nulu somewhat responsive?" he asked then.

The native girl nodded.

"Although she appears weaker than Tama," she answered, "I'm sure she is recovering somewhat. Her forehead doesn't appear to be so hot and she swallows the
coconut milk I give her without difficulty. When she
opens her eyes there seems to be a questioning look in
them. She doesn't recognize me."

The bronzed giant's dark eyes were kindly.

"After we have finished eating," he said, "I'll try and
talk with her. Perhaps I'll make her realize who I am."

Some few minutes later, Bantan stepped into the hollowed log and knelt near Nulu. He gently stroked her
forehead and softly spoke to her, calling her by name.

"Nulu, please open your eyes."

The unconscious girl heaved a deep sigh and her eyelids fluttered momentarily before opening. Since the
bronzed giant's body blocked the sunlight, the girl's eyes

could not thereby be blinded by the bright rays. Her hazel eyes studied the handsome features above her filled with concern for her welfare, then a light sob escaped her fevered lips as recognition of his identity was forced into her awry faculties. A semblance of a smile touched her trembling lips and she whispered his name so faintly he could hardly hear it. Her hands folded upon her bosom sought to lift toward him, but lack of strength resulted in them dropping again.

"Nulu," he murmured, "get well soon."

Moisture gathered in the girl's eyes, and looking down at her, Bantan saw that her fevered lips were moving somewhat.

"Kiss me, Bantan to make me strong," was what he read in her eyes that her voice couldn't speak.

A choked sob escaped his lips as he lowered his face and his mouth covered hers, hoping that the contact would give her renewed strength. She breathed deeply and strongly. As his lips left hers and he watched her for a reaction, he felt elated to see that Nulu had indeed gained new strength, as though the contact of their lips had transferred energy from his healthy body to her weakened one.

With a long drawn breath Bantan then turned his attention to Tama. To his surprise the native's eyes were open, and recognition was apparent in their depths. A slight smile touched his fevered lips.

"You are stronger now, Tama," the bronzed giant said observingly with a smile.

"Much better, Bantan, my friend," was the answer in a faint voice. He then turned his head and looked at the silently watching Mauria. "With such a wonderful nurse I don't want to die."

Moisture instantly rose in the native girl's dark eyes at being paid such a fine compliment.

"I'll continue caring for you until you are well, Tama," she promised in a slightly trembling voice. "All my life I'll want to care for you."

An awed expression came into Bantan's eyes, and he was glad that Mauria had expressed herself thusly, for he realized now for the first time that she could transfer her affection from him to Tama, as he had hoped she would. His eyes thanked her silently as they met and held for a long moment. A smile touched his lips as he turned to Tama.

"You are a lucky man, Tama," he said, "to have Mauria speak like that of you."

The native only smiled and closed his eyes, sighing wearily.

"I'm hoping to sight an island soon," Bantan added. "And this time I'll be hoping it will be an uninhabited one so that you and Nulu will have plenty of time to regain your strength before we continue on to Marja."

Although Tama did not open his eyes, he nodded his head to indicate he had heard.

Before exchanging places with Mauria, Bantan knelt near the unconscious Nulu and again kissed her fevered lips. Although she did not open her eyes, he was aware of a slight responsiveness in the girl's lips moving against his. Then he covered her folded hands with one of his for a long moment.

Presently he was again plying his paddle with alertful eyes ever scanning the horizon, and the native girl, once more in the hollowed log, tended to their patients with loving solicitude.

CHAPTER XIII

Tama's Story

IT WAS NOT LONG thereafter that a gentle breeze stirred in the paddler's favor and he was grateful that the increasing heat of the sun was tempered. Bantan constantly inquired of Mauria the condition of her patients, and was assured their fever appeared to be steadily abating. Otherwise, with only brief rests, he continued to ply his paddle faithfully, and the canoe and the trailing hollowed log with its human cargo moved steadily over the slightly undulating surface of the mighty South Pacific Ocean.

The bronzed giant's tiring eyes were suddenly given reason for renewed hope, for slightly to his right the waterline appeared broken, and he was positive another island was to be seen. He joyfully called the native girl's attention to his discovery and she was elated to learn of it.

"Want me to help you paddle?" she asked with eagerness. "Our combined efforts will increase our chances of reaching it before nightfall."

"Do you feel Nulu and Tama will be all right?" he asked in return.

"I'll give each some more coconut milk first," she said in answer.

While administering to her patients, Mauria was relieved to notice that their foreheads appeared much cooler, but they still remained in a somewhat lethargic state.

In a few minutes she joined the bronzed giant, and with her assistance their progress was much better in the

144

direction of their goal. To their eager eyes with the passing minutes the island appeared to loom more prominently in the distance. When a couple of hours of steady paddling had passed they could easily distinguish the foliage that clothed it. It appeared to be about the same size as the one occupied by the mermaids.

For the first time since earlier morning some sea gulls could be discerned near the island they approached. A glance at the sun nearing the waterline assured the two paddlers they would be on land before darkness completely enveloped them. Most of all, they earnestly hoped the island would prove to be uninhabited; and if so, their joy would be complete.

The bronzed giant's tired eyes scanned the beach that was evident for any sign of canoes, indicating inhabitants. As well, he studied the foliage for possible sight of a village concealed within; but he saw nothing, and for that reason felt they could beach the canoe without danger. From beyond the breaking waves he carefully sniffed the air with his delicate nostrils, hoping in that manner to determine the presence of humans through their effluvia. The pleasing aroma of the foliage and numerous flowers was all that he was aware of.

Mauria turned about, meeting his tired eyes.

"Is it going to be safe to go ashore?" she asked.

He nodded with a tired smile.

"I can obtain no scent of humans," he answered. "Before we enter the surf, I'll leave you to navigate the canoe alone. I'll manage the hollowed log for the safety of Nulu and Tama."

Arising, Bantan unfastened the towline and drew the hollowed log alongside the canoe. Picking up his paddle he carefully selected a place so that he would not disturb the two still unconscious patients lying therein. He nodded to the native girl, indicating for her to paddle ashore.

The hollowed log would be a more difficult matter, but the bronzed giant was confident of his ability to reach shore without shipping too much water. He watched Mauria as she expertly guided the canoe through the gentle surf, and he had to admit his admiration for her ability. When she had disembarked and drew the canoe out of the water, then did Bantan follow.

The unwieldly craft rocked and tossed somewhat erratically in the surf, but the paddler was ever ready with strong strokes to keep it from turning broadside or capsizing, and within a couple of minutes the blunt prow grated upon the sandy beach. No water had been shipped to add to the inconvenience of Nulu and Tama. The native had stirred somewhat and his eyes opened through curiosity as the rougher water was encountered. Recognizing the bronzed giant as the navigator he sighed and closed his eyes, confident that all would be well.

Bantan stepped out of the hollowed log and drew it a short distance up on the beach with the ready and willing Mauria's assistance. Then pausing, he looked toward the fringing foliage and again his keen nostrils sniffed the scented air. The native girl's eyes studied the foliage as well. With a sigh he turned to her and smiled.

"Gather some grass for pallets," he said to her. "I'll carry Nulu and Tama to the edge of the foliage."

The native girl was off on her mission at once. Then Bantan reached within the hollowed log and slipped his arms about Nulu's back and legs and carefully lifted her. She stirred and a plaintive protest was unconsciously uttered, but she did not recover her senses while he carried her up the beach. Placing her gently upon the sand, he then did likewise for Tama.

The bronzed giant then went to the water and dragged

the canoe to the foliage's edge, then returned for the hollowed log. Because it was heavier, he experienced more difficulty with it, but doggedly kept at the task until it, too, was alongside the canoe.

Mauria had brought sufficient grass by this time and pallets were quickly fashioned. Nulu and Tama were moved upon them for greater comfort. The native opened his eyes meanwhile and in a weak voice offered his regrets that he was such a nuisance. Both Bantan and Mauria assured him that he would have been willing to act accordingly had their positions been reversed.

With moisture in her eyes the native girl assured Tama she would care for him uncomplainingly until he had regained his lost strength. She asked if he cared for some fruit or drink, and he answered that he did feel that he might. And so she gave him drink and fed him to his want.

Meanwhile, the bronzed giant knelt at Nulu's side and managed to restore her to consciousness. When she looked with awe about her surroundings she realized in some miraculous manner she was now upon land. As well, she appeared to recognize Bantan. A weak smile touched her lips and there was a glow in her hazel eyes.

"Bantan!" she whispered.

Inclining his face nearer the girl's, he smiled gently as he noted her fevered lips moving and suspected what favor she was silently asking. He pressed his lips tenderly upon hers. One of her arms managed to encircle his neck. When their lips parted, she smiled again and her glowing eyes thanked him.

"Do you feel like drinking some coconut milk and eating some fruit, Nulu?" he asked.

She nodded weakly.

Bantan obtained a coconut from the canoe along with some other fruit. He lifted the girl to a seated position,

supporting her with his strong right arm while he offered her drink with his left. Nulu drank almost greedily
as a result of her fevered body demanding liquid to
quench its fire, but she ate sparingly of the fruit he
offered. When she had partaken of what she wished, he
then eased her back upon her pallet. He remained at her
side, holding her hands even though they did not speak.
Within minutes she fell asleep. Looking toward Mauria,
he saw that she appeared very happy as she and Tama,
still conscious, were talking quietly.

The bronzed giant then partook of food and drink.
Since twilight would soon be upon them, he decided to
gather more grass for pallets for himself and Mauria.
Arising to his feet he informed the native girl of his
intentions, and both she and Tama nodded. Before the
sun had set he had gathered sufficient for their needs.
With the coming of twilight Tama fell asleep. Bantan,
meanwhile, arranged a pallet in the canoe and another in
the hollowed log. Mauria drew near him. As he straightened and became aware of her presence, he smiled.

"Do you know, Mauria," he said, "I am very happy
that we rescued Nulu and Tama?"

"I, too, am, Bantan," she replied. "I realize now that
I can learn to love Tama very much, and later will be
a devoted mate to him."

He placed a gentle hand upon the native girl's shoulder
and looked at her for a long moment.

"I am happy for you," he murmured. "Now that Nulu
has come back to me, I find I am happier, too. You've
been a fine companion to have shared the adventures we've
undergone and you command my highest admiration."

The native girl's eyes became moist. She reached for
the hand that rested upon her shoulder and held it in
both of hers. She lowered her head and kissed its back.
Looking up at him, she smiled apologetically.

"I know I've been a nuisance to you in the past," she said in a low voice, "and I hope you'll forgive me. As my 'dream man,' my heart was yours from the beginning if you had wanted it as I've told you so many times. But I'm sure from now on Tama will occupy my dreams."

Upon an impulse Bantan freed his hand from hers and he placed both of his arms about her, drawing her close to him.

"Mauria, you'll never know how close I came to accepting your love," he confessed. "But I'm sure as matters have developed you and Tama are going to be very happy, and Nulu and I will be very happy as well." With his peroration the bronzed giant pressed his lips upon the center of her forehead, then released her. "So long as I live I'll always feel proud to have known you."

Mauria choked back a threatening sob.

"And I'll always feel the same toward you, Bantan," she answered fervently.

Before retiring for the night, the bronzed giant placed Nulu in the canoe and Tama in the hollowed log as a precaution against dampness from the sandy beach. He and Mauria brought the pallets they had lain upon and placed them near the water crafts. Though Bantan waked a number of times during the night, to his relief he saw that their patients continued to sleep soundly and their breathing was quite regular.

In the morning when the bronzed giant woke with the rising sun, he again checked Nulu and Tama and found they were still asleep. Their color was much better and he felt the fever had been broken. Mauria awoke almost at the same time. They indulged in a brief swim before returning ashore to partake of their breakfast. After they had eaten, they roused the blonde-haired girl and the native. Both appeared much brighter and in better spirits, and while the fever had left them, both were very weak.

After being given their morning meal, they were able to talk more and stated they were feeling stronger. But it would be several days before either would have regained a semblance of their normal strength.

After they had eaten, Bantan asked if they would like to be bathed, telling them they would feel much more refreshed. Each was reluctant to be treated as a helpless babe, but the bronzed giant knew what was best for them. He carried Nulu out into the surf. Mauria accompanied him and bathed the blonde-haired girl. Returning with her to the edge of the foliage, he then carried Tama into the water. Since the native was strong enough to stand, he was allowed to do so, steadying himself with one hand on Bantan's shoulder while he was being laved. Afterwards, he was carried to where Nulu was basking in the warm sunlight. Both admitted they felt much more refreshed after their bath.

Bantan and Mauria sat near them, happy that their patients were so much improved on this morning and of apparently alertful faculties.

"Tell me," the bronzed giant said to Tama, "what happened to you and Nulu? After the sea monster upset the canoe, when I came to the surface I called to all of you. Only Mauria answered. We saw the overturned canoe and the hollowed log with fruit and nuts floating about. I righted the canoe and retrieved the two paddles, my bow and arrows, and collected what fruit and nuts we would need. I continued to call to both of you. Since no reply was heard and darkness was fast settling, we paddled toward the east. Just before the sea monster upset the canoe I was sure I had sighted an island—which proved so. Tell me, just what happened?"

The native smiled wryly with recollection of the horror his memories resurrected.

"At the mission school I attended I learned much of

the sea monsters that inhabited the ocean depths," he explained. "What upset the canoe is known as a manta ray. They are not dangerous—like a shark for instance. The manta ray just happened to come along and we happened to be in its way. Just before the canoe was upset I heard you shout a warning, and for a reason I cannot explain I seemed paralyzed—but not with fear.

"Both Nulu and I were flung side by side into the water and we became draped over the front edge of one of the manta ray's large flippers. I was half dazed, but was fortunate I had instinctively filled my lungs with air before going overboard. As soon as I could collect my dazed senses I tried to worm away from the flipper. I was aware that Nulu was at my left side, but she appeared to be unconscious. Gripping one of her arms I continued to worm myself free, dragging her with me. The pressure of the water hampered me and I knew the manta ray must have borne us a considerable distance before I managed to free ourselves and floated to the surface. I was so exhausted that I couldn't call out, and I was worried because Nulu appeared so lifeless. But I did remember the direction the manta ray had been swimming, so with Nulu I swam in the opposite direction, hoping to find you and Mauria.

"It seemed a long time had passed and darkness had completely settled when I bumped into the overturned hollowed log. By this time I was breathless and couldn't have shouted—try though I did. It was difficult to right the hollowed log and keep Nulu afloat at the same time, but finally I managed to do so. I don't know how I was able to lift her unconscious body in the boat, but I must have done so somehow. Then with difficulty I drew my self in as well.

"Although I was very weak, my first concern was for Nulu, fearing that she had expired. But I was aware that her heart was beating, so felt she was merely stunned. It was then that I tried to call out, but my voice was very weak and I don't imagine I was heard. Then I turned my attention to Nulu and tried to revive her, but couldn't bring her to consciousness. I finally collapsed after awhile, and must have been unconscious all the while we drifted aimlessly until you found us."

"And we found you both in time," Bantan commented. "Do both you and Nulu wish to hear what happened to Mauria and I?"

"You mentioned an island," the blonde-haired girl said. "There was one?"

"Yes, there was an island," he answered, nodding. "It would have been a lovely island except it was inhabited by mermaids."

Of course Nulu had never heard of such mythical creatures, and for that reason she appeared puzzled. But apparently Tama had heard of such. He whistled softly beneath his breath.

"Mermaids!" he murmured. "It has long been considered that mermaids were creatures of the imagination and never really existed. You both really saw such creatures?"

A soft laugh issued from Mauria.

"That they exist Bantan and I have seen actual proof," she declared, then shuddered momentarily. "We were lucky to escape with our lives."

"They were vicious creatures?" Tama asked unbelievingly. "I have learned that they were supposed to be very lovely and enchanting."

"They are lovely in appearance," the native girl added. "One of them told me all of their males were lost in a terrible storm while they were upon an annual pilgrimage. Since that time they have lived without males. There are about twenty in number and their queen is known as Sirena. I was first captured by them and was a guest, then later a prisoner. Bantan rescued me. They stole our canoe, and had it not been possible to retrieve it I don't know what might have happened to us. As for me, they had no use; but from my talks with Sirena I know they would have welcomed any form of male so that they might perpetuate their race. Bantan was fortunate he was not captured by them, for I doubt if he would have escaped. They would have guarded him well."

"It's unbelievable!" Tama murmured, looking toward the bronzed giant and shaking his head.

Bantan smiled ruefully.

"It may be unbelieving to you, Tama," he said; "but having seen the mermaids I know they exist. I would not wish to be a captive of their queen. I believe she would be crueller than Zarna." And with his peroration he shook his head.

Since Nulu did not know what mermaids were, she asked about them. Mauria explained their physical characteristics, and when she had described them, the blonde-haired girl could only shake her head in disbelief.

"They have no legs and feet," she murmured. "I can hardly believe such creatures exist."

The native girl smiled mollifyingly.

"I'll hope we never again have the occasion to see them much less than be captured by them."

Nulu appeared to shiver and a wry expression overcame her features.

"I can't believe such creatures live," she murmured again.

"We have talked enough for now," Bantan said then, for he noticed that both Nulu and Tama were struggling to remain alert when their utter weariness was only too apparent upon their features. "Both of you must rest often until your strength returns. Later, we can talk more. As it is, I fear we have talked too much."

Tama smiled wearily.

"I am a long way from what I was," he agreed. "I don't ever remember when I felt so weak as I do now."

Mauria drew close to him.

"Lie down and rest," she said solicitously. "You have nothing to worry about while Bantan and I are around."

The native lay back and sighed.

"The fever made me weaker than I can ever remember any other sickness did," he murmured.

Mauria inclined her face toward his and kissed him.

"Sleep, Tama," she murmured.

Meanwhile, Bantan drew near Nulu who also lay back. He, too, kissed her, bringing a smile to her lips and a glow in her eyes.

"The sooner you and Tama regain your strength," he said to her, "the sooner we can leave for Marja Island."

"I want very much to go to Marja," she said softly, then closed her eyes.

"And you shall," he promised.

Within a few minutes both Nulu and Tama were again sleeping peacefully.

CHAPTER XIV

The Temple of the Sea God

BANTAN AROSE to his feet and looked at Mauria.

"Remain with them," he said. "I haven't forgotten about the leak in the canoe's bottom, so I'll search for the pitch I need."

The native girl smiled and nodded.

The bronzed giant entered the foliage which was not too thick or tangled, and without difficulty threaded his way through it. His sharp eyes were anxiously seeking what was required. Within fifteen minutes he found what he sought, and half an hour later he had returned to the landing and performed a more thorough repair job on the canoe's bottom.

Mauria watched him in silence while Nulu and Tama continued to sleep undisturbed.

"Now," he said, turning to the native girl, "I'll test it by paddling around the island to be assured that we are its only inhabitants."

"I'll hope we are," Mauria answered.

The bronzed giant nodded. Without further delay, he turned and momentarily paused to glance at the sleeping Nulu and Tama, then dragged the canoe to the edge of the water. Within a few minutes he was paddling through the calmer water a short distance from the surf. From the edge of the foliage Mauria watched him. She waved as he looked in her direction, and he waved in return.

Bantan's eyes for the most part constantly focused upon the island shore and foliage as he circumnavigated

155

it. Having landed upon the west shore, he was now paddling southeast. Occasionally sea gulls were flying about, and whenever one passed near him, it would screech as though in protest that an alien had come to its domain.

As he rounded the southern side of the island the bronzed giant noticed little change in its regular contour nor did the beach appear different. His eyes looked constantly for evidence of humans, but he could detect nothing to indicate such. He was hopeful that no sight be obtained, for in the past upon such peaceful looking islands their human inhabitants had always been enemies. But presently, when approaching the eastern shore, he was acutely aware of the changing scenery.

The tropical foliage gave way to a rough cliff and the beach ended where the rocky surface continued into the water. The face of the cliff was honeycombed with numerous caves of various sizes. In many of them terns were crouched. The bronzed giant was relieved that the blinding sun no longer faced him as it had since starting out. He was leisurely paddling so that his sharp eyes might more carefully scan the cliff and its summit. In his mind there was something familiar about the scenery presented to him, and recollection of the mermaid island was visualized. Slightly ahead he noticed a cove, and as his eyes followed it, he observed a larger grotto at the base of the cliff. He nodded now.

"So much like the mermaid island," he soliloquized. "I wonder what the grotto will reveal?"

The water in the cove was slightly ruffled, and Bantan glanced down at it but could not see bottom. A number of small colored fish were to be seen swimming about, but his sharp eyes saw no octopus lurking in the depths. No sharks appeared to be in the nearby vicinity.

The grotto's opening was of sufficient size to easily permit the canoe's passage. Slowly plying his paddle, the bronzed giant propelled the canoe within the aperture, his sharp eyes missing no detail of the interior. The walls were rough above the apparent high-water line. Below, the erosion of water had smoothed them somewhat. There was several feet clearance to the rough ceiling. At the present time the tide appeared to be at the half-way level, and from the dampness of the walls just above, it was obvious the tide was receding.

Peering straight ahead in the darker recesses of the grotto, Bantan was aware about a couple hundred yards farther there was to be seen a faint glow. He continued to paddle slowly and the canoe must have covered at least a hundred yards when its prow grated upon the rocky floor. Stepping out, he drew it half out of water, remembering as he did that the tide was receding. Then with his right hand clutching the handle of his dagger he advanced slowly along the passageway toward its end where the faint glow was becoming greater in intensity.

As the bronzed giant reached the end he came to a halt and surveyed the interior of the amphitheatre, the walls and ceiling of which glowed with phosphorescence, so that no detail was missed. It closely resembled the one on the mermaid island except there were no corridors leading from it other than the one he had traversed, nor was there a pool of water that the other had.

What arrested his attention was directly opposite him upon a dais. There was a smooth, rock altar some ten feet in length. Upon it was a life-size statue fashioned by the hand of man. It was reclining upon its right side, facing him, stretching full length. From the waist up it represented a man, but from there down it was of fish-like proportions.

Recollecting what Mauria had been told of the mermen going upon an annual pilgrimage, Bantan now felt this must be the island to which they had come. This must be the temple where they had worshipped this sea god that reclined upon the altar.

Through curiosity he now advanced toward the altar of the sea god until he stood before it and examined it more carefully. The bronzed giant realized the artisans who had fashioned it were excellent craftsmen, for the features appeared so real that one would have been positive they were alive. Even the gray eyes had been polished so that they appeared life-like. The features, stoic though they were, bore traces of slight wrinkles on the forehead, otherwise they were smooth. The lips were slightly parted, revealing strong teeth, and the nose was firm and acquiline.

After some few minutes had passed, Bantan shrugged and turned about to retrace his way to his canoe. His curiosity had been satisfied, and since there was nothing else within the temple to attract his attention, he had no further reason to remain. At the opening he paused to once more look about, then with another shrug returned to where his canoe now lay completely out of the water because of the receding tide. In a few minutes he had turned it about and pushed it into the water and was plying his paddle leisurely.

Once again in the open, the bronzed giant resumed his way around the island shore. An examination of the leak he had repaired revealed his task had been perfect, for no slightest seepage was evident. Several hundred yards from the cove the cliff gave way to the heavily foliaged tropical growth. There appeared no apparent change in the island's contour as the paddler continued his way until in due time he was within sight of the landing place. Mauria was to be seen with her two patients. They were seated now, having awakened from their nap.

Nulu espied the canoe shortly after it rounded the

shoreline, and her hazel eyes were brightened with joy at sight of her beloved one.

"There is Bantan," she said, indicating the canoe and its lone occupant.

Mauria and Tama looked in the direction the blonde-haired girl pointed and were pleased to know he was returning so soon.

When the bronzed giant had beached the canoe and approached his companions, he smiled in greeting, as they did, and expressed his happiness to find Nulu and Tama awake. Unashamedly he kissed the blonde-haired girl.

"Do you know," he then said, straightening, "that this island must be the one to which the mermen came on their annual pilgrimage?"

Without awaiting any comment, Bantan related what he had discovered in the grotto. Then looking at Mauria, he added:

"The mermaid who told you about the mermen—did she say they knew where they went?"

The native girl shook her head.

"She told me none of the mermaids knew where they went on their pilgrimage," she answered. "None of the mermen ever told."

Bantan's lips were touched with a smile.

"Perhaps it is well that the mermaids don't know," he commented. "Otherwise, we wouldn't be too safe here. My trip around the island assures me that we are its only inhabitants. We shall remain here, of course, until Nulu and Tama are completely well before we set out for Marja."

"That Nulu and I were only in full possession of our strength now," Tama murmured with a shake of his head.

"For two people who were so near death," the bronzed giant said consolingly, "you both are doing very well.

Be at peace with yourself, Tama. Everything will be all right from now on."

"I'll hope so," the native answered with an apologetic smile. "It makes me feel so helpless to know I am partly responsible for our delay in reaching our ultimate goal."

Bantan approached Tama and rested a gentle hand upon one of his shoulders.

"We are upon a beautiful island with plenty to eat," he said, "and we have nothing to worry about, so don't fret. In due time you will have regained your strength, as Nulu will, then we shall set out upon our delayed trip."

The native placed a hand upon the bronzed giant's that rested upon his shoulder.

"Thank you, Bantan," he said. "You say things so nicely it makes me feel good to know you for the true friend you are."

The bronzed giant winked to Mauria, who had been watching them with moisture in her dark eyes, then he returned to Nulu's side. The blonde-haired girl placed a hand upon his arm and smiled sweetly.

"It's good just to be alive," she murmured. "Thinking how near death Tama and I were gives me more reason now to want to live."

Later that day Bantan busied himself constructing an ample lean-to for the comfort of all. Mauria rendered him a hand—happy as always that she was able to be of assistance.

For a change in diet, the bronzed giant fashioned crude nets. Out beyond the gentle surf his patience was rewarded with catching some fine fish. Wild yams had also been found growing nearby during his incursions within the island. While the native girl proved her ability in cleaning the fish that had been caught, Bantan prepared a fire. The girl also welcomed this opportunity to prove herself a fine cook. The baked fish and yams were indeed delicious and much more staple food than what they had been existing upon.

During the passing days Mauria gathered material and industriously fashioned herself and Nulu as well new articles of apparel. Both the bronzed giant and Tama complimented her.

While Nulu and Tama continued to improve, Bantan explored various parts of the island which was in keeping with his adventurous spirit, and always he returned with arms ladened with fruit and nuts, or material with which to fashion spears and arrows.

With greater improvement, Nulu and Tama were up and around more often and for lengthier periods. They even indulged in brief swims accompanied by the bronzed giant and Mauria. Before a week had passed, so rapid his recovery, Tama asked that he might join Bantan in a trip to visit the grotto of the sea god.

"As well it will give me a chance to see how well I am regaining my strength," he added.

Nulu and Mauria were asked if they cared to join them, and they were quite agreeable.

The canoe was launched into the gentle surf and soon the bronzed giant and the young native were leisurely paddling until they neared the cove. Mauria remarked of its similarity with the one on the mermaid island.

The canoe was maneuvered within the grotto. The tide was about the same level as the previous week when Bantan alone had come hither, but since it was rising now, upon disembarking, the canoe was drawn several yards up on the rock floor.

Later, when examining the stone sea god as it reclined upon the altar, Tama expressed his wonder that mermen and mermaids indeed existed.

"We learned at the mission school that such a race existed only in a study known as mythology and never actually were in a state of living existence," he explained. Having noted the perfection of the sea god's construction, he added: "It is evident that the artisans of their race were very skilled, considering the crude tools they must have possessed to have done such a fine job."

Nulu and Mauria remained silent, but the native girl's experiences with the mermaids made her realize how fortunate she and Bantan had been to successfully escape from their island. She hoped to never see any of them again, for unquestionably they would be ruthless enemies.

"I imagine Dr. Zarwood would be very interested to know of the existence of the mermaids," Bantan remarked. "If he were to subject one of them to the retrovider he created, in all probability he would be able to trace their ancestry to the very beginning of their race." The bronzed giant then sighed. "It is unfortunate that his mind had to become unbalanced, for in actuality he is a very brilliant man."

"You mentioned that to me before, Bantan," Mauria said with a quizzical expression upon her features.

"It is true," he admitted, nodding. "Dr. Zarwood's ability fascinates me. And to think he is capable of prolonging one's youth for an indefinite period." He sighed deeply.

Tama merely stared at the bronzed giant, but offered no comment pertaining to the fabulous Dr. Zarwood.

"Since there is nothing further of interest here," Bantan said presently, "we might as well return outside."

In accord, they left the temple of the sea god and returned along the passageway to find that the incoming tide had already reached the canoe. Its position was reversed and in a few minutes was being paddled toward the outside of the grotto's entrance. Tama assured the bronzed giant he was of sufficient strength to continue around the island. And so they did.

When the canoe was beached at the landing, the young native assured Bantan with the passing of a few more days he felt he would be capable of undertaking the trip to their ultimate goal.

"During the next few days I'll paddle some more to get in better shape," he added with a smile.

"That will be fine," the bronzed giant said in answer.

During his paddling exercises in the days following, Tama was accompanied by Mauria, who also paddled; and each day in turn found the young native becoming stronger and anxious for the time when he could announce he was capable of embarking upon their final destination.

Meanwhile, Bantan and Nulu would walk along the sandy beach, and in this way the blonde-haired girl became aware of her returning strength. During these walks, they would talk of life upon Marja Island, and the bronzed giant assured Nulu that though living conditions would be utterly different from what she had experienced thus far, she would soon become accustomed to the new life that awaited her there. The girl's hand held in his tightened her fingers upon his.

"So long as you will be there, Bantan," she murmured, "I'll be happy enough. It seems I can hardly wait until we reach your home island to be your mate."

Although the bronzed giant smiled down at the girl, inwardly he wondered what Wanya, his foster sister, and Lori, to whom he owed a debt of gratitude, would think and what their reaction would be when they were told that Nulu was to be his mate in the near future. With a shake of his head he would banish such thoughts, for he knew he could not foretell future events. He resolved it would be better to wait until the time came and hope matters took care of themselves.

During the last few days they intended to remain upon the island, Bantan gathered nuts and placed them in the hollowed log, leaving the more perishable fruits to be gathered the day before they left.

Mauria and Nulu gathered tough grass and braided strong ropes, one to be used as a towline, and the other for a spare in case in some unforeseen manner the first one might be broken.

The bronzed giant even fashioned another bow, and from the intestines of a sea gull provided a string for it. Although it seemed they had lots of time on their hands, there was always something to be accomplished, and in this way time passed more speedily.

Two weeks had now passed since they had first come to the island, and on the morning of this day at breakfast Tama announced that he felt fit to take up paddling chores with Bantan in their search for Marja Island. The bronzed giant evinced his pleasure at this announcement, although during the past few days he had been expecting the young native to mention his fitness, for he appeared in the best of physical condition. Nulu, too, had regained her former strength and she had acquired a lovely tan. She smiled at Tama's statement.

"I, too, am glad that we are going to leave," she added. "It is beautiful on this island, but I'm sure we would not want to live here all of our lives."

During the day all four joined together gathering the fruit that would be necessary for their trip and stored them in the hollowed log. After the evening meal and darkness had fallen, they remained upon the beach awhile.

"Many times when on Beneiro, and later on Marja," Bantan explained, "I would study the heaven and know just where certain stars would appear. They change positions as the moon waxes and wanes, but every thirteen moons those certain stars would be in their places again. As people of civilization would say—everything repeats

itself—but we of course are that much older. When I left
Marja on that sun that now seems so long ago, I paddled
westward for over four suns before reaching Mandoes
Island. In what direction the cliff-encircled island is from
there has me puzzled. We do know that the mermaid island is not too far from there, and this island is about
the same distance. I believe paddling east slightly to the
south should bring us within three suns at the most somewhere in the vicinity of Marja. Only when that time has
come to pass will we know for sure."

"And until only a short while ago," Nulu murmured,
"I never knew about the sun, moon, and stars. How I
have loved to watch them since."

"Tomorrow, then, we shall start," Tama said. "We
have fruit and nuts for a longer period than three days
in case we miss our objective."

"Each night I will check the position of the stars,"
the bronzed giant added. "In that way I am convinced
we should not go far astray."

During the short silence that ensued, Nulu linked an
arm with Bantan's.

After some little while had ensued and further discus-
sion was of the probable location of Marja, each had
become aware of their weariness as a result of the day's
activities and so they decided to retire.

"Let's hope our sleep tonight will be refreshing," the
bronzed giant said as they prepared to retire beneath the
lean-to. "The next few nights will not be so comfortable."

Bantan and Tama lay at one end of the shelter while
Nulu and Mauria were upon the other, and it was not
many minutes later that all four were asleep.

CHAPTER XV

Captives of the Mermaids

BANTAN WAS AWAKE shortly before the sun rose above the waterline. Arising without disturbing the others who were still sleeping, he went at once to the water's edge and indulged in a brief swim. Returning to the edge of the foliage, a glance assured him that his companions had not awakened. He went to the canoe and inspected its bottom which had been caulked in a number of places. He regretted now that he hadn't obtained a greater supply of pitch for a future use during their trip to Marja.

However, he felt it would be better to be on the safe side by having a supply on hand. Resourceful by nature, the bronzed giant decided for the safety of all concerned he would do well to obtain more of it. The time it would take to do so would be negligible compared to what delay might result without it. With a nod he turned about, thinking he had heard a sound behind him.

Mauria had arisen and was watching him in silence for a moment before approaching. A smile was exchanged between them.

"Nulu and Tama are still sleeping?" he softly asked.

The native girl nodded.

In a whisper Bantan then informed her of his intentions.

"I shall be gone only a short while," he explained. "By the time I return I'm sure they will have waked. After we eat we can leave the island. With the pitch I'll gather we'll have no further worry over a leaking canoe.

It has served well these past moons, and when we reach Marja I'll fashion another."

Mauria could understand his resourcefulness, knowing him so well, and she nodded, urging him to be on his way without further delay so that he would return the sooner.

"Should Nulu and Tama wake while you're gone," she added, "I'll explain to them where you are."

With a smile to the understanding native girl, the bronzed giant was on his way. Owing to the heavy dew that had settled upon the foliage during the night, he threaded his way more carefully so as not to be drenched with moisture. For that reason it required longer to reach his objective.

With a slab of bark to be used as a container for the viscid pitch, Bantan mounted the giant tree where some twenty feet from the base an enormous burl was to be reached. With his feet firmly planted between two giant limbs, he hacked away at the pitch with his dagger until he had a generous supply that would be sufficient to caulk a number of leaks. He allowed the bark container to drop to the ground and it landed perfectly without disturbing its contents. He then rubbed the sticky dagger against the bark of the tree until he had removed most of the viscid pitch adhering to the blade, then he dropped it alongside the bark container. He lowered himself from the crotch and in a few minutes was upon the ground. His first duty was to thoroughly clean the dagger until the steel blade shined as it formerly had. Then he returned it to its sheath.

Picking up the bark container, the bronzed giant returned through the foliage the way he had come. He visualized the hasty swim he would have before eating his morning meal. Some insects clung to him annoyingly in the stickiness of the morning dew, and he knew a plunge into the gentle surf would relieve the uncomfortable feeling.

Altogether he couldn't have been gone more than three-quarters of an hour at the most. By this time he assumed Nulu and Tama would have waked and bathed. The ever efficient Mauria would have their breakfast prepared. Perhaps they might already be partaking of it rather than wait for him.

The dew-drenching foliage was now thinning. The sound of the gentle surf was soothing to Bantan's ears. With a smile upon his handsome features, he now parted the foliage to step out upon the beach. Words of greeting were upon his lips. But as he appeared, his smile altered to wondering concern. The canoe was missing. He dropped the bark container with the pitch heaped upon it at his feet. Though the hollowed log was upon the beach, Nulu, Mauria and Tama were nowhere about!

Bantan's eyes sought the shimmering expanse of water before him. A couple of hundred yards from shore he saw the canoe moving away from the island. Brilliant sunshine flashed upon dipping paddles. Shading his eyes from the glare of the sun now a short distance above the horizon, he saw that Tama and Mauria were wielding them. He also distinguished the blonde-haired Nulu in the forward end. But the fourth proudly seated in the aft portion of the canoe—who was that person?

His first instinct was to cup his hands to his mouth and shout to them. Then his sharp eyes detected a disturbance to each side of the canoe, keeping clear of the dipping paddles. Sunlight gleamed upon naked, flashing arms. His shoulders drooped and his features became saddened with the realization that the mermaids had come during his short absence and taken his companions prisoners, unknowingly leaving him alone with the hollowed log ladened with fruit and nuts as his only means of transportation.

As the bronzed giant stood there helplessly, the shock of the situation gradually subsided. By what strange coincidence had he decided to leave his companions earlier to procure pitch? He wondered had he remained with them, would he as well have been taken a prisoner? With a shake of his head, unable to determine, he knew had he been present when the mermaids had come, he would have given them stiff opposition before being taken a captive. He could not help but wonder if Tama especially had submitted without a struggle—and Mauria. Nulu had apparently been so surprised, her bewilderment would not have aroused much protest on her part—that was understandable. Then, too, there was the possibility the mermaids had taken them by such surprise that there had been no opportunity of offering resistance.

Bantan was unalterably determined that he would rescue his friends. But first, he had a few problems of his own to solve before doing so. He would have to fashion a paddle. That was paramount to all else. First, he would take a hasty plunge, and then satisfy his craving for food. Returning from the water he felt much refreshed. From the hollowed log he brought forth what he required to eat. He noted the refuse from fruit and nuts and knew from the amount scattered about that not only his friends, but the mermaids as well had partaken of the stores. Meanwhile, he continued to watch the canoe as it became smaller in the distance.

His breakfast completed, he lost no time seeking what he required to fashion a paddle. His incursions within the foliage during the past two weeks had familiarized him the likely place to search. Within half an hour he returned to the beach with a piece of branch that suited the purpose. With his keen dagger where it had been located, he had cut it to the required length. And now he busied himself whittling upon it. With the passing minutes becoming hours the piece of branch was rapidly taking shape. And while he assiduously busied himself thusly, the canoe disappeared from sight.

Never in his past life had the bronzed giant been occasioned to fashion a paddle in the record time that it now took to feel his task was completed to his satisfaction. It was about noonday, with only brief pauses, that he was ready to give pursuit. He emptied the hollowed log of most of its contents, leaving the choicest fruit and nuts for his own consumption during the trip. Quickly he partook of his noonday repast, then without further delay dragged the hollowed log to the water's edge. It was much more difficult to breast the surf, gentle though it was, with the cumbersome craft, but mighty muscles plying a crude but stout paddle, forced it through to the calmer water beyond. Setting his course through memory, bronzed arms flashed beneath the sunlight and the hollowed log moved across the shimmering surface as fast as could be expected.

🖝   🖝   🖝

When the mermaids under the superb leadership of Sirena had come to the island, the queen had been the first to espy the lone figure of the native girl standing near the lean-to at the edge of the foliage. Presently a bronzed man appeared from the shelter. He and the girl conversed. All the while the swimming mermaids continued to near the surf. And then from the lean-to appeared another young woman, much lighter skinned than the other and with blonde hair. She joined her companions, not one of them looking in the direction of the gentle surf.

Sirena nodded and with a wave of her hand indicated her companions were to follow her. It seemed the gentle surf had no more than received them when all were ashore. Spreading fanwise, they slithered speedily up the beach. Armed with a trident as each was, their stoic features unchanged, the mermaids represented a grim group.

Mauria uttered a cry of distress as she was first to recognize the presence of the mermaids, and the grimness stamped upon Sirena's features made her realize she was a ruthless foe indeed.

To say that Nulu was surprised is putting it mildly. She was speechless, and her fear was second only to her bewilderment at seeing the creatures whom they had discussed. Now she had reason to know them for what they were.

Tama appeared dumbfounded at sight of the mermaids that mythology had mentioned, but at the same time he had scoffed at the idea of their possible living existence in the present.

Ever since the escape of Bantan and Mauria, Sirena had silently vowed vengeance upon them. Looking at Tama, she mistook him for the bronzed giant of whom the native girl had spoken so highly. As chance would have it, Ano and Majane, the only two mermaids who had actually seen Bantan, for some reason were not in the present group that had accompanied their queen. None of the others present, including the queen, had ever seen him in person, so it was only natural that Sirena assumed this handsome, bronzed giant was he.

For days and nights the queen had hesitated leaving her island in search of them; but at last her determination to follow and recapture them, if possible, could be denied no longer. And so they had come and were timely in recapturing the escaped fugitives. She now looked at the handsome native as she menaced him with her trident.

"So, Bantan, you thought you could escape me," she mocked. "The sea gods for some reason must have prevented you from doing so."

The native was surprised to be addressed as "Bantan." He turned to Mauria but read no encouragement upon her horrified features. Then he looked at Nulu, but her bewilderment was still apparent and no encouragement was to be obtained from her. Then he faced the queen of the mermaids and drew himself erect. He looked down upon her with steady eyes.

"Why have you followed us?" he demanded.

Sirena laughed bitterly, but did not reply at once.

"We have done no harm to any of you," Tama continued. "We only wish our freedom."

The mermaid queen's hazel eyes were hard with no slightest touch of softness.

"You are in no position to ask favors, Bantan," she answered. "I am queen of our island. You, Mauria, and the other light-haired female are our prisoners. We are going to return to our island."

"We have no desire to return to your island," the native declared. "We wish to go to Marja Island."

Again Sirena laughed bitterly.

"Your wishes are contrary to mine," she stated. She menaced him with her trident. "Come, let us lose no time. Prepare your canoe for launching."

Tama had hoped to prolong the conversation with the mermaid queen, hoping that Bantan would return in the meantime. He was sure the bronzed giant would be able to foil the mermaids in their designs. He hesitated deliberately.

Sirena prodded him with her trident.

"Don't try my patience," she warned. "I want to return you to my island alive. But if I can't have you alive, I shall not hesitate to kill you."

The native looked at Mauria and the sympathy he read in her dark eyes made him realize for her sake and Nulu's he had no other choice. Flashing a glance at Nulu, he could see that she was still bewildered by these fish-like women.

All of the mermaids were hungry after their lengthy swim from their island, and the fruit and nuts in the hollowed log attracted the attention of one of them. She called the queen's attention to her discovery, making her realize that she was very hungry.

"We shall eat to our fill," Sirena said. "And then we shall return to our island without further delay."

And so all partook of fruit and nuts, including the three prisoners, but several of the mermaids kept strict watch upon them. When some fifteen minutes had passed all had eaten to their fill. Then the queen spoke to one of her handmaidens. In another moment the mermaid and a companion transferred fruit and nuts in the middle of the canoe. Sirena watched them and told them when to stop. Then she spoke to Tama.

"The canoe," she said in commanding tones. "Push it into the water."

Reluctantly Tama went to it with the queen close behind with her menacing trident. Pegra and Beta slithered to each side of him. Mauria now stepped forward to help him push the canoe into the water. The mermaid queen offered no protest. She turned to the two guards covering Nulu and indicated for them to follow.

The canoe was pushed into the water. The blonde-haired girl was forced to sit in front. Pegra was to guard her for awhile, and the others would be given turns to relieve them of the weariness of swimming. Mauria was then told to enter and take up a paddle. Sirena spoke to several mermaids to hold the canoe until the male and herself embarked. After Tama entered and took up a paddle in readiness with the native girl, the queen then drew herself within and sat in the aft end.

"Now," she said.

The paddles moved expertly as the mermaids holding the canoe released it, and within a few minutes they had breasted the gentle surf and were in the calmer water beyond. If the mermaid queen felt any fear while they passed through the surf she gave no indication. While the water craft moved speedily along, swimming mermaids leisurely remained to each side. A smile of satisfaction touched Sirena's lips. With admiration she looked upon the smoothly tanned back and shoulders of the well-muscled paddler kneeling in front of her.

So comparatively easy the recapture of the prisoners had been, the mermaid queen could hardly believe it had been so. Now she could relax. Already she was formulating how she was going to placate the handsome "Bantan" when they reached her island, for in her heart she did not want to kill him. She realized that she could easily learn to love him very much.

The blonde-haired girl! For the first time Sirena gave a thought of her. Where had she come from? She remembered Mauria had told her that Bantan loved a white-skinned girl but he and his sweetheart had lost their lives. It was obvious that Mauria had lied about the bronzed giant meeting his death and that the native had been the one instead who had not survived. Loving Bantan as she did, the native girl was not one to relinquish him to the blonde-haired girl. She felt it would be amusing to bait Mauria and thereby lessen the monotony of the trip.

"Mauria, when I speak to you, you need not stop paddling to answer me," she said. "Tell me—where did you find the white-skinned girl?"

The native girl looked meaningly at Nulu, who had not spoken as yet, and she felt she understood she was to maintain silence.

"Bantan and I found her upon the island," she answered. "We have tried to speak to her, but she either does not understand or cannot talk."

Nulu had overcome her bewilderment by this time, and when Mauria had looked at her meaningly, intelligent girl that she was, she understood that she was to pretend to be voiceless. She merely blinked her eyes as she heard Mauria answer the mermaid queen. In a dazed manner she had heard Sirena address Tama as Bantan, and since her beloved was not present, she knew when he returned from the island's interior and found them gone, in some way he would follow and rescue them. No matter what the odds or how difficult the situation, in some miraculous way he would appear. Only too well she remembered how he had spared her upon two previous occasions from ignonimy from Tarnaz, the aborigine. She was positive he would rescue her again.

Sirena frowned to know the white-skinned girl was a mute, and for that reason she would have little use for her when they returned to her island except to let her perform the menial tasks that were necessary.

"When we reach our island, Mauria," the mermaid queen then said, "I shall place the white-skinned girl in your care, and you will see that the menial tasks of the grotto are taken care of. I shall instruct one of my handmaidens to teach you what you should know."

The native girl did not answer to this, for she realized only too well that her status and Nulu's would be that of slaves, and unless they did what was demanded of them they would be punished, and perhaps killed.

"You do not answer me," Sirena said chidingly.

"I have nothing to say," was the answer. "You are the queen and I am merely a slave."

The mermaid queen smiled with smugness.

Meanwhile, Nulu was keeping a watch of the island shore that had been left behind, and now that the canoe was some little distance away, her sharp eyes espied the bronzed figure that appeared at the edge of the foliage. She recognized him at once, and with a glance at the mermaid who was guarding her, she knew she could not permit the expression of happiness enter her eyes that ordinarily would under other circumstances. But as she watched him, she was positive he had sighted them and would understand that they were being forced to return to the mermaid island. She knew she could not enlighten Mauria or Tama of her discovery at the present, but just as soon as opportunity provided she would tell them that she had seen Bantan, and then they would understand.

At intervals as the time passed, the mermaid who guarded Nulu was relieved by a tiring swimmer, and she in turn by another, and so on until all of the swimmers had had an opportunity to rest. Sirena, however, asserted her prerogative as queen and did not offer to spell a swimmer. She enjoyed being transported in the canoe, and as well to concentrate her unceasing admiration for the bronzed paddler whom she believed to be Bantan.

Tama and Mauria were permitted brief rests and were allowed to partake of the fruit and nuts that had been brought so as to keep their strength at normal. But as the hours wearily passed, their strokes lagged somewhat. It was well along in the afternoon before they finally guided the canoe into the cove, and both paddlers, though wearied, were relieved that they had come to their journey's end, only in turn to be apprehensive as to what lay in store for them.

CHAPTER XVI

Daring Rescue

WHILE BANTAN PADDLED the hollowed log toward the mermaid island, the first couple hours were not too difficult; but as the brassy sun passed his zenith and gradually moved westward in the cloudless heaven, the brilliant rays hampered his vision. The heat was quite intense for awhile until tempered with a gentle breeze. He compared the retarded speed of his cumbersome water craft with that of the canoe, and he realized it would require considerably longer to reach his objective. Darkness would have enveloped the water by several hours before he spanned the intervening distance. However, he was not one to complain overly much, feeling that the hollowed log was better than nothing—much better than an unwieldly raft, and more preferable by all means than swimming the distance intervening.

To reach the mermaid island in utter darkness would be to the advantage of the paddler, since, should any sentries be on watch duty, they would not be able to sight him. The monotony of the wearisome trip was relieved upon several occasions. Once he sighted a turtle swimming parallel to his passage a hundred yards distant. Upon another occasion he encountered a school of flying fish that fairly bombarded him.

The bronzed giant paused once to rest and partake of the fruit and nuts he had taken with him and quenched his thirst with the milk of a coconut. During the last couple of hours he plied his paddle with head lowered to avoid the brilliant rays of the sinking sun. As the red ball of fire finally sank beyond the mermaid island he was relieved, and it was then that he distinguished it looming prominently well within view. With the passing of a couple more hours after darkness had descended he should easily reach it.

Before the mantle of night had fallen the paddler could discern the cove with clearness. As the evening stars began to appear in the canopy above, there was a brilliant one of the first magnitude directly in line some little distance above it. With this beacon there was no danger of going astray.

The bronzed giant continued to paddle his cumbersome craft with wearying arms, but each stroke brought him that much nearer to his goal, and for that he was thankful.

As the land mass loomed darkly before him, and his alertful ears could hear the slapping of the gentle surf, Bantan's eyes were quite accustomed to the darkness to distinguish near objects. He beached the hollowed log a short distance to the right of the cove facing him. Remembering that there was a passageway that led to the amphitheatre, he wanted to be as near it as possible. He had every reason to believe the mermaids would have taken his canoe there, and in all probability would have guards stationed close to it as a matter of precaution.

Without too much difficulty he drew the cumbersome water craft up the sandy beach, wearied though he was, and concealed it within the fringing foliage. Breathing deeply for a few minutes, he then crept along the edge of the foliage until he reached the aperture leading into the cliff.

Pausing, Bantan's delicate nostrils sniffed the air, but he was aware there appeared no fresh effluvia to be detected of the mermaids being in the near vicinity. Peering within the opening, at its end where it bisected another corridor, he could distinguish the faint glow of the phosphorescence that emanated from the other corridor walls and ceiling. With his right hand clutching the handle of his dagger, he passed through the opening, his keen eyes watchful and his sharp ears alerted for any alien sounds.

In due time he reached the end of the passageway, and at its end he paused to peer to each side of the bisecting corridor for signs of mermaids. There were none, but from his left which led to the amphitheatre he heard muffled voices, and he suspected an audience was being held there.

Without further pause, he stealthily advanced in that direction, regretful that the corridor was softly bathed from the phosphorescence in the walls and ceiling, for he would have preferred to traverse it in pitch darkness. Time and again he paused to look to his rear to ascertain no one was sneaking up behind him. Closer he drew to the end of the corridor.

About twenty yards from the amphitheatre, Bantan was in a position to espy his canoe near the edge of the unrippled pool. He could hear harsh voices, but as yet he could not see who spoke. Now, edging forward a little more toward the end of the corridor, he could see the other side of the pool. As well, he could see a number of mermaids armed with tridents surrounding Nulu, Mauria and Tama. The prisoners were standing and their hands were bound behind them. Their heads were lowered because of the hopelessness of their position.

It was the queen's voice that was so harsh and, craning forward a trifle more, the bronzed giant could see Sirena's features contorted in rage.

"Mauria, you tricked me!" she all but screamed as she pointed a condemning hand at the native girl. "You let me believe this native was Bantan. Ano and Majane were quick to tell me that the male was not Bantan, as I believed, for they both had seen you and Bantan together."

The native girl stood erect, remaining silent, realizing there was nothing she could say to help in her present position.

"Where is Bantan?" the queen then demanded. "I will offer you and the blonde-haired girl your freedom—with some restrictions—if you will tell me where Bantan is. Will you tell me?"

Mauria merely stared at Sirena with no emoton registering upon her blank features.

The mermaid queen motioned to Pegra and Beta. At once the two mermaids prodded the native girl's legs with their tridents.

"Down upon your knees before the queen," Pegra commanded.

Mauria dropped to her knees.

With an angry toss of her head, the reddish hair sweeping to the right and left of her naked shoulders, Sirena's features were contorted with ungovernable rage. But now, strangely, a sneer curled her thin lips.

"You love Bantan so very much you would rather die than betray him," she charged. "Admit that I speak the truth."

The native girl looked directly at the sneering mermaid queen.

"I do not love Bantan, nor does he love me," she answered in a steady voice. "I respect him very much—but I am not in love with him. I love Tama. I speak the truth."

Sirena's sneer faded. She could easily determine the native girl spoke the truth. She looked wonderingly up at Tama who was looking down at Mauria with unmistakable lovelight glowing in his dark eyes.

The queen shook her head almost wildly and her hazel eyes blazed angrily.

"Tama, is it true what Mauria says?" she demanded.

The native removed his eyes from the object of his devotion and faced Sirena.

"It is true," he replied. "I love Mauria very much and want her for my mate."

The queen's features were stern and unrelenting.

"Tama, where is Bantan?" she then asked.

The native shook his head.

"I do not know where he is," he answered.

Sirena shook her head angrily.

"Was he upon the island where we took you captives?" she demanded.

Tama merely looked at the queen, but made no effort to answer.

Sirena then glared at Mauria.

"Was he?" she asked insistingly of the native girl.

Mauria remained silent.

For a moment the queen looked at Nulu, but recollecting she was a mute, she did not feel like wasting time putting questions to her. Her stern eyes then went from Mauria to Tama. Her thin lips tensed.

"Bantan *must* be upon the island," she said emphatically. Her lids narrowed to mere slits. "And you, Tama, allowed me to believe you were Bantan."

The native's poise was one of humbleness—as though he realized he had no excuse to offer.

Sirena's bosom rose and fell heavily because of her pent emotions. "I should have you tortured to death, Tama," she hissed. "Instead, I'm going to turn you over to my handmaidens. Before they are through with you, you will probably wish you were dead." Then she turned glaring eyes upon Mauria. "And because you shared Tama's guilt," she added in bitter tones, "I will have you witness the treatment my handmaidens will inflict upon your loved one."

The native girl's eyes closed and she pressed her lips together to choke the protesting cry that otherwise would have been uttered.

Looking about at the mermaids, the queen noted their gleaming eyes and eager faces as they looked up at the male captive. Then Sirena looked toward the silent Nulu, wondering what she was to do with her. Although she was blameless of the crimes charged to Tama and Mauria, the fact that she had been with them when they had been captured indicated she must be considered a friend of theirs—and a friend of Tama and Mauria must be considered an enemy.

"The one that doesn't speak, my queen," Pegra asked, interrupting her meditations. "What shall we do with her?"

Sirena's eyes were resentful as she flashed a look at the silent, blonde-haired girl, and then she turned to the mermaid.

"She will be of no use to us," she answered. "But there is no need to dispose of her now. Bind her legs and leave her here so she can't escape. Later, I'll decide what is to be done with her."

The mermaid obtained thongs from the sleeping chamber. Nulu was made to lay down and her ankles were securely trussed. She put up considerable opposition during the operation. Pegra than looked toward the queen.

"And now may we take Tama to our sleeping chambers?" she asked.

The queen nodded with the flourish of an arm.

"Do with him what you wish," she said. "But—don't kill him."

Pegra assured her queen they would not kill the male prisoner; then, assuming command, she indicated for

Tama and Mauria to proceed in the direction she pointed. All of the mermaids gathered about them as they slithered along the smooth floor.

Sirena looked toward the silent, blonde-haired girl lying upon the floor, then she slithered toward her private chambers.

A silent witness to the proceedings within the amphitheatre, Bantan's keen eyes missed no detail and his alertful ears had heard everything that was spoken. Time and again his right hand would tighten upon the handle of his dagger in reflection of contemplated actions. Realizing were he to announce his presence, he was aware the outnumbering mermaids would overwhelm him, however valiant his efforts, even though he might manage to slay several of them with his dagger. His eyes would narrow to mere slits and the muscles of his jaw tensed while he tried to formulate a plan for rescuing his sweetheart and his two native friends.

Sirena's choice of Tama's punishment with Mauria to be a helpless witness made the bronzed giant understand the queen's depraved state of mind. Now that she had retired to her private chambers, and the mermaids herded the unwilling Tama and Mauria into their sleeping chamber, this was the moment the unknown watcher awaited. He looked toward the silent Nulu, lying upon the floor at the edge of the unrippled pool. Since the canoe containing his weapons was upon the opposite side, he nodded. His plan was formulated, and now was the time to carry it out.

Without further hesitation, Bantan raced silently toward the canoe, flashing glances toward the queen's private chambers and then toward the opening of the one the mermaids had entered. Reaching the canoe, a look within ascertained his weapons were there. He withdrew the two bows and the two groups of arrows. With them clutched in his left hand, he quickly raced around the pool until he reached the side of his sweetheart.

At sight and recognition of him, Nulu would have shouted aloud in delirious joy as a happy expression radiated her features and eyes. But the bronzed giant cautioned her to maintain silence. Placing his weapons upon the floor, with his dagger he quickly severed her bonds. As they arose to their feet he handed her a bow and some arrows and nodded in the direction of the sleeping quarters where babbling voices were to be heard quite distinctly.

"We must rescue our friends, Nulu," he whispered to her. "We can't leave them behind."

The blonde-haired girl nodded grimly in understanding.

With an arrow affixed to their bow, the others being clamped between their left arm and body, they silently advanced toward the opening through which Tama and Mauria had been forced to enter. Looking within, Bantan's dark eyes glinted with anger.

Tama was being reluctantly forced to attain a kneeling position with several mermaids menacing him with their tridents. Mauria's ankles had been trussed and she stood against the wall, her features saddened at her sweetheart's mishandling. A mermaid stood near her with a menacing trident. Bound hand and foot, the native girl was helpless to interfere. Tears filled her eyes.

Pegra had assumed command of the situation. Beta was close beside her with glittering eyes and fast rising and falling bosom. None of the mermaids gave a thought to look toward the doorway of their quarters. Had they, less enthusiasm in their undertaking would have been displayed.

For there, with arrow affixed to his bow and ready to discharge if necessary, stood a grim, bronzed giant. Just behind him stood an equally grim-faced, blonde-haired

girl. The first intimation the mermaids had of the presence
of aliens was when a low, chilling voice spoke.

"Release the prisoners."

The chattering voices became silent upon the instant,
and awed faces turned to the doorway from whence the
grim voice had spoken.

Tama's features were astounded, as were Mauria's,
to see Bantan standing there with tensed bow and arrow
ready for release at the slightest provocation. And they
could see the determined Nulu just behind him similarly
armed.

Pegra's surprised features altered to contorted rage,
as did Beta's, and the other mermaids as well revealed
their displeasure at this interruption. But whatever con-
templations they considered upon enactment were paralyzed for the time being because of the threat that faced
them.

Tama drew himself to his feet with a smile of relief
and, since his ankles had not been bound, he moved
toward the doorway. From the lips of Pegra and Beta
he heard hisses of rage. But because Bantan's sharp eyes
watched them they dared not strike at the native with
their tridents in an effort to halt him.

As soon as Tama reached his savior, Bantan stepped
within the doorway but did not remove his eyes from the
snarling features of the mermaids. He spoke softly to
Nulu to use his dagger to cut the native's bonds. Quickly
the girl did so. Tama then accepted the dagger, and Nulu
also stepped within the opening with her bow and arrow
in readiness again.

A grim-faced native passed among the mermaids as
he went to the now smiling Mauria. Bantan's dagger was
tightly clutched in his right hand. Quickly he severed
the bonds at her ankles, then as she turned about, he

cut those about her wrists. Watchfully the two returned
to the doorway.

The bronzed giant spoke in a soft voice to the native.

"You and Mauria take the canoe through the passageway in which you came to the cove. Paddle to the left.
I have the hollowed log concealed in the foliage and will
join you as soon as possible. Place my dagger in its
sheath and hurry. Nulu and I will remain here until
you are well on your way."

Heartfelt thanks were uttered by both Tama and
Mauria, and without further hesitation they were on their
way. The bronzed giant heard the soft scraping of the
canoe bottom on the rocky floor as the two rescued prisoners were obeying his instructions. In the tensed minutes
that passed the sound became fainter. After they had
pushed the canoe into the passageway, no further sound
could be heard.

In the meantime the mermaids were drawing closer together. Bantan was keenly aware they were plotting something rash and he realized he would not be able to maintain them in subservience much longer. During his lifetime he had never slain a member of the opposite sex,
though some had been deserving. And though these creatures could not be classified as humans, they were female,
and he was reluctant to slay one if at all avoidable. He
whispered to Nulu.

"Join Tama and Mauria," he bade her. "You heard me
tell them what I would do."

"I don't want to leave you," she protested tearfully.
"Let me stay with you."

"You must," he insisted. "Go quickly now."

The blonde-haired girl muffled a sob. Quickly stepping
to his side she kissed his cheek, then ran toward the
passageway into which Tama and Mauria had disappeared
with the canoe.

Pegra and Beta were looking at the bronzed giant with glowering expressions and they were acquiring a menacing attitude. Whispering among themselves, in a concerted mass they slowly moved toward the doorway where the grim-faced Bantan stood with tensed bow and gleaming eyes that kept shifting from one snarling face to another. From a distance of twenty feet they had drawn nearer almost half that distance.

By this time the bronzed giant calculated Nulu must have joined Tama and Mauria, and they should have launched the canoe into the water. Within a few minutes thereafter they should emerge into the cove. He felt the time had come for his own escape and he did not doubt his ability to easily outdistance the mermaids, however fast they slithered after him in pursuit.

Bantan now took a forward step with snarling features, and the mermaids drew to a concerted halt, fearful for the moment that he would discharge an arrow into their midst, possibly to be followed by others. His bluff was successful, then he wheeled about in a flash and passed through the doorway at a swift run. His eyes were upon the opening of the passageway he would traverse to freedom.

Too late he saw the mermaid queen appear as from nowhere. With a shriek of rage she dived for his fast-moving legs and managed to clutch one of them with her strong hands. Caught off balance as he was and his dash for safety suddenly arrested, Bantan's reflexes were as quick as lightning. He released the bow and arrows and prepared himself for a quick fall. Landing upon his hands, he gave a mighty surge with his imprisoned feet and succeeded in breaking Sirena's grip. At the next moment, snatching up his discarded bow, but having no time for the scattered arrows, he heard the enraged queen shriek to her handmaidens as they appeared in the doorway.

"Don't let him get away!" she screamed.

But the agile Bantan had regained his feet and was running at top speed toward his objective.

Several tridents were hurled at him, but missed their aim, owing to the haste with which they had been cast.

The bronzed giant's keen ears were aware he was increasing the distance between him and his foes, and once he paused briefly to cast a fleeting glance over a shoulder to ascertain this fact. The mermaids with the queen in the lead were giving him swift pursuit, but he knew they would be unable to overtake him. He did wonder whether he would be able to launch the cumbersome hollowed log before they could prevent. And with this thought in mind he ran at top speed to the corridor and along its length to the one that bisected and would lead him outside.

CHAPTER XVII

Marja Bound

UPON REACHING the bisecting corridor, Bantan paused momentarily to look backward. He could see the pursuing mermaids entering the opening, and the metallic sound of their tridents as they clashed upon either wall or floor could be heard as they slithered along the rocky floor.

Without further pause, the bronzed giant then dashed in the direction of the corridor's outer opening. Although he was wearied from the day's activities, he forced his powerful legs to remain at top speed in his flight. He regretted now that he had dragged the hollowed log to the edge of the foliage, for he realized precious minutes would be consumed to drag it to the water and launch it. Had he been able to foresee how easy the rescue of his sweetheart and two native friends would have been, he would most assuredly have left it near the water's edge.

Breathing somewhat hard, Bantan presently reached the open. Unerringly he went to the hollowed log in the darkness, thankful that he had turned it around when leaving it there. His heart was beating like a trip hammer as he dragged it from concealment onto the beach and from thence toward the water's edge. It seemed now, owing to his weariness, to be twice as difficult as when he had dragged it up on the beach. With straining muscles he endeavored to keep it moving, momentarily expecting to hear the first sounds of the pursuing mermaids.

Gasping harshly, he now felt the soothing wetness laving his feet and ankles as he backed into the water. An-

189

other mighty tug he gave and the cumbersome, hollowed log was half into the water. Quickly, though staggering somewhat from his herculian effort, he moved to the rear of the water craft. Pushing upon it with all his strength, he shoved it free of the sand and almost fell within. His groping hands grasped the crude paddle, and in a kneeling position with sweeping strokes, he forced it into the gentle surf.

At that moment he heard the first sounds from the opening in the corridor, and he knew the pursuing mermaids had at last appeared. The voice of Sirena in the lead was clearly to be heard.

"We must find him!" she shouted. "He must not get away!"

Other voices intermingled, and the paddler could hear them moving about swishingly. So intent his attention was upon the sounds, his paddle struck the side of the hollowed log with a seemingly loud thud. The sound was heard by his pursuers, for the queen's voice again was heard.

"In to the water!" she shouted. "He must be escaping in a canoe."

By this time Bantan had fortunately breasted the gentle surf and his progress was much better, but not as great as it would have been had he been paddling his lighter and much less cumbersome canoe. He knew the pursuing mermaids could not see him in the darkness any more than he could see them, and for that reason he took care to prevent his paddle again coming in contact with the side of the water craft.

The bronzed giant paddled straight outward, his ears listening intently for sound of the canoe Tama, Mauria, and Nulu were escaping in; but strain his eyes as he did, to no avail were his efforts to see them. He risked calling softly to them, hoping they would hear him. Straining his ears, he could hear nothing, however. By this time they must have managed to easily reach the cove.

As Bantan drew away from the gentle surf and the sound of breaking waves as they rolled swishingly up on the sandy beach and retreated, his keen ears were better able to hear sounds in the immediate vicinity. Occasionally he would pause briefly in his paddling and concentrate upon the swirling of water to indicate a body moved through it. Such sounds would apprise him that the mermaids were not too far behind him. A fleeting backward glance availed him no sight of them owing to the almost pitch darkness that enveloped the immediate surroundings.

Stroke after stroke followed as the paddler's tiring arms continued to wield his paddle as an automaton. Still his sharp eyes looked about for sign of the canoe and its occupants, and his keen ears were alerted to any alien sounds.

It was well that the bronzed giant's eyes were on the sharp lookout, for suddenly a dark object loomed just ahead of him slightly to his right. He knew it must be the canoe.

"Tama?" he called out softly.

"Bantan?" was the questioning answer.

"Keep going," he bade. "The mermaids are right behind me."

At once the paddles of Tama and Mauria were heard dipping into the water, and behind their combined efforts the lighter canoe moved away from the slower craft Bantan was paddling. But his tiring arms continued to move as rapidly as was humanly possible.

With the passing of a few minutes he became aware the hollowed log appeared to be losing momentum. At once he turned and could distinguish a pair of wet hands grasping the aft portion of the water craft a scarce yard from where he knelt. Quickly he slapped the flat side of the paddle to one side of them. The wet hands disappeared at once and he felt a slight tremor pulse the length of the hollowed log. With greater effort he again plied his paddle and was assured nothing was clinging to it since its speed increased somewhat. Unless he was mistaken he thought he heard a sound of frustration issuing from the darkened water just to his rear.

Bantan's alert ears could hear the swirling water as a swimmer moved through it, and the sounds appeared to be coming from his right—and were closer. Even while he wielded his paddle he was positive a mermaid in the lead of her companions had overtaken him. He had every reason to be discouraged, but so long as he could continue paddling he would not complain. But he was constrained to admit that his present prospects were not too bright.

And then he heard a sudden swishing of water near where the pursuing mermaid was, and almost hopefully he believed the fate that controls the destinies of human beings was intervening in his behalf. He heard a muffled gasp from the lips of the mermaid and there was a splashing of water as though she beat her hands upon the surface in a determined effort to scare away some molesting demon of the deep.

The paddler called upon reserve strength to at least maintain his present effort and happily was able to do so. With attentive ears upon the disturbance to his right —just behind him now—more gasping sobs sounded to indicate distress. And then the voice of the mermaid queen was heard as she shouted to her less able followers to hurry and render her assistance, for a shark was molesting her. From nearby encouraging voices answered Sirena's cry for help, accompanied by a more audible splashing of arms coming in contact with the surface as greater speed was called upon.

The plight of the mermaid queen did not cause Bantan to suffer any qualms of conscience, for, as an enemy, he felt under no obligation to render her assistance. Had she been a total stranger under similar circumstances he wouldn't have hesitated to render help in her behalf.

In the passing minutes while the mermaids came to the assistance of their queen, the paddler took advantage of the delay in their pursuit to increase the distance that spanned. Once again he called softly to Tama, and from a short distance ahead he heard the native reply.

"Are you all right, Bantan?" Tama asked, a trace of anxiety noticeable in his tones.

Bantan gave assurances that he was all right.

Tama and Mauria desisted paddling until the hollowed log neared them. In a hushed voice the bronzed giant acquainted them with the distress the mermaid queen had encountered.

It was decided to attach the towline to the hollowed log. Bantan entered the canoe. All could take turns at paddling during the night. He pointed out the stars to follow before he lay down to rest. Nulu begged so insistently to be allowed to paddle and thereby give Mauria a much-needed rest that she was permitted to do so.

"I didn't paddle during the afternoon as you did," she said as the native girl handed her the paddle. "While I may not be as strong and as capable as you, you need some rest."

While Tama and Nulu paddled, Bantan and the native girl rested. Their progress was as good as could be expected with the hollowed log in tow. The native was beginning to show the effects of weariness in a little while, since he, too, had been compelled to paddle to the mermaid island that afternoon, and his strength was not at peak form as he had thought.

No further pursuit developed from the mermaids. Had

they known of the utter weariness of the escaping fugitives, they unquestionably would have endeavored their utmost to overtake and recapture them. In all probability they might have been successful in their effort.

During the long night, the four took turns at the paddles, and in the interim the others would rest and catch a short nap. Since there had been some fruit and nuts in the hollowed log which Bantan had not consumed, they were grateful for this sustenance.

With the coming of daylight all were relieved to observe the island toward which they paddled was not far distant. They should easily reach it by mid-morning. Studying the slightly ruffled surface to their rear no sign of pursuing mermaids was evident. The bronzed giant wondered if Sirena had escaped death from the shark that had molested her. With a shrug he hoped he had seen the last of the mermaids.

He now contemplated their immediate future. More fruit and nuts would have to be gathered before they left the island. He could only hope the mermaids would give up their desire of recapturing them, but of course there could be no certainty on this. He resolved that in turn they would keep watch for their possible return, and in the event they were seen approaching the island, sufficient warning would be obtained to give them an opportunity of acting to the best of their interests.

Before the canoe reached the calmer water beyond the surf, Tama and Mauria, who were paddling, desisted doing so at Bantan's request. He unfastened the towline and drew the hollowed log alongside the canoe and stepped into it.

"I'll paddle it ashore to avoid any damage to the canoe," he explained.

The native and his sweetheart nodded in understanding.

"May I go ashore with you, Bantan?" Nulu asked with appealing eyes.

He smiled and nodded. The blonde-haired girl stepped into the hollowed log and crouched within. She smiled thankfully up at the bronzed giant.

"I don't like being separated from you," she murmured.

Within a few minutes each water craft was beached without mishap. Wearied as all were, they dragged the canoe and the hollowed log to the edge of the foliage.

"There, that is done," Bantan said with relief. "Had the mermaids not come, at this time we would have been a sun nearer to our goal. Let us hope we have no further interruptions."

A similar hope was expressed by his companions.

The bronzed giant realized Tama's utter weariness, as well as Mauria.

"Why don't you both rest beneath the lean-to awhile?" he suggested. "I know both of you are very tired. A little later I'll rest as well. While you are doing so, I'll examine the fruit and nuts I discarded and see what can be reclaimed."

"I'm not tired, Bantan," Nulu said with a smile.

"You can keep an eye upon the stretches of water just in case the mermaids decide to follow us again," he said to her.

Tama and Mauria retired to the lean-to.

While Nulu seated herself at the edge of the foliage near Bantan, and kept her eyes fixed upon the water beyond the surf and as far as she could see, the bronzed giant examined the fruit and nuts. Hermit and land crabs had despoiled some, but the larger portion had not been touched. This was deposited into the hollowed log. When he had completed his task, he was aware only several armfuls would be required for their future need.

Remembering the bark container with the pitch he had

gathered, the bronzed giant found it where it had been dropped and was none the worse. With it, he checked the canoe bottom, and any place that appeared to have any weakness was given a generous application of pitch.

All the while he busied himself thusly, Nulu retained a careful watch of the stretches of shimmering water within her scope of vision. Upon a number of occasions she would look at Bantan with eyes of gentleness, and many were the sighs that found their way to her lips, loving him so much as she did.

After he had finished patching the canoe bottom, the bronzed giant placed the bark container of pitch in the forward end of the canoe. With a smile as his eyes met those of the blonde-haired girl, he went to her and seated himself. Placing an arm about her shoulders he smiled wearily.

"I am so tired," he murmured, "I could close my eyes and sleep."

Nulu brushed his cheek with her lips.

"Sleep then, Bantan," she murmured. With one hand she stroked his forehead gently. "I know you are very tired. Have no fear, I'll keep watch while you sleep. I'll get you a pallet for your comfort."

Nulu quickly arose and went to the lean-to where Tama and Mauria were fast asleep. She took the pallet that had been hers and returned with it to where the bronzed giant was lying.

"Be more comfortable," she murmured.

As he stretched himself upon it, the blonde-haired girl leaned over and kissed him gently. With a smile Bantan closed his eyes and almost immediately was asleep.

Shortly after noonday Mauria was first to waken, and feeling much refreshed, arose and joined Nulu who was faithfully watching the ocean surface while at her side Bantan was slumbering peacefully.

The native girl smiled and the blonde-haired girl responded similarly, then she went to the water's edge and indulged in a brief swim. Afterwards, she returned to where Nulu was seated.

"I'm hungry," she said. "Want me to prepare something for you as well?"

A nod was the answer. While they were eating, Tama appeared from the lean-to, and seeing the two eating made him realize that he, too, was hungry. He smiled to them.

"After I have a brief swim I'll join you," he said.

Some fifteen minutes later as the three were finishing their meal, Bantan stirred and opened his eyes. Having slept for several hours he felt surprisingly fit. He arose and said he would have a swim, and afterwards, he, too, would have something to eat. By the time he returned from the water fruit and nuts were prepared for him and he ate to his fill. Meanwhile, he explained what they would do before setting out upon their delayed trip to Marja.

"Tama and I will gather more fruit and nuts," he said. Looking at Nulu and Mauria, he added: "You two may remain here and keep watch. If it is agreeable to all, later, when the sun's heat lessens, we can start for Marja. I would prefer to wait until another sun, giving us a chance to have a good night's sleep; but thought of the possible return of the mermaids makes me feel we should not wait until another sun. I'm sure we would not wish to be captives of them again, although I have been fortunate to remain uncaptured. We can paddle slowly to conserve our strength, and we can take turns while the others rest and sleep."

Tama nodded agreeably.

"It would be best that we do as you say," he said.

Mauria was in accord as well.

Nulu shrugged.

"It is lovely here and I would be content to pass my entire life on this island," she said. "But whatever Bantan thinks best is what we should do."

The bronzed giant and Tama smiled. Then, with parting words, they departed to gather fruit and nuts. They were not gone long before returning with their first armful and depositing the assortment into the hollowed log. Again they were on their way for a final armful. Not much more time was consumed in the gathering, and then the two men joined the two girls at the edge of the foliage. The bronzed giant smiled as he placed an arm about Nulu's shoulders.

"It has seemed a long time since I left Marja," he said with a shake of his head. "All that has happened since is hardly credible. And it all started with me seeking Amar, who had been indirectly responsible for the death of poor Nao. Since then Mauria came into my life. Then there was Dr. Zarwood, Luane, you, Tama, Zarna, and then Mena, and Nulu, not to forget the mermaids. Living on Marja is going to be very tame compared to the adventures I've had since leaving the island. I hope all have been well and will be happy at my return with the new friends I have acquired."

Nulu looked inquisitively up at the handsome, bronzed giant.

"Do you suppose Wanya and Lori will be pleased with me?" she asked.

He uttered a deep sigh.

"I'm sure they will, Nulu," he said with a smile, and his arm tightened a trifle about her for added assurance. "You are of my race, and that is most important of all. I'm sure Father Lasance would have no reason to reproach me."

The blonde-haired girl snuggled her head in the hollow of his shoulder and her arm about him tightened as well.

"I'll be very pleasing to you, Bantan," she murmured. "If not, you can beat me."

"I don't think that will be necessary," he said with a soft laugh.

Tama and Mauria smiled to one another, and though the native girl's eyes were a trifle moist, she reached for one of her companion's hands and held it tightly in hers.

"We'll be very happy, too, Tama," she murmured.

When a couple of hours had passed and the sun's heat was lessening, Bantan at last arose to his feet and stretched.

"The time has come," he announced. "We'll have something to eat and be on our way."

Half an hour later they were ready to depart. The canoe and the ladened, hollowed log was dragged to the water's edge. The bronzed giant had been considering the best method of launching the heavier water craft and this he informed Tama.

"We'll let Nulu and Mauria paddle the canoe to the calmer water," he said. "The surf is gentle and you and I can swim alongside the ladened, hollowed log until we reach the calmer water. We should have no great difficulty."

Nulu and Mauria stepped into the canoe and took up their paddles. They were shoved into deeper water and within a few minutes the two paddlers had reached beyond the gentle surf.

Then the heavier craft was pushed into the water. With a hand upon each side of the gunwale slightly to the front from amidship, Bantan and Tama guided it, not without some difficulty, however, through the breaking water until at last they reached the calmer water where the canoe was awaiting them. In turn, each drew himself within. The towline was attached to the hollowed log. The bronzed giant and the blonde-haired girl were to take up the first session of paddling. The slack in the towline was taken up, and then with dipping paddles they moved away from the island, their course eastward slightly to the south.

CHAPTER XVIII

The Castaways

BY THE TIME the sun had set, the paddlers had changed places twice. A slight breeze aided them all the while for which they were grateful. Bantan and Nulu had just been relieved by Tama and Mauria. The canoe with the hollowed log in tow were quite a few miles from the small island they had left. The bronzed giant looked back at it and a whimsical smile touched his lips.

"We've done well so far," he said. "By tomorrow morning we won't be able to see the island."

Tama and Mauria nodded, but offered no comment.

Bantan and Nulu rested, meanwhile, and awaited the coming of darkness and the appearance of stars to be their guide during the night, for it was their intention to continue taking turns so as to cover as many miles as possible. Furthermore, during the coolness of the night there would be less discomfort in plying their paddles than during the heat of day. It was fervently hoped the present good weather would prevail, for they had no likening to have a tropical storm overtake them.

With the coming of dawn, true to Bantan's surmisal, no sight of the island they had left was to be obtained. After partaking of fruit and nuts, the bronzed giant and Nulu were ready to take up the paddles and resume their progress. They exchanged places with the wearied Tama and Mauria who lost no time obtaining some sleep before it would be their turn again to resume paddling. Each couple would paddle approximately two hours before being relieved.

The bronzed giant's keen eyes swept the horizon before the sun appeared above the waterline, and as far as his scope of vision permitted he could detect no sight of land. Even bird life appeared non-existent, which fact indicated they must be a considerable distance from any island. The day appeared to be a very nice one and, doubtless, as the sun rose higher, would be a hot one, for not the slightest breeze stirred at the present.

With spirits that were high Bantan and Nulu plied their paddles in unison, and their progress was good. The brilliant sun facing them was annoying even though they kept their heads lowered. The inconvenience of this was lessened with the glowing thought that Marja was their goal, and with the passing of a couple more suns and all went well they should reach the island.

The sun was two hours high when Tama and Mauria, having waked from their nap, partook of fruit and nuts and exchanged places with the two paddlers. A few words were exchanged before Bantan and Nulu rested and managed to catch a nap before the rising sun became too unbearable.

No denizens of the deep were about the immediate vicinity, for which the occupants of the canoe were grateful, though upon a couple of occasions turtles were seen at a short distance as they paddled methodically on their way to some unknown destination that an instinctive nature beckoned them.

By the time the bronzed giant and the blonde-haired girl relieved the native and his sweetheart, the sun was much higher. Though the burning rays were more intensive, the paddlers could now face the direction in which they were headed with no difficulty.

Bantan's sharp eyes first discerned the floating object

slightly to the right of their direct course, and his curiosity was aroused. It did not appear to be a boat of any kind, but more like a raft. Upon it he could distinguish several objects that appeared like the huddled bodies of human beings. At once he called Tama's attention to his discovery. The native studied the raft for long moments, as did Mauria.

"Those objects do look like bodies," Tama agreed, convinced. "A ship must have been wrecked and they are survivors."

"We'll have to investigate," the bronzed giant said. "It is the humane thing to do. It may be possible that they are still alive; and if so, we will have to render them assistance. Should they be dead—" and he shook his head, "—that is another matter."

"Of course," the native agreed.

Mauria remained silent as did Nulu, for each realized they had no say in the matter whether or not they favored the choice.

As the canoe drew nearer the floating raft a disturbance in the water about it was to be noticed.

"It appears sharks must sense the helplessness of the raft's occupants," Bantan commented.

Even though a half mile intervened, the disturbance in the water caused the raft to bob somewhat since the surface of the ocean was relatively calm with no breeze to ruffle it. The bronzed giant's sharp eyes distinguished four bodies upon the raft, and while he continued to watch them intently, he observed no movement. It was quite possible they had expired from want of food and water, but he would know for sure only when he had examined them.

As the canoe drew closer, the sharks—there were three of them—became more daring. A plan evolved in Bantan's mind. He put down the paddle and reached for his

bow, affixing an arrow to it. With it in readiness to discharge, he awaited the propitious moment, and when it
came a twang of the bowstring was to be heard. The
arrow imbedded its sharp point in the shark's neck. With
a thrashing of water the creature dived beneath the surface close to the raft. In doing so, the arrow was dis-
lodged from its neck, leaving a trail of blood in its wake.

The two remaining sharks instantly sensed the plight
of their companion and became maddened at the scent
of fresh blood. The water churned as, forgetful of the
helpless human beings upon the raft for the time being,
they followed the wounded shark, intent upon slaying
and devouring it.

With a smile and a nod, Bantan placed his bow in the
bottom of the canoe.

"That takes care of the sharks for the present," he
said. Studying the inert bodies for a long moment, he
shook his head as he added: "They don't seem to be
alive, but we'll know shortly."

Nulu continued to paddle easily until the canoe drew
alongside the raft. It was about twenty feet in length
by some fifteen in width and was covered with sheathing.
It was fairly buoyant in smooth water and none of the
huddled forms thereupon appeared to have been wetted
by waves washing over it.

Bantan placed a tentative foot upon an end of the raft
and bore his weight upon it, assuring himself of its sta-
bility before stepping upon it.

"Be careful, Bantan," Nulu murmured.

He assured her that he would.

In another moment he was upon it, the raft tilting
slightly beneath his weight, but in no way were the huddled bodies upon it disturbed. In the center there was
an open space between outflung arms and legs and the
bronzed giant sought it; then he bent and examined the

first of the bodies which appeared quite still. The man, as the others, was clad only in a pair of dungarees and an undershirt. His face was unshaven and the pallor of death appeared to stamp it. A hand placed over his still chest ascertained he had expired.

Without further pause, Bantan then examined another. This man was younger—slightly over twenty—and though several days' growth of reddish beard covered his sunburned face, his features were not of the pallor as the first. He appeared to be breathing very slowly. A third man, much older than the first two, also had expired. The fourth was a man of about thirty, black hair covering his ugly face and upper lip. He was stoutly built, and an examination revealed that he lived.

"Two are alive and two are dead," he said with a shake of his head as he looked at his companions in the canoe. "It is our duty to look after the two who are living and do for them what we can."

"Shall we take them aboard the canoe?" Tama asked.

The bronzed giant nodded.

"We can't tow the raft along with the hollowed log," he said.

"But what about those who have died?" Mauria asked.

"We'll leave them on the raft," was the answer. "It would be inhuman to heave their bodies into the water, knowing full well that there are sharks nearby."

Transferring the two helpless bodies into the canoe was a delicate task, but at last was successfully accomplished without any mishap. The canoe was somewhat overcrowded as a result, and Bantan was undecided for a few moments just what they should do.

Nulu shuddered as she looked upon the two castaway's bewhiskered, sunburned features.

"And now what?" Tama asked. "Shall we continue on to Marja?"

The bronzed giant was constrained to admit the problem was a delicate one, overcrowded as the canoe now was. To reach Marja would consume another two suns at the least—perhaps more than three. To return to the island they had left would be much less. Thought of the mermaids returning was also in his mind. It was so much closer, and adequate attention to the two rescued castaways could more quickly be provided if their lives were to be spared.

"Much as I dislike the decision," he said with a shake of his head, "I think our best course is to return with the castaways to the island we left."

Tama nodded and looked at Mauria for her assent. She had been watching the two unconscious castaways with a slight frown, as though inwardly wishing they had not come into their lives. But as her sweetheart touched her bronzed arm, she appeared startled momentarily.

"It is agreeable to you that we return to the island we left?" he asked.

"Of course," she assured him. Then, looking at the bronzed giant, she added: "Whatever Bantan thinks we should do I have no objection."

Nulu had been watching the two castaways and she looked up and nodded her willingness that they return to the island.

Since it was Tama and Mauria's turn at paddling, Bantan administered to the two unconscious men. Upon each in turn he managed to force some coconut milk between their bearded lips, and with a handful of water he bathed their foreheads and necks. And when it was his and Nulu's turn to relieve the two natives, Tama administered to them.

Before sundown no further sight of the raft upon which the two dead bodies reposed was to be seen.

The canoe and the hollowed log in tow made good

progress during the balance of the afternoon, and all during the night this progress was maintained. The two castaways still remained in a coma; but the following morning when the island toward which they were paddling was well within view, Bantan was aware the pallor of the two men's faces was healthier than on the previous day, and for that reason he believed they would recover with reasonable care.

The bronzed giant's keen eyes studied the island shore when they were ready to beach their water crafts, and he could see that it was as they had left it. He could not determine whether the mermaids had returned during their brief absence. He had informed his companions that he would navigate the ladened, hollowed log ashore, and now he did so with no mishap. The canoe followed, and after it was beached, Bantan and Tama carried the two unconscious castaways to the lean-to where they gently placed them. Then they dragged the canoe and the hollowed log to the edge of the foliage. The beach was carefully surveyed for recent traces of the mermaids having been here, but there were no such indications. It had been mentioned that at all times a careful watch, as previously, would be maintained for their possible return, and this assignment fell to Nulu and Mauria.

Meanwhile, Bantan and Tama administered to the two castaways, and late in the afternoon they were rewarded, for both of them regained partial consciousness. Though at first there appeared no awareness in their eyes of their whereabouts, or recognition of their benefactors, it was a good sign that they had emerged from the coma that had claimed them since they had been found.

Several hours before sunset it was apparent another lean-to must be constructed, and Bantan and Nulu gathered the required material and one was hastily erected.

Pallets of grass was also fashioned for the comfort of the rescued castaways.

The next morning Bantan was awake before his companions. His first duty was to check the condition of the two castaways. The younger of the two was still asleep, but the other was lying with eyes open as though in wonder at his present whereabouts. As the bronzed giant looked down at him, an awareness appeared in the man's dark eyes. In silent curiosity he looked up at his benefactor who smiled.

"You are awake." The bronzed giant spoke in English.

The man merely stared up at Bantan with no expression.

"If you can understand me just nod your head," Bantan said. "I know you must be very weak. Do you feel like having something to drink?"

The man merely nodded.

The bronzed giant at once left the lean-to and returned within a couple of minutes with a husked coconut. Squatting upon his haunches, with his dagger he bored a hole into one of the eyes. With a strong right hand beneath the man's shoulders he raised him to a seated position.

"Open your mouth," he said.

When the man did so, Bantan held the coconut above his lips and allowed the milk to trickle into his mouth. With no apparent difficulty being experienced in swallowing, nearly half of the coconut's contents was consumed before he closed his mouth, indicating he had enough for the time being. He was then eased back upon the pallet of grasses upon which he had lain. The castaway continued to regard his benefactor in silent wonder with no semblance of a smile upon his lips.

"Feeling better?" he was asked.

The man merely nodded, but uttered no words.

The bronzed giant then turned his attention to the

other, younger man. He placed a hand upon his forehead, but detected no fever. It was then that the castaway's eyelids fluttered before finally opening. His eyes were blue. He looked up in wonder at his benefactor, unable to believe his present whereabouts in consideration to the memory of his last conscious recollection, and that he now was alive. His mouth slightly opened and he murmured unintelligible words.

"You are still too weak to talk," Bantan said to him. "Would you like something to drink?"

The castaway weakly nodded with a trace of eagerness in his eyes.

The bronzed giant helped him to a seated position and held the coconut so that he was able to drink the contents remaining with brief pauses. Easing him back to his pallet of grasses, a grateful expression was in the young man's eyes as he looked up at his benefactor. He again tried to speak, but his words were not coherent.

Bantan smiled and cautioned him not to exert himself because of his apparent weakness.

"Rest," he bade him. "Later, I'll feed you some more."

The bronzed giant was aware of the young man's gratefulness, and because of that admirable trait he did not regret any service performed in his behalf. With a slight frown he turned his attention to the older man who had not appeared grateful. Looking down upon him, the man's eyes were still open and he was watching his benefactor with indifference.

"Would you like some more coconut milk?" he asked.

A nod of the man's head was his answer.

"I'll get another coconut," Bantan said. "Your friend drank what was left in this one. I'll be right back."

He went to the hollowed log for another coconut. Looking toward the hastily constructed lean-to where Tama, Nulu, and Mauria were, he saw that they were still sleeping. With the coconut in hand, a sweeping glance at the stretches of water within his scope of vision revealed no menace of any kind, and then he returned to the lean-to where the two castaways were. Squatting upon his haunches, he husked the nut, then bored into one of the eyes with his dagger point. The older man's eyes still watched him with indifference, and, if anything, a slight sneer touched his lips.

More coconut milk was given the castaway and he consumed over half of the nut's contents before indicating he had enough. As he was eased back to the pallet, Bantan noticed the peculiar expression that appeared in the man's eyes as his attention became riveted upon something behind him. Turning about, he saw that Nulu was silently standing a few yards away. She was looking from one castaway to the other with some concern. She smiled in greeting as her eyes met the bronzed giant's.

"They are improving," she said, diviningly.

He nodded as he arose and joined her, placing an arm about her shoulders.

"With the passing of a few more suns there should be marked improvement in them," he said.

Looking toward the two castaways who were watching them, Bantan smiled.

"I'll be back shortly," he said.

He and Nulu returned to the other lean-to where Tama and Mauria had now arisen. Naturally they wanted to know how the two castaways were faring and they were enlightened. Before making preparations for their breakfast, all four indulged in a brief swim.

Afterwards, Tama and Mauria approached the lean-to where the two castaways were lying. The two men looked at the newcomers in silence. There was a certain shyness apparent in the younger man's eyes as he looked at the lovely native girl, whereas his companion revealed no such emotion. If anything, his eyes were bold in staring, and this was not unnoticed by both Tama and Mauria. An uncomfortable feeling passed through the native girl, making her feel uneasy. She drew closer to Tama.

"Feeling better now?" he asked in English.

The younger man nodded and the semblance of a smile touched his lips. His companion merely blinked his eyes, but the boldness of them still persisted as they rested upon the comely native girl. Presently Bantan and Nulu appeared, and the older man's eyes opened a trifle wider and his boldness in staring at the blonde-haired girl was more apparent, even to the extent of causing the bronzed giant to wonder if the man, when well enough to be around, would be trustworthy in the presence of Nulu and Mauria should he and Tama chance to be absent.

CHAPTER XIX

A "South Seas Tarzan"

LATER IN THE MORNING a short distance from the landing and away from Nulu and Mauria, Bantan and Tama discussed the castaways between them.

"The larger and older of the two men I believe is not to be trusted," the native said, shaking his head. "I noticed the boldness in his eyes when he looked at Mauria and Nulu."

The bronzed giant nodded slowly and his lips tightened a trifle as he spoke.

"When they become well and strong, we must not leave Nulu or Mauria alone around them. The younger man appears trustworthy, however."

"He doesn't reveal boldness in his eyes," Tama agreed. "He appears grateful for what we have done for him. But the other—"

"Let us see if we can have them bathe," Bantan then said. "We can carry them to the water if necessary."

Returning to the lean-to they found both castaways were now seated. The younger man smiled pleasantly in greeting, though the older man's features remained impassive—almost hostile.

"Feeling better?" the bronzed giant asked them with a smile.

The younger man nodded, whereas his companion merely blinked his eyes.

"Would you like to bathe in the surf?" Bantan then asked. "Perhaps you'd like to have your clothes washed, and after they have dried you'll feel more comfortable."

Again the younger man nodded with eagerness and spoke in a soft, faltering voice.

"I don't think I have strength enough to go to the water's edge," he said. "If I were helped I would appreciate the opportunity of bathing in the surf."

The bronzed giant then looked at the older of the two men who was watching him with a peculiar expression in his black eyes—an almost hostile look.

"How about you?" he asked.

For the first time the older man spoke, and his voice was of a discordant nature. He indicated his companion with a thumb.

"Baby Bob first," he said. "I can wait."

Neither Bantan or Tama appreciated the surly answer that had been given. Even the younger man did not appear to like the manner he had spoken. The bronzed giant's eyes met those of the castaway for a long moment and held them unwaveringly, then he turned to the one addressed as "Bob." The native was at his side.

"All right, Bob," Bantan said. "We'll help you."

They helped him to his feet, and with the weakened man between them, the two assisted him down the beach. At the water's edge they paused and helped him remove his undershirt and dungarees, leaving only his shorts to cover his nakedness. The young man appeared somewhat abashed, but he was assured he had no occasion for embarrassment. Wading into the gentle surf with Bantan and Tama at his side supportingly, Bob appeared to delight in laving himself with the refreshing water, and a smile radiated his features.

Though the sun was quite hot, the water seemed much colder than it actually was with the result within ten minutes Bob's teeth were chattering and he was shivering. His thin body was sorely in need of more healthy flesh clothing his bones. He was led ashore, and while Tama supported his trembling form, the bronzed giant rinsed his soiled clothing and wrung them out. Without further delay they assisted the young man back to the lean-to. His damp clothing was placed over a limb to dry.

"Thanks," Bob said smilingly to his benefactors. "I feel a lot better already."

Bantan and Tama smiled and nodded then turned their attention to the older man. He appeared somewhat resentful as they helped him to his feet and to the water's edge and repeated what they had done for Bob. When they returned him to the lean-to, although he appeared much refreshed from his bath he offered no word of thanks as his companion had. A sour expression had now come upon his features as though he disliked being babied, although he would have been physically unable to have performed alone what his benefactors had helped him.

Leaving the two castaways, Bantan and Tama returned to where the canoe was beached and they seated themselves. While they had bathed the two men, Nulu and Mauria had taken a convenient stroll along the beach.

"Bob is agreeable," the native said in low tones. "But the other—I don't know what to think of him."

"Yes, I know," the bronzed giant agreed. "We'll keep an eye upon him for the good of all."

"It would be best," Tama said. "I'll tell Mauria to keep out of his sight as much as possible. You'll tell Nulu the same?"

"I will tell Nulu," and Bantan nodded.

And this they did when they returned from their walk.

Bantan and Tama brought the noonday meal to the two castaways at their lean-to. Their damp clothing had dried and they had donned it. Bob was smiling as the two approached with fruit and nuts. His companion still refrained from smiling or even appearing grateful.

The bronzed giant addressed both men, though he looked at the younger of the two when he spoke.

"Would you like to bathe again in the surf later?"

"I'd like that very much," Bob answered with glowing eyes. Then he turned to his companion. "How about you, Mike?"

That surly expression appeared upon the older man's face as he answered in his unpleasant tone of voice.

"We'll eat first and then think about it."

The smile upon Bantan's lips remained as he nodded to Bob, but it faded as he looked at "Mike."

"We'll see you later, then," he said.

The bronzed giant and the native returned to the vicinity of the lean-to they occupied where Nulu and Mauria had prepared their meal, and they ate it, speaking in soft voices.

Later in the afternoon Tama was left with Nulu and Mauria while Bantan assisted Bob to the water's edge for his promised bath. The bronzed giant asked questions of him, for he wanted a more thorough knowledge of the younger of the two castaways toward whom he had taken a likening.

"What is your entire name, Bob?" he asked.

Horwath," was the reply.

"I am called Bantan, and Tama is the name of my native companion," the bronzed giant volunteered. "Have you known Mike long?"

"A couple of months," was the answer. "He is not very sociable I'll admit. I think you are aware of that without me telling you."

A light laugh escaped Bantan's lips and he admitted the fact.

"What is his entire name?"

"Mike Decker," was the answer. "Both of us come from the U.S.A., which is United States of America. I was born in Monessen, Pennsylvania. Mike comes from New York. The vessel we were working upon must have struck a mine that has been floating around ever since the end of World War II. She sank awfully fast. I don't know how many were saved. I owe my life to Mike. He's a much stronger swimmer than I, and had he not kept me afloat I'd have been a goner. He got me aboard the raft where two other men were. They must have succumbed when you found us."

"Yes, two were dead," Bantan admitted. "We left them on the raft rather than cast them into the water. When we came upon the raft, sharks were about. After they were driven away I examined the bodies, and you and Mike were transferred into our canoe."

"I want to thank you for saving our lives, Bantan," Bob said with sincerity. "I'll speak for Mike as well, as I doubt if it would occur to him to thank you."

"That's all right, Bob," was the bronzed giant's reply. "I appreciate you mentioning it."

"I know you must be of white origin," the young man said. "Have you lived in this vicinity long?"

"Nearly all my life," was the answer. "My real name is Arthur Delcourt; but I've been known as Bantan ever since I was a child, and I sometimes forget my real name."

"Do you know," Bob added with a wholesome grin, "that back in America I've read a lot of books and seen motion pictures about a fictional character known as Tarzan? He was born of English parents in the African jungle and was brought up by savage apes. He became a sort of king in the jungle and a righter of wrongs. Somehow you remind me a lot of him in appearance."

The bronzed giant laughed softly.

"I have never heard of the Tarzan you speak of," he said. "But I like your expression of comparing me with him. It's too long a story to tell now, but I, too, have righted a few wrongs in this region—sometimes with the help of native friends."

Bob laughed good-naturedly.

"That would make you a regular South Seas Tarzan," he declared. "But you speak good English for having lived in this region nearly a lifetime."

"I owe my first knowledge of English to a missionary with whom I was marooned for several months upon an atoll," Bantan explained. "Later, Americans, who were friends of my parents, searched for traces of their disappearance, and myself as well, and I was established as the son of their friends. I would have returned to America with them—but that is too long a story to tell now. I have a feeling your friend Mike may become impatient for his bath if we remain here much longer."

"You'll tell me more about yourself another time, Bantan?" Bob asked with eagerness.

"Perhaps," was the answer.

Accompanying Mike Decker for his bath was not as sociable an affair as with Bob Horwath. Since the man was reluctant to speak voluntarily of himself, the bronzed giant was not one to press him for details. And so, except for only a few words, the bath was completed and the castaway was returned to the lean-to where the younger man greeted them with a good-natured smile.

"I'll be hoping to hear more about you, Bantan," Bob said hopefully.

Mike Decker looked curiously at the bronzed giant at the mention of his name. With a nod as he turned and left, Bantan heard young Horwath speak to his companion about him, reminding him of a South Seas Tarzan, and a smile touched his lips as he returned to join his companions who had just returned from a walk. The smile was still upon his lips and Tama's curiosity was aroused to the extent of inquiring the reason for such a pleased expression.

"Did the older castaway finally become sociable?" he asked.

"I find Bob very sociable," was the answer. "He mentioned to me how I reminded him of a book and motion picture character known as Tarzan, who reigns in the African jungle as a ruler of some kind. He said I was somewhat of a South Seas Tarzan."

Books and motion pictures were not comprehensive to Nulu and Mauria, and for that reason they stood as though awed. A knowing smile touched the lips of Tama, who did have such knowledge.

"Do you know, Bantan," he said, "that I agree with Bob. At the air base where I was taught to become a pilot, we would have motion pictures shown, and I've seen some of the Tarzan films. Where he was the undisputed lord of the jungle, I'd say you have been somewhat of a leader in the islands in this vicinity. Tarzan was the favorite of my companions at the air base as well as of myself."

Bantan smiled deprecatively as he turned to Nulu.

"Come," he said, "let's take a little walk."

The blonde-haired girl smiled happily as she joined the bronzed giant and linked her arm with his.

Tama smiled to Mauria and they seated themselves and kept a watch upon the seemingly endless stretches of water while talking of matters pertaining to themselves and their future.

Later in the afternoon after Bantan and Nulu returned, Tama and Mauria decided upon a stroll along the beach. They had no more than disappeared around a bend in the shoreline when young Horwath appeared from the lean-to he shared with Mike Decker. As his eager eyes rested upon the bronzed giant and the blonde-haired girl seated near their lean-to, he felt a trifle abashed because of the girl's presence, but he managed to muster sufficient courage to approach them, although with some hesitation.

"I hope I'm not intruding, Bantan," he said.

A smile touched the bronzed giant's lips and he indicated a place beside him.

The young man moved forward and seated himself.

"Bob, this girl is Nulu, my sweetheart," he said in the nature of an introduction. "She cannot speak English, so I'll speak to her in the tongue she understands and let her know what we are saying." With his words Bantan spoke to Nulu in the native tongue he had taught her.

The young man shyly looked at the blonde-haired girl and a flush mounted to his cheeks. As he saw the girl smile and nod to him, he, too, smiled and nodded. He watched the bronzed giant as he spoke further to Nulu, and she nodded to what was said. Bantan turned to young Horwath.

"It may seem difficult for you to believe, Bob," he said; "but Nulu was rescued from a cliff-enclosed island where primeval conditions exist and huge monsters of a long-ago age still roam. She was brought up among a tribe of aborigines from whom I rescued her. The fact that she was white-skinned—but tanned somewhat now —was due to a huge cloud that covers the entire island's interior, so that the inhabitants never see the sun, moon, or stars. It was there that I found Tama. He was a pilot in the late war and, while chasing a Jap plane, was forced to abandon his plane because of low fuel and he landed within the island."

"Gosh!" Horwath murmured, somewhat astonished at what he had been told.

"Would you like to know how I happened to reach that island?" Bantan asked with a smile.

"I'd like very much to know," the young man said with glowing eyes, now that his astonishment had been mastered.

The bronzed giant told him of Dr. Zarwood upon Mandoes Island and the miracles he was capable of performing. And all Bob Horwath could utter was "Gosh!" And this was repeated as Bantan would pause during his narrative. Incredible as the events were, when mention of the mermaid island was made, the young man was fairly speechless.

"It can't be possible!" he exclaimed at length, his eyes wide. "Mermaids!"

But the bronzed giant smiled and assured him it was so, adding hopefully that Bob wouldn't have the occasion to make their acquaintance, for he would be a sorrier and wiser man for such an experience. Shortly afterward, with the return of Tama and Mauria, young Horwath arose to rejoin his companion. He was smiling and shaking his head with incredulity.

"It just don't seem possible," he murmured. "But it must be so. Bantan would have no reason to lie to me. I wonder what Mike will think when I tell him?"

When Bob Horwath appeared at the lean-to where Mike Decker was seated, the latter was quick to observe the young man's enthusiasm.

"What are you bubbling about?" he asked rasply.

Young Horwath seated himself with a smile.

"Do you remember how I told you that Bantan was somewhat of a South Seas Tarzan?" he asked with glowing eyes.

"Well, what about it?" was the surly, answering reply.

"Let me repeat to you what he has just been telling me," Bob said.

In ebullient spirits the young castaway went on to relate Bantan's adventures. When he had completed the telling, Decker laughed ridiculously, though resentfulness was all too apparent in his dark eyes.

"Dr. Zarwood!" he fairly exploded. "A primeval land where prehistoric monsters still roam! Aborigines! Warrior women! And last of all—mermaids! Say, baby Bob, do I look so stupid as to believe that hogwash? Look at me—do I look that stupid? Who do you think you're kidding?"

The larger man gripped the younger man's arm in a ham-like hand and crushed it so hard that Bob fairly winced with pain.

"Please, Mike, don't squeeze so hard," he moaned. "But, honest, what I've been telling you must be true! Bantan doesn't appear to be the type of man who would have any reason to lie."

Decker laughed uproariously, but he released Bob's arm, much to the latter's relief.

"Bantan must be some sort of hero to you now," he snarled. "If he is an American like he says, for what reason would he want to remain in these island regions? I think he's a nut."

Young Horwath rubbed his sore arm, but he was very serious as he spoke.

"He told me he had an opportunity to return to America with friends of his long-lost parents who sought them," he asseverated. "He told me he'd tell me later on about his choice to remain in the tropics."

Decker laughed again in ridicule.

"And no doubt you'll swallow his line of bull just as you did about Dr. Zarwood, primeval land, prehistoric monsters, aborigines, warrior women—and—and mermaids! Come on, baby Bob, grow up. Remember—you're living in the twentieth century—not back in the middle ages." And then with a burst of stentorian laughter in accompaniment to his thoughts, he slapped his leg with a ham-like hand. "Mermaids!" he finally uttered. "Boy, that nearly kills me. Mermaids!" And again peals of laughter issued from his wide-opened mouth.

Bob Horwath surveyed his companion in unmitigated disgust.

"Laugh if you want to, Mike," he said. "But Bantan expressed the hope I would never be captured by the mermaids. They are not the lovable creatures you might think them to be. They are vicious."

Decker's laughter subsided, and for a long moment he looked at his younger companion in seeming awe.

"Say, baby Bob," he remarked at last. "You've got it bad. Are you sure you aren't touched with fever?"

"Listen, Mike," Bob said seriously. "The blonde-haired girl was rescued from the primeval land. She can speak no English, only a native language Bantan also speaks. She was rescued by him from a tribe of aborigines. The native, Tama, was a pilot during World War II, and he had to parachute into the primeval land where Bantan found him. If you don't believe what I'm telling you, I suggest that you ask Bantan about it when he brings our evening meal. I'm positive he can tell you more convincingly than I can. I dare you to mention the subject to him."

Decker's brow furrowed and, though his features were resentful, he nodded.

"Yes, baby Bob, maybe I'll do that," he said. And then, as though speaking to himself: "Who does this Bantan think he is? If he gives me the line of crap he gave Bob, I'll tell him off. Yes, that's just what I will do." Turning to the young castaway, he grinned maliciously. "Just watch and listen to me when this would-be-Tarzan comes with our evening meal."

"I'll be watching and listening," Bob promised with eagerness. "I can hardly wait."

CHAPTER XX

To Convince a Doubter

A short while before sundown, Tama appeared at the lean-to with the evening meal for Horwath and Decker where both had been lying down. The older man looked up in surprise at the native, for he had been anticipating the bronzed giant.

"I hope you both are continuing to feel better," Tama said with a smile.

The younger of the two castaways was disappointed because Bantan had not come in his stead.

"Where is Bantan?" he asked disappointedly.

"Yes, where is he?" Decker gruffly wanted to know, not waiting for Tama to answer young Horwath.

The smile upon the native's lips vanished on the instant and he critically regarded the older man.

"Do you wish to see him about something?" he asked politely.

"What about the baloney he's been telling baby Bob?" Decker demanded in his unpleasant tones. "A Dr. Zarwood who can perform miracles, a primeval land where prehistoric monsters roam, warrior women, aborigines, and last of all—mermaids!" He laughed emphatically with the utterance of the word "mermaids." "Yes, come to think of it, he told Bob that you were found on the primeval island. Is that true?"

A tolerant smile now touched Tama's lips and he nodded.

"It's true," he declared. "Strange as it may seem—Bantan did not tell your friend anything but the truth."

Decker regarded the native in exasperation.

"Are you trying to tell me what Bantan said is true?" he demanded. "What do you think I am—stupid? Or, do you know the meaning of the word?"

Tama's tolerant smile persisted.

"I was on the primeval island," he said quietly. "I've seen the prehistoric monsters, the warrior women, and the aborigines. I've also been a captive of the mermaids. Do you think I would have any reason to lie about such a matter?"

Decker's features became incredulous with surprise.

"Listen, you know we are living in the twentieth century, or don't you?" he asked with apparent sarcasm.

"I am well aware of that," was the quiet answer.

The unbelieving castaway shook his head violently. The native's tolerant smile was irritating to him.

"Listen," he said. "Bantan might convince baby Bob about all that baloney, but you're not going to make me believe any such crap. I think you and Bantan must be a couple of nuts to tell the fairy tales you do—and expect a sane person to believe them."

Tama laughed almost mockingly.

"There is a saying about 'seeing is believing'," he said after a moment. "For your sake, I hope you don't have to be convinced that way."

And with his words the native bowed politely and turned to depart. Decker called after him, bringing him to a halt. Tama turned about again with impassive features, but his eyes were critical.

"When Bantan has the time," the older man said, "tell him I want to have a talk with him."

Tama forced a smile to his lips.

"I'll tell him," he promised.

Decker then proceeded to eat of the fruit and nuts. He met Horwath's troubled eyes.

"I guess I told him off, didn't I?" he grunted.

The younger man could only shake his head in despair.

"Mike, I think you should be grateful that our lives were spared," he said.

The older man shrugged and grunted. His mouth was too full to speak.

"Mike," Bob added, "if you are looking for trouble, I think you are picking on the wrong guy if you pick Bantan as your object."

Decker raised a ham-like fist threateningly. He shook it at his companion.

"Do you think I'm afraid of that teller of fairy tales?" he demanded.

"I think he is to be highly respected—not threatened," Bob answered in a low voice.

The older man's disgust was apparent.

"Says you," he grumbled. "I saved your life, and now you are trying to tell me off. Who in hell do you think you are?"

"Listen, Mike," Bob said in a pleading tone of voice. "I admit you saved my life and I'm grateful to you for having done so. But don't forget that Bantan and Tama saved both of our lives."

Decker regarded his companion critically before he spoke.

"But that doesn't give either of them the privilege of trying to entertain us with fairy tales—and expecting us to believe them. We don't have to listen to that kind of crap, and I for one won't hesitate to let them know it."

Young Horwath shrugged hopelessly.

"Do as you like, Mike," he said, evidently depressed. "But don't say I didn't warn you."

Decker granted, then his normally ugly features took on a menacing expression.

"Now look here, baby Bob," he warned, "don't try and give me any advice. I'm old enough to know what I'm doing."

Horwath merely shrugged.

"Have it your own way," he said.

Thereafter, they resumed eating in silence for the most part. Occasionally Decker would mutter such words as, "Dr. Zarwood," "primeval land," "prehistoric monsters," "warrior women," "aborigines," and "mermaids." With this final utterance, he burst into a peal of laughter and rocked to and fro for nearly a minute, ending with slapping one of his thighs with the palm of his ham-like hand.

"That does it!" he muttered. And then again he laughed aloud. "Mermaids!" he repeated. "Boy, that is a rich one. Talk about some of the star TV comedians! Bantan has them all beat with his fairy tales."

Young Horwath regarded his fellow castaway with an expression bordering upon unmitigated disgust.

"Say, Mike," he said, "are you all right?"

Decker's laughter ceased and he turned to his companion. He started to laugh again, then ridicule was to be read in his dark eyes.

"If you were to kiss me, baby Bob," he said with a silly grin, "I could believe that. But—mermaids—" Once again he burst into stentorian laughter and rocked to and fro, clutching his stomach with both hands. "Oh, boy—oh, boy—" was all he could utter. After his laughter had subsided, an expression of evil appeared in his eyes. "Lead me to the mermaids. I think I could love them all."

At that moment Bantan appeared without warning around the end of the lean-to. No smile touched his lips and there was a peculiar glint in his dark eyes. He looked directly at Decker.

"Tama tells me you wanted to see me about something, Mike," he said.

Bob Horwath maintained a respectable silence, but a slight smile touched his lips and his blue eyes were filled with admiration toward his benefactor.

The older man looked at the bronzed giant mockingly.

"Baby Bob has been telling me some of the fairy tales you told him," he said. A silly grin spread over his ugly features as he added: "Were you telling those stories so that you might impress him that you are something of a South Seas Tarzan? Baby Bob is easily impressed, but I'm not."

Bantan's eyes narrowed a trifle and an ironical smile touched his lips.

"I understand, Mike," he said in crisp tones, "that you don't believe I was telling the truth."

The older man's features were still enwreathed with a silly grin.

"Now look," he said. "Just because Bob and I owe our lives to you and your native friend doesn't give you the privilege to tell baby Bob such fairy tales so that he'll look up at you as a hero."

The ironical smile on Bantan's lips faded.

"You do not believe anything that I told Bob?" he asked.

Decker's silly grin was replaced with disgust.

"Of course I don't," he answered. "I've been around this world too long to believe such crap. Although I'm not from Missouri, I'm one that has to see for himself to believe."

The bronzed giant regarded the castaway with critical eyes for a long moment before speaking.

"Sleep well tonight, Mike," he said. "If you are well

enough tomorrow, I'll take you to a place on this island that may convince you of something that words can't."

Decker laughed with sarcasm.

"On this island?" he repeated. Then he nodded emphatically. "I'll be ready in the morning. I'll have to be shown to believe."

"After we have our morning meal, then," Bantan said.

"May I go along, too, Bantan?" Bob asked anxiously. When the bronzed giant looked at him with a shade of disappointment in his eyes, the young man added hastily: "It's not that *I* don't believe you. I want to see Mike be convinced."

A slight smile now touched Bantan's lips and he nodded.

"All right, Bob," he agreed, "you may accompany us."

And with his words he turned and left.

A scowl was upon Decker's face as he watched the bronzed giant silently walk away. When he felt he was beyond hearing, the older man turned to face his companion.

"I told you I'd tell him off," he said smugly.

A complacent smile touched the younger man's lips.

"We'll decide that tomorrow," was all he said.

Decker regarded Bob Horwath with a quizzical expression.

"What he wants to show me wants to be mighty convincing," he mumbled, and he lay back and covered his eyes with his forearms.

When Bantan returned to his companions, Tama was aware of the glint in his dark eyes.

"Did you convince Mike of something?" he asked with a slow smile.

The bronzed giant shook his head.

"He has to be shown to be convinced," he replied. "I

promised that I'd show him something tomorrow morning after breakfast that might convince him."

After breakfast the following morning, Mike Decker and Bob Horwath felt surprisingly fit after a sound night's sleep. Tama brought their breakfast, and without a word left them. The two castaways had no more than finished eating when Bantan appeared.

"All ready?" he asked.

Decker and Bob nodded and followed the bronzed giant to the water's edge where he had dragged the canoe. They were told to enter, and after they had done so, Bantan pushed it into the gentle surf. He then leaped within agily and in another moment had snatched up his paddle. With powerful strokes he forced the canoe through the breaking water into the calmer area beyond. Since the rising sun faced the paddler, he lowered his head so as not to be inconvenienced by the blinding rays.

Bob Horwath sat in the bow, facing the paddler, and Decker sat about amidship. Over the shoulder of the larger man, the younger marvelled at the expert paddling of the bronzed giant. Meanwhile, his companion was scanning the island shore. An insolent expression was upon his face.

In due time they rounded the shoreline and now Bantan could raise his head. He avoided looking at Decker, though once when his eyes met those of Bob's, the trace of a smile touched his lips.

Soon the canoe was nearing the cove, and as the paddler guided it toward the grotto's opening, Bantan noted the peculiar expression that now had come upon Decker's face. Bob, too, was aware of what the paddler intended and he looked with interest as the canoe continued toward the opening.

"Are we going in, Bantan?" the younger man asked with eagerness.

The bronzed giant merely nodded, and a moment later they had passed through the opening. The paddler noticed the high-water mark on the side of the passageway and he was also aware of the present status of the tide.

Straining his eyes, Bob could see a faint glow ahead. As well, he could distinguish the end of the water some distance ahead where it gently lapped the smooth, rock floor.

Decker turned his head upon one occasion after the canoe passed through the grotto's opening, and he wondered not a little what it was that was supposed to change his opinion of his benefactor.

Soon the canoe's prow grated upon the rock floor and came to a halt.

"We'll have to get out here and walk the rest of the way," Bantan said quietly.

In a few moments with the bronzed giant in the lead, the trio advanced toward the phosphorescent lighted amphitheatre. As they reached the end of the passageway, the leader stepped to one side so that the two castaways could see the stone figure of the sea god that reclined upon the altar. He pointed toward it as he looked at Decker who was staring in open-mouthed wonder at the object directly across from where he stood.

"This is the temple of the sea god," Bantan said. "It is here—so one of the mermaids told Mauria—that the mermen came once each year to worship their deity. Examine it carefully and you will see from the waist down it resembles a fish. Come, let us approach closer so there can be no doubt as to what it represents."

As he spoke, the bronzed giant advanced toward the altar with Bob Horwath at his side. Decker trailed behind with mouth now closed, but wonder still apparent in his eyes. When they stood before the altar, the younger man appeared excited and his blue eyes were eager.

"Such a fine piece of stone work," he murmured. "Whoever fashioned it must have been extremely skilled in his art. It is perfect." As he spoke, he trailed a hand over the features.

Decker's dark eyes looked upon the stone figure with a trace of awe. Then he remembered that no previous mention had been made of the mermen who had come here on an annual pilgrimage as being alive at the present. Only of the mermaids had Bantan mentioned. The awe in his eyes faded and he now grunted as though unconvinced.

"What happened to the mermen who came here?" he asked.

"Mauria was told by one of the mermaids that a terrible storm had raged after the mermen had left their island," the bronzed giant answered. "It is obvious they must have perished, for none returned."

Decker again grunted.

Bantan then caught the older man's doubting eyes with his and held them for a long moment.

"Are you convinced there *were* mermen, Mike?" he asked. "And that the mermaids are still in existence?"

The man shrugged.

"This may be a temple of the sea god," he admitted. "It is possible centuries ago mermen and mermaids existed; but I still doubt their existence at the present time."

"If they once existed," Bantan said, "why couldn't they exist at the present time?"

Decker again shrugged, then he forced a grin to his face and his eyes expressed ridicule.

"I see a temple and a stone figure of a sea god upon an altar," he stated. "But I would have to see the mermaids in person before I'd admit they exist at the present time." He turned to Bob Horwath and noted his evident excitement. He added: "Baby Bob here believes almost everything he's told, and no doubt he has swallowed this story hook, line, and sinker. Isn't that the truth?"

The younger man looked despairingly at his fellow castaway. He shook his head regretfully.

"It is too bad that you are so stubborn, Mike," he said sadly. "I'll admit I do believe Bantan's story about the mermen and the mermaids." And with his spoken words he looked at the bronzed giant with a hopeless smile.

Decker shrugged noncommittally.

"Until there's living proof of the mermaids," he declared, "I'll still stand corrected."

A pitying expression passed over Bantan's features.

"Come," he said peremptorily, "we are only wasting our time here. Let's return to the canoe."

He left the altar of the sea god with quick strides and headed for the opening in the passageway. Bob followed close behind, almost panting in his effort to keep close, while Decker with an insolent grin upon his lips followed more leisurely in their wake.

In due time the canoe was being paddled through the passageway and presently appeared in the sunlight. Wordlessly a grim Bantan wielded his paddle, trying to avoid the insolent features of Mike Decker. In absolute silence the canoe was paddled back to the landing and was beached. After the two castaways stepped out, the bronzed giant dragged the canoe to the edge of the foliage where Tama, Nulu, and Mauria were standing. Young Horwath and Decker returned to the lean-to they occupied.

As Bantan straightened, his companions were aware of his grim features. Tama shook his head sadly.

"Decker was not convinced," he said diviningly.

The bronzed giant shook his head with apparent disgust.

"He is not convinced," he admitted.

"But Bob was?" the native asked.

A nod was the answer.

"It is too bad that some people must see something with their own eyes to believe what another has," he said, shaking his head sadly. "I am almost determined to take Decker to the mermaid island and leave him there. Perhaps he'll be convinced then."

An expression of dismay possessed Mauria's features while Nulu appeared surprised. Tama merely nodded.

"It would serve him right," he declared.

"I dislike being called a liar," Bantan added with a note of disdain in his voice.

"We should leave Mike here alone, taking Bob with us," Mauria suggested. "Maybe the mermaids will return to this island and would find him."

A smile touched the bronzed giant's lips.

"What you say has possibilities, Mauria," he said. "However, we'll wait a few more suns before we decide what to do."

And so it was agreed they would do this.

CHAPTER XXI

A Change of Heart

LATER IN THE FORENOON, Bob Horwath left the lean-to. Standing at the edge of the beach he looked toward the other lean-to. Bantan and Tama were seated by the canoe while Nulu and Mauria were a short distance from them. The bronzed giant saw the young castaway with a forlorn expression upon his features, and he called to him indicatingly. A smile touched the young man's lips, and he at once went toward his benefactors.

"Sit down, Bob," Bantan said. "You looked lonesome."

Young Horwath smiled to Tama and seated himself at the bronzed giant's side. The native excused himself upon some slight pretext, feeling they would rather be alone.

"How is your friend Mike?" Bantan asked with a smile.

"He took a walk," was the answer. "I might have gone along with him, but didn't feel like it."

"Both of you are recovering nicely," the bronzed giant remarked.

"Thanks to you and Tama," Bob agreed.

A deprecative smile appeared on Bantan's lips.

"Please don't mention it."

"You told me yesterday you would tell why you rejected the opportunity of returning to America with friends of your parents," Bob then said. "Would you care to tell me?"

A nod was the answer. Briefly, the bronzed giant related what young Horwath wanted to know.

"Under the circumstances, Bantan," the young man said, "I think I would have done the same thing. In America, without a job or money, life can be difficult."

The bronzed giant merely nodded.

"When we rescued you and Mike," he said, "we were on our way to Marja Island. I have been away for a number of months. My adopted people will be wondering what has happened to me, since I have never been absent for so long a time."

"Finding us on a raft has altered your plans somewhat," Bob divined. "I am sorry, please believe me. Last night before falling asleep I was wondering about the immediate future. But of course I couldn't reach a definite conclusion. I suppose when news of our ship sinking reaches other ships they'll probably be around looking for survivors. I'm sure Mike and I could get along here alone until we are rescued."

"Only having a canoe as we do," Bantan added, "it would be difficult to grant both of you passage to Marja. I am not so sure you both would be as safe here as upon Marja. I haven't forgotten about the mermaids and the possibility they might return."

"If we saw them first," Bob said, "we could hide. At least, we have legs, whereas they haven't."

"That is true," the bronzed giant admitted. "When Mike comes back from his walk, talk over with him your plans for the immediate future."

"I'll do that," the young man promised. "There he is now."

Young Horwath arose to his feet. Looking toward Tama, Nulu, and Mauria who were nearby, he smiled and nodded—they doing likewise—and he returned to the lean-to.

Mike Decker had thrown himself upon his pallet of grasses and was breathing deeply from the exertion of walking along the beach. At Bob's return he looked up and grunted.

"Been listening to more of Bantan's fairy tales?" he asked with sarcasm.

The young man seated himself near Decker.

"He was telling me why he renounced the opportunity of returning to America with friends of his parents," he said. "I'll have to admit I admire him. He did start back with them, but radio contact with America was made and he learned the trustees of the estate that was his to claim had been squandered. Rather than be a pauper, he chose to remain in the tropics where money did not matter."

The older man grunted, but offered no speech on the matter.

"And, Mike," Bob added, "he told me the day we were found on the raft that he and his companions were enroute to an island known as Marja. He had left the island and his native friends several months ago. Because of our helpless condition they returned here where they could take better care of us. He asked me if I had been thinking of the future, and to talk matters over with you. Because of the limited accommodations of their canoe, they can't very well ask us to go with them to Marja. Furthermore, we stand a better chance of being rescued from this island which is nearer to where our ship was wrecked and we were picked up."

Decker had risen to a seated position while his companion was speaking and a dour expression had overcome his features.

"So, we delayed Bantan's homecoming," he remarked. "Well, that's too bad. We didn't ask them to rescue us."

"Look, Mike, it was the humane thing to do," Bob

said placatingly. "Just reverse the situation. Suppose we found Bantan and his friends in a similar state. Wouldn't we have done as much for them?"

The older man shook his head uncertainly.

"I don't know," he admitted. "No one ever did anything for me. I've always had to make my own way. I told you once before that I always had a hard row to hoe in life."

"Let's not go into the past," his companion protested. "Let's discuss the immediate present. Now, we know Bantan and his friends would like to be on their way as soon as possible. Do you feel well enough to face the future by ourselves and look for an early rescue?"

The dour expression on Decker's face softened and a malicious one replaced the other.

Young Horwath noticed the change in his companion and at once suspected of what he was thinking.

"No, Mike," he pleaded, "don't entertain such thoughts. I know what you have in mind."

The older man looked at his companion and the tip of his tongue licked his lips. An unholy light had appeared in his dark eyes. He spoke in a low voice.

"Do you know, baby Bob," he said, "if we had those two babes to ourselves to wait on us hand and foot we'd be living in paradise."

The young man shook his head in disgust.

"They are already spoken for," he declared. "The blonde-haired girl, Nulu, is Bantan's sweetheart, and Mauria is Tama's. That's that, and there's no changing the situation."

Decker continued to lick his lips and the unholy gleam in his eyes did not lessen.

"Boy, could I go for that blonde-haired babe," he remarked. "And the native girl is not a bad dish either."

"I hope Bantan never knows of your thoughts," Bob stated.

Decker uttered an exclamation of disgust.

"There you go—mentioning the would-be-Tarzan again," he snarled. "Do you think I'm afraid of that teller of fairy tales? Do you?"

Young Horwath shook his head sadly and did not answer. The older man seized one of his arms in a crushing grip until the younger man winced.

"Don't you think I could beat him up in a fight?" he demanded. "Do you think I've been so weakened that I couldn't do it?"

"I don't know," young Horwath almost cried, pulling his arm free from the man's crushing grip. He rubbed it gently. "I wish you wouldn't grab me that way again. My arm is almost numb. I don't think you know your strength."

A silly grin overcame the larger man's face. He reached out and patted his companion's head gently.

"All right, baby Bob, I'm sorry," he said mollifyingly. "Does that make you feel better?"

Young Horwath arose to his feet with tears of frustration in his eyes. He left the lean-to and started walking along the beach, still rubbing his tender arm.

Decker watched him leave, then laughed softly as he lay back again and closed his eyes. The vision of the comely native girl appeared in his thoughts, but he banished her features from his mind almost instantly in preference to Nulu. The longer he entertained thoughts of her the greater his desire to possess her. Whenever the vision of Bantan sought to obtrude upon his delirious imaginings of the blonde-haired girl a scowl would overcome his features and he would clench and unclench his ham-like hands repeatedly. He could almost feel them smash time and again into the handsome features of the

bronzed giant as he battered them into an unrecogniz-
able mass of flesh and blood.

Nearing noonday young Horwath returned to the lean-
to to find his companion somewhat impatient.

"I wonder if we are going to have anything to eat,"
he muttered. "I'm getting hungry."

"Didn't you know they have a fire going?" the younger
man asked. "I think something special is being cooked."

Earlier, Bantan had caught some fine fish and these
were being cooked by the efficient Mauria. Presently
Tama appeared with a large cooked fish along with some
fruit and nuts on a crude platter.

"Something special today," he said with a smile.

Bob Horwath smiled his thanks. His companion merely
grunted and reached for a piece of the fish with his fingers. Tearing off a generous chunk he tasted it and found
it delicious. Smacking his lips, he grinned at the younger
man.

"Boy, this is good!" he remarked. "Dig into it, baby
Bob, or I'll eat it all by myself."

Young Horwath shook his head despairingly.

"I wish you would leave out the 'baby' when you
speak to me, Mike," he said.

Decker looked at his companion in astonishment for
a moment.

"O.K., ba—, Bob," he corrected himself. He laughed
at the next moment. "I guess it's just a habit of mine.
I'll try and remember. But, boy, oh boy, this fish is the
best I've ever tasted. I wonder whether Nulu or Mauria
cooked it?"

"I imagine Mauria must have done so," Bob answered.
"Most native girls are trained from early childhood to
be good cooks in preparation for the time when they are
mated."

Thoughts of Nulu in the older man's mind vanished at

once and the now glowing features of Mauria became prominent instead. As he finished swallowing another generous mouthful of fish, he looked at his companion with glowing eyes.

"Say, ba—, Bob," he again corrected himself with a short laugh, "you know I might go for a native girl if all of them can cook as well as Mauria. I wonder if your hero might reconsider making room for us in the canoe and take us to Marja? The native girls there who are unmarried might be willing to cook for us. We could live the life of Riley then."

Young Horwath smilingly shook his head.

"No, Mike, I don't want to go native," he answered. "While what you say sounds appealing, I still do not forget I am a white man."

"Sure, kid," the older man said, smiling, "I know it. But the way this fish is cooked sure gets me. Come on, dig in before I eat it all. I don't want to be greedy, but I just can't help myself." He chuckled. After swallowing another generous mouthful, he nodded emphatically. "After we get through eating, I'm going to ask who did the cooking of this fish. I'll thank whoever it was. Yes, sir, whoever did it deserves to be thanked. I could kiss her hands even."

A surprised light appeared in young Horwath's eyes.

"By God, Mike," he exclaimed, "you are a human being after all."

It was Decker's turn to be surprised. He looked at his companion in apparent awe for a moment, then he laughed.

"Eating such wonderfully cooked fish makes me feel good," he said, as he reached for another generous portion. "Yes, sir, I could kiss the hands that cooked this."

Bob could not refrain from laughing.

The outcome of the cooked fish dinner was much in

Decker's favor, for he had consumed at least three-quarters of it; but his younger companion had not minded since it resulted in a happy frame of mind for the older man, and for that reason Bob was grateful. He disliked constant bickering and, being of a passive nature, did not want trouble with the larger man. He hoped most sincerely he would make no improper advances toward either Nulu or Mauria to incur the wrath of Bantan and Tama. He knew Decker was a bully because of his size and strength, and he could be vicious and belligerent, and to keep him pacified would be to the best interests of all.

When the last morsel of their delectable meal had been consumed, the older man wiped his mouth with the back of a hairy hand.

"I know I said I'd thank whoever cooked that fish," he said in a low voice. "But if I did it would prove I was getting soft. Forget that I said what I did. You will, ba—, Bob, won't you?"

"Sure, Mike, whatever you say," his companion agreed with a disappointed expression overcoming his face.

Decker sighed deeply, and after an eructation he drew a deep breath and reluctantly exhaled. Then his brow furrowed in serious thought.

"I wonder if the mermaids are good cooks?" he asked aloud.

Bob Horwath shook his head despairingly, but a slight smile touched his lips as he realized how his companion's thoughts without warning could leap from one subject to another.

"But I thought you didn't believe in mermaids," he said remindingly.

A silly grin came over the older man's ugly features that seemingly humanized them.

"Yes, I did say that, didn't I?" he answered. "But

just think of the possibliities. If there are no mermen, we could be like kings. We'd rule a harem. Say, do you know it's worth thinking about. Boy, I can imagine myself sitting on a throne with those beautiful dolls swishing around in answer to my every wish. I'll tell you what, Bob. The next time you talk with your hero, ask him the direction of the mermaid island. Maybe we could build a raft, erect a sail, and go there." He rubbed his hands briskly and nodded repeatedly. "The more I think of the idea the better it seems."

Bob arose to his feet.

"I've got to take a walk," he said. "I'll leave you with your mermaid thoughts."

"Remember, if you see your hero don't forget to ask him," the older man added.

The young man nodded.

"I'll do that for you, Mike," he answered.

"Thanks, ba—, Bob," the older man again corrected himself. "You're my pal. The best ain't none too good for you."

As chance would have it, young Horwath met Bantan shortly. A smile touched the young man's lips.

"You're happy about something, Bob?" the bronzed giant observed.

The castaway shook his head, though the smile still lingered.

"Mike feels so good about the fish dinner," he answered, "that he even believes in mermaids now. He was wondering if mermaids could cook as well."

Bantan laughed softly.

"But I thought he didn't believe in their existence," he averred.

Bob's eyes were filled with humor.

"He asked me to ask you in what direction their island is located," he added. "He's thinking of building

a raft and sail there. He seems to think they would welcome him."

"And you?" the bronzed giant queried. "Do you wish
to go, too?"

The young man shook his head.

"If I thought Mike was serious about going to the
mermaid island," Bantan said, "I'd have Tama help
me paddle him there. Incidently, the mermaid island lies
due west from here."

Bob Horwath shook his head sadly.

"Mike has had a hard time in life," he said. "He's told
me no one had ever given him a helping hand, and for
that reason he appears inconsiderate when anyone does
him a favor."

"I can understand that," the bronzed giant said with
a nod.

"As for myself," Bob added, "I'd like to remain here
and await rescue which should result in the wake of our
ship that was wrecked. As for Mike—" and he shook his
head dubiously, "—I can't answer for him."

Bantan smiled in understanding as they parted.

When the bronzed giant rejoined his companions, a
smile still lingered upon his lips. He looked at Mauria
and nodded.

"Mike appreciated your cooking," he said to her. "Bob
was telling me."

The native girl smiled.

"It is nice to know something pleased him," she answered. "He is a strange man."

The bronzed giant winked to Tama.

"He even wants to go to the mermaid island," he added.
"Bob doesn't, however. He would rather remain here
and await rescue."

"I would be happy to paddle Mike to the mermaid is-

land," the native said with a touch of eagerness in his
tones. "Do you think he is serious?"

"He talked to Bob about building a raft to get there,"
Bantan added. "He wanted to know the location of the
mermaid island and I told him where it was."

Mauria laughed softly.

"It would be hoping for too much of a good thing that
Mike did go there," she declared. "But would Bob want
to remain here—alone?"

"He says he would," Bantan answered.

"Maybe we could induce him to return to Marja with
us," Tama suggested.

"If Mike is serious about going to the mermaid island," the bronzed giant said, "I'll ask Bob if he would
care to accompany us. I'm sure we could make room
for him in the canoe. He's not so large as his companion."

Even Nulu, who had been silent, nodded her head, as
did Tama and Mauria.

CHAPTER XXII

A Request Is Granted

WHEN YOUNG HORWATH rejoined his companion, Mike had been lying flat upon his back with eyes closed, trying to envision himself upon the mermaid island as the undisputed ruler. He opened them now and sat up.

"Did you ask your hero the direction of the mermaid island?" His first question was uttered with eagerness.

"Due west from here," was the answer.

Decker rubbed his hands together briskly and smiled with glowing eyes.

"Thanks, ba—, Bob," he said, again correcting himself. "Boy, you are a pal. Are you sure you don't want to go with me?"

The young man shook his head emphatically.

"Thanks for the invitation, Mike," he answered. "But the answer is still no."

"But, Bob, you don't know what you'd be missing," the older man protested. "Just think of those beautiful babes waiting on us hand and foot. Doesn't that mean anything to you?"

Young Horwath shook his head.

"It doesn't appeal to me," he replied.

Decker arose to his feet and stretched his powerful arms.

"Well, I've got to look around for logs to make a raft," he said. "I wouldn't know how to build a canoe."

"If you are serious about going to the mermaid island," Bob said, "it won't be necessary to build a raft."

"How else am I going to get there—swim?" the larger man demanded.

"I think Bantan and Tama might be willing to paddle you there—if you are serious," was the answer.

The older man's lower jaw dropped in surprise and he gaped at his fellow castaway for a long moment.

"Do you mean it, ba—, Bob?" he demanded.

The young man nodded solemnly.

Decker appeared in deep thought, then nodded and spoke as to himself.

"I guess they are anxious to get rid of me," he mumbled. Then he straightened to his full height of over six feet, and he shook his head almost violently. "No, sir, I'm not going to be indebted to them by any means. I'll build my own raft with my own two hands. I won't even ask you to give me a hand."

And with his words he stamped indignantly away from the lean-to.

Bob watched him go and shook his head hopelessly.

In a little while Mike Decker returned to the lean-to. The afternoon sun was hot and he was apparently exhausted. His fellow castaway had fallen asleep, but at the return of the older man he awoke and sat up. He yawned.

"Back already, Mike?" he asked in surprise. "Did you find any material with which to build your raft?"

The older man dropped wearily upon his pallet of grasses and heaved a deep sigh.

"There's all kinds of trees," he muttered. "But I don't even have a jacknife. What's a guy going to do? Whew, but it's hot."

Young Horwath shook his head dismayingly.

"Then I guess the idea of building a raft is out of the question," he commented.

"Don't worry, ba—, Bob," Decker said with assurance.

"I'll figure out a way yet to get to the mermaid island. Don't bother me now. I'm about pooped."

"Sure, Mike, just as you say," was the answer. The young man looked at his companion for a long moment, then again lay back, resting his head upon his folded hands. Shortly both fell asleep.

They were thus when Tama later appeared with their late afternoon meal upon a crude platter. Seeing that both castaways were asleep, he decided not to waken them, but left their food, knowing they would notice it when one or the other waked from his nap. As silently as a ghost the native returned to his companions.

"How's Mike?" Bantan asked with a smile.

"Both are sleeping," Tama answered. "I didn't waken them."

"A little later I'll have a talk with Mike," the bronzed giant said.

"If Mike really wants to go to the mermaid island, Bantan," Mauria asked, "would you take him there?"

"Only if he insists," was the reply.

An hour before sundown the bronzed giant took a walk to the other lean-to. Both castaways had waked and had partaken of their meal. Decker appeared glum and his younger companion had been trying to cheer him up.

"Hello, Bantan," Bob spoke up.

The bronzed giant nodded and smiled.

"How is Mike?" he asked, looking at the older man.

Decker looked up and shook his head disgustedly.

Bob shook his head warningly at Bantan, silently cautioning him of his companion's peculiar mood, though it could easily be observed. Since the bronzed giant did not wish to provoke any unpleasantness, he picked up the platter and turned to depart.

"I'll see you both in the morning," he said.

Decker wanted to say something and then shook his

head, deciding otherwise. Bantan hesitated momentarily, hoping the man would speak, but since he looked away, he shrugged and continued on his way. After he was beyond hearing, Bob spoke to his companion.

"You wanted to say something to him," he said in a low voice. "Why didn't you? I think he wanted to talk with you."

The older man shrugged and made no reply. He arose and strolled out on the beach. The sun was near setting. With his head lowered to avoid the blinding rays, he walked slowly along the shore. Time and again he would shake his head as though to dispel some thought that came into his mind. To have looked at him one would have felt he had not a single friend in the world, and that precisely was how Decker felt. Stubbornness is a difficult trait to slough, and not infrequently in the past he had felt exactly as he did now. Hopelessness is not a pleasant emotion. It was dark when he finally returned to the lean-to. His companion was asleep, so he, too, lay down on his pallet of grasses. It was a long while before he slept, however.

In the morning Tama brought breakfast for the two castaways. They had been awake for the past hour and had gone to the water's edge and bathed. Bob Horwath was as cheerful as ever, but Mike Decker appeared preoccupied. As the native spoke in greeting to them, the younger man replied good naturedly. The older man looked up, and though no smile touched his lips, for the first time there was a trace of friendliness in his dark eyes, which was not unnoticed by Tama.

"A little later," Mike said, "if Bantan isn't too busy, would you ask him if he might drop by? I'd like to speak with him."

The native smiled.

"Of course, Mike," he answered. "I think he wanted

to speak with you late yesterday afternoon, but you appeared indisposed."

The older man merely nodded and Tama left.

Bob appeared pleased at his companion's words, and the two men ate their breakfast.

"It's nice to have our meals brought to us like this," the young man remarked. "I'm going to miss this service when we are alone."

Decker merely grunted, but offered no comment.

Half an hour later Bantan appeared at the lean-to. A smile touched his lips as he spoke in greeting to the two castaways. Bob was cheerful in his response whereas Decker merely nodded.

"You wished to speak with me, Mike?" the bronzed giant then asked.

The older man again nodded.

"Bob has told me how saving our lives has interfered with your plans," he said. "I'm sorry about that. I know I haven't been acting very grateful for all you and Tama have done for us, but down deep inside I know I have you to thank for my life. You must understand that no one had ever done anything for me in my life before, and for that reason I hardly know how to thank anyone who has done something for me."

"That's all right, Mike," Bantan assured him. "I have a feeling you would have done the same for me had our positions been reversed."

Mike looked up at the bronzed giant with a peculiar expression in his eyes.

"Bob said the same thing to me," he commented. "Somehow it started me thinking that our first impressions of people are not really what they seem to be."

The bronzed giant smiled deprecatively.

"Let's not mention it," he said. "I know my stories to Bob, as he told you, sounded wild and impossible. But one has a right to believe what they wish. However, we won't speak any more of that."

Decker shrugged and the semblance of a smile came to his lips.

"We'll forget about that," he agreed. "But, honestly, do the mermaids exist that you were telling about?"

Bantan nodded.

"And they are white-skinned?" the castaway asked.

The bronzed giant again nodded.

"The queen has long red hair," he added.

Decker appeared a little uneasy, as though hesitant to speak what was on his mind. Bantan waited patiently. Finally Decker spoke.

"Ever since I served a two-year hitch in the army," he said, "I've been knocking around the U.S.A., and my prospects for employment were not too promising. I'd have a job for a little while then I'd get laid off. I didn't have a chance to specialize in any particular craft. It was in sheer desperation that I hired out on the ship that resulted in me being here. I haven't much to return to were I to be rescued. I've read a lot of supposedly true stories that were published in various magazines following World War II about members of various branches of the service being isolated among native tribes. Some of them were fortunate—and others not. I'd be willing to take my chances and settle among some tribe if it were possible—even mermaids."

"But the mermaids may not be friendly to you," Bantan said with a note of caution. "If their queen liked you, you would be fortunate. If not—" He shook his head.

"But returning to America doesn't hold any bright prospects for me," the castaway said protestingly. "Without a job, the country can be a cruel place to live in. I've heard about mermaids and always thought they were the figment of man's imagination. If you say they really exist, I know I'll never rest content unless I have seen them with my own eyes."

A slight smile touched the bronzed giant's lips.

"You would really want to cast your lot with the mermaids?" he asked seriously.

The man shrugged and the semblance of a smile touched his ugly face.

"What have I got to lose?" he asked.

Bob Horwath had been an attentive listener, but had not offered a word of protest. Now he spoke up.

"Count me out of that deal, Mike," he said, shaking his head. "No mermaids for me."

"That's O.K. by me, Bob," he was assured. "If you want to wait and be rescued to return to nothing, that's your business. But as for me—I've had it. I'll take my chances—even with mermaids."

Realizing the man was determined, Bantan nodded decisively.

"I'll talk it over with Tama," he said. "If it is agreeable with him, we'll paddle you to the mermaid island. But remember, you'll be on your own once you are ashore."

"That's agreeable to me," Decker replied with eagerness.

"You'd want to go today?"

The man nodded, determined.

"I'll be right back." And with his words the bronzed giant left the lean-to.

Bob looked appealingly at his fellow castaway.

"You're serious, Mike," he remarked. "You can't be."

The older man nodded.

"I've been kicked around long enough," he declared. He nodded his head decisively. "If I have a chance for a life of ease I'm going to take it."

Young Horwath shook his head despairingly.

"I can't argue with you on your choice, but it lets me out," he said. "All I can hope is that you won't regret it."

A peculiar smile touched Decker's bewhiskered lips.

"What have I got to lose?"

Bob regarded him for a long moment.

"Have you thought about your respect as a white man?" he asked.

"That all depends on how each individual considers it," was the reply. "I don't figure I have any respect to lose."

"If you didn't want to return to America," Bob declared, "we could remain upon this island and live in the temple of the sea god. I'd be willing to do that, because, like yourself, I have very little to return to America for."

Decker shook his head impatiently.

"The only way I'd remain on this island is if Bantan and Tama do not agree to take me to the mermaid island," he declared. "You're still young, Bob, but I'm a man who doesn't want to live forever without women. In America, one must have a good-paying job to afford one. In this region it doesn't matter so much. Somehow I think Bantan has the right idea. Money and position doesn't matter here. A man can live a full, rich life."

Bob only shook his head despairingly.

"I never want to forget I am an American," he stated.

"That's your privilege, Bob," Decker admitted. "But as for me—I've had it."

At this juncture in their conversation Bantan returned to the lean-to. He looked at the older man in earnest.

"Are you serious about wanting to go to the mermaid island?" he asked.

The castaway nodded emphatically.

"I was never more serious in my whole life," he declared.

"Tama and I have talked it over with our sweethearts," the bronzed giant said. "We'll leave Nulu and Mauria here and we'll start right away. You'll come along for the ride, Bob?"

The younger man nodded.

"Bob and I will help paddle," Decker stated. "O.K., Bob?"

Young Horwath again nodded.

Without delay they left the lean-to.

Tama had dragged the canoe to the water's edge and returned to Mauria and was talking with her. Moisture was in Nulu's eyes as Bantan approached her while Decker and young Horwath went to where the canoe awaited them.

"I wish I were going with you, Bantan," the blonde-haired girl said in a trembling voice.

The bronzed giant smiled and placed his arms about her and kissed her gently.

"We'll be back later tonight, Nulu," he murmured. "And then there will be nothing to prevent us leaving for Marja."

"Hurry back," she said with wistful eyes.

Bantan turned and, with Tama, went to the water's edge.

With moist eyes Nulu and Mauria watched their beloved ones launch the canoe with the two castaways aboard. When they were beyond the surf, the two paddlers turned and waved to the two girls standing at the edge of the foliage, and they waved in return. Turning about, Bantan and Tama then plied their paddles with expert strokes and the canoe moved rapidly over the calm surface.

In due time Decker and young Horwath took turns

with the paddles. Each had watched how their predecessors had paddled, and though they were somewhat clumsy at first, gradually they acquired the knack of making each sweep of their paddle equivalent to the energy expended thusly. The older man was much stronger than his companion, but their strokes were so regulated that good progress was maintained.

When the bronzed giant and the native relieved the two castaways, the keen eyes of the former espied the mermaid island upon the horizon and he indicated it for Decker's benefit. Tama had not neglected to place fruit and nuts in the canoe, and of these when hungry or thirsty, the four men partook at their convenience.

Desultory conversation was exchanged. The sun was a blazing ball of fire in the heaven above, but a gentle breeze rose in their favor to temper the heat and all were grateful for this.

With the appearance of the mermaid island, Bantan indicated their course would be slightly to the right, so that they might keep from view of any possible watchers on shore. It necessitated paddling extra miles, but they were more assured of not being seen.

It was mid-afternoon when the canoe drew close to the breaking waves on the southern shore of the island. Bantan's sharp eyes had studied the edge of the foliage for some little while, and now he was positive it would be safe to land. With a nod to Tama, they plied their paddles and within a couple of minutes the canoe's prow grated in the soft sand.

Mike Decker stepped out upon the beach. He looked at Bob Horwath and extended a ham-like hand. A smile touched his lips.

"Sure you won't change your mind, Bob?" he asked with a twinkle in his dark eyes.

The young man grasped the extended hand and shook his head.

"Not a chance, Mike," he answered. "The best of luck to you."

Decker nodded, then as his hand and Bob's unclasped, he turned to Bantan. He extended his hand to him.

"Thanks," he said. "This is the end of the trail for me. I hope some day I might be in a position to render you assistance should you need it."

The bronzed giant clasped the man's hand.

"The mermaids occupy the grotto at the cove on the east shore," he advised. "I hope you will find the contentment that you have been looking for on this island."

Decker thanked Bantan. He then turned and shook hands briefly with Tama.

"Your girl is a very good cook," he said. "Don't let her get away from you."

He was assured such would not come to pass.

And then with good wishes again expressed by all, the canoe was launched into the gentle surf. Bob waved to the man standing on the beach watching them, and Decker waved in return.

"And now," Bantan said, "back to the island we came from. Mike has our good wishes for a happy and contented future."

Bob Horwath was aware of a slight lump in his throat, but with a shake of his head, he knew there was nothing to be said or done to alter his recent companion's decision. He did hope with sincerity that all would be well for him.

"If you wish to accompany us to Marja, Bob," Bantan said, "you would be welcome."

"I hardly think so," was the answer. "I'll remain upon the island and wait for rescue. I'll make out all right." He nodded with confidence.

"Just as you say," the bronzed giant added. "If you should change your mind at the last minute don't hesitate to let me know."

"I'll do that," Bob promised. "But I wish to return to America. I'm still young, and perhaps things will be different when I get back than they were when I left."

CHAPTER XXIII

Grim Pursuit

LOOKING SHOREWARD, young Horwath saw Mike Decker walking along the beach in the direction of the cove. A slight sigh escaped his lips as he silently wished his erstwhile castaway friend the best of luck in his choice. The young man's trend of thought was then interrupted as he heard an exclamation of surprise from Bantan. He looked at once toward him.

"Look, Tama," the bronzed giant said. "The mermaids are aware of us!"

The young native paused momentarily to glance toward the cove. From that place and headed in their direction the brilliant sunlight glistened upon flashing arms and rapid movements in the water as heads bobbed.

Although the paddlers had felt they had not been observed when skiriting the east end of the island, from the summit of the cliff a pair of watchful eyes had espied them in the distance. Quickly this information had been brought to the mermaid queen. For what reason the canoe had approached the island, Sirena could not guess; but at once she was determined that the occupants must be captured. Quickly word was circulated among all the mermaids, and by the time the canoe had appeared in view again, the queen was in the lead of her subjects, all being armed with tridents, and they were swimming rapidly at an angle that they hoped would enable them to capture the occupants of the canoe.

"A watcher must have seen us as we approached the

island," Bantan said with a grim nod. "The last time we escaped them we had the darkness of night in our favor. Now, we are not so well favored."

Tama nodded with grimness as he looked toward the sun which was several hours from setting.

"We could not be so fortunate this time to leave the island undetected," he murmured disappointedly, shaking his head.

Young Horwath was speechless and his eyes appeared mesmerized by the swimming creatures. Even from the distance he noted their speed, and for a reason he could not define he became aware that he trembled strangely.

Meanwhile, Bantan and Tama plied their paddles with mighty strokes, and while the canoe forged ahead with unabating speed, it soon became apparent that the speedy mermaids were intent upon cutting them off. Deviating their course from due east almost south, the paddlers could only hope this longer route would soon tire their pursuers and make them realize the futility of their chase.

The keen eyes of Sirena perceived the three male figures in the canoe, two of whom she recognized. Where the two females were, she could only guess they had been left upon the other island for some unknown reason. She now conceived a plan that could not fail. She called to Pegra and Beta who were near her.

"Pegra, with Beta and two other strong swimmers," she said, "swim to the island from which they came and take the two females prisoners. I shall continue with the others to pursue the canoe."

And so it was that four mermaids lost no time swimming in an easterly direction, leaving the queen and her followers to continue their present course.

Upon the beach, Mike Decker was standing in apparent awe. His sharp eyes had sighted the swimmers who had emerged from the cove and were headed for the canoe

Bantan and Tama paddled. A curse was emitted from his bearded lips.

"Damnation!" he exclaimed. "They do me a good turn and now they are in trouble. And the saddest thing of all—I am in no position to help them. But, there may be a chance that I can help them."

Cupping his hands to his mouth he uttered stentorian shouts that could not fail to be heard.

Bantan's keen ears heard the sound from the shore. Quickly he looked in that direction to see Decker shouting in an endeavor to either warn them of impending danger else detract the attention of the mermaids.

"Mike is grateful after all," he commented with a nod.

Sirena, too, heard the shouting from shore and, turning, her sharp eyes espied the burly figure of a large male standing there. With a shake of her head, she dismissed thought of the unknown man for now. He could wait, for there was no escape for him. She was not to be thwarted in her present objective. It was Bantan who appealed to her, willing or not though he be. He was the one she wanted to capture for her own.

Though some of the queen's subjects were aware of the unknown male upon the beach, shouting to them, and they appeared to hesitate, the leader screamed for them to continue their present course.

"Mike is trying to help us, Tama," Bantan said. "But it appears that Sirena is not to be halted in whatever designs she has upon us."

The native nodded with grimness stamped upon his features.

Young Horwath was still trembling and he appeared seemingly frozen. Time and again he shook his head violently in an effort to rid himself of the uncontrollable paralysis that gripped him.

Bantan was not unaware of the young castaway's condition, and he fervently hoped he would not go berserk to add to the difficulties that already confronted them.

"Steady, Bob," he cautioned the young man. "We are in no danger."

With a violent effort, young Horwath dispelled whatever disturbing emotion that gripped him. His smile was more of a grimace, and he nodded to the bronzed giant.

"I'm all right now, Bantan," he said in a faint voice. "It was a good thing you spoke to me when you did. I don't know what overcame me at sight of the mermaids, but the assurance in your voice was all I needed to snap out of it."

The bronzed giant smiled and nodded encouragingly.

"Just keep hoping everything will be all right," he advised.

"I'll try," the young man promised.

Mike Decker, standing upon the beach, realized his shouting was in vain. There was no question in his mind that he had been heard and seen, and why more attention wasn't accorded him, he couldn't understand. He was tempted to plunge into the surf and swim toward the mermaids. The only thing that deterred him was the fact he realized as a swimmer he was no match for them. Better to remain here and await them, for he was sure they would soon realize the utter futility of attempting to circumvent the two paddlers.

But Sirena was of no such mind. Continually she exhorted her less capable followers to exert themselves to their utmost in overtaking the canoe with its three males. In a vague way she now wondered where the third male in the canoe had come from, and what the one upon the beach was doing there. Of course she had no means of knowing; but with the glowing thought of four males upon their maleless island she could envision the perpetuation of their tribe which, without any males, was surely doomed to extinction with the passing of time.

Such promising thoughts of the rosy future induced the mermaid queen to excel herself in pursuit of the canoe with its three male occupants. She was continually drawing ahead of her less capable followers. Repeatedly she called to them to hasten their progress; and only by stupendous efforts her subjects managed to do so.

The mighty strokes of the two paddlers lagged somewhat now, and drops of perspiration continually were rolling pathways down the faces of Bantan and Tama as they continued to wield their paddles unceasingly. The merciless sun was some little distance from the western horizon and the heat was keenly felt. No breeze whatsoever stirred.

Young Horwath was now moaning piteously beneath his breath as he was a silent witness to the gradual lessening of the distance that spanned the canoe and their grim pursuers. More distinctly could he see the determined faces of the mermaids. The one nearest with the reddish hair and beautiful features appeared to be the leader, for she was performing superbly in the water.

"That I could only help, Bantan," he murmured, as his worried eyes caught the attention of the bronzed giant.

A smile and a reassuring nod was his answer.

"Just keep hoping all will be well, Bob."

At the next moment Tama uttered a moan of despair. He ceased paddling and turned to Bantan with agonizing eyes.

"I've developed a cramp in my right shoulder," he said, shaking his head mournfully.

The bronzed giant nodded to young Horwath.

"Your chance to help has come, Bob," he said. "Take Tama's paddle and do your best."

Quickly the young castaway exchanged places with the native and took up the paddle.

"I know I'm no match for you, Bantan," he said apologetically. "But," with a determined shake of his head, "I'll do my best."

"More than that cannot be expected," was the reply.

While Tama massaged his right shoulder with the fingers of his left hand, the bronzed giant and young Horwath continued to wield their paddles. The neophyte could not hope to equal Bantan's power and ability, but he was all willingness, and determination was clearly stamped upon his sweat-streaked features.

Owing to the now slower progress of the canoe, the mermaids continued to gain upon their quarry, and from all indications of their seemingly untiring strokes it was clearly apparent it would require many miles before there would be any lessening of their present speed.

The watchful eyes of Sirena, still in the lead of her followers, had noted a change in one of the paddlers, and thereafter, as a result, she was well aware of the canoe's reduced speed. In jubilant spirits she again urged her subjects to hurry more so that they sooner overtake and capture their quarry.

The disappointment that Bantan felt because of their reduced speed was not reflected upon his features. In no way did he upbraid himself for having brought Mike Decker to the mermaid island which had resulted in the present dire situation. Looking toward Tama, who was continuing to massage his cramped shoulder, he spoke gently to him.

"Your shoulder is still painful?" he asked solicitously.

The native nodded glumly.

"Something like this would happen when my services are needed most," he added with a shake of his head.

"Bob is doing well, though," the bronzed giant added.

"But I fear we are steadily losing the race. The mermaids appear to be tireless. Already I can observe a gleam of triumph in Sirena's eyes—as though she senses we are losing speed."

And now to add to Bantan's dismay, Tama uttered a moan of despair.

"The canoe has sprung a leak," he announced. "But, I'll hold a foot over it to prevent water from entering."

And this he did. But shortly another patched seam appeared to be weakening, and water seeped within. This the native managed to cover with his other foot, fervently hoping no other patched seams would weaken to admit water at this most crucial time.

Almost frantically Bob Horwath was plying his paddle with the result many of his strokes lacked the power of propelling the canoe in exchange for the amount of energy that was expended. Bantan was only too well aware of the young man's state of jumbled nerves, and he spoke to him in a low voice, cautioning him to relax and not tire himself needlessly.

"We are quite a distance from the mermaids," he added. "Take it easy."

"I'll—I'll try, Bantan," Bob answered with a nervous laugh.

Thereafter, plying his paddle more methodically, he became aware he did not tire so easily and the canoe appeared to make better progress. Perspiration streamed from his brow and formed pathways upon his cheeks.

The bronzed giant heaved a relieved sigh now, realizing that young Horwath's better control would prolong the chase just so much longer. Were immediate darkness only to favor them, there undoubtedly would be a better chance of eluding their grim pursuers; but a glance at the brassy sun revealed several hours must yet elapse before that time would come.

A couple hundred yards now spanned the canoe from the leading mermaid. With gleaming eyes, Sirena never for a moment abated her progress, and while she continued to exhort her followers to greater speed, a triumphant glow pulsated through her entire being as she gained yard after yard upon her quarry. She was aware nothing short of a miracle would prevent the recapture of the three males.

Tama continued to massage his cramped right shoulder, and not infrequently he noted the steadily decreasing distance that spanned the canoe from the flashing arms of Sirena as she cleaved the smooth water with well-measured strokes. The calculated thrashing of her tail fin added considerably to her speed as would be natural.

The native regretted that all weapons had been left with Nulu and Mauria for their own protection in case of need. Had they a bow and some arrows, or even a single spear, it would now be to their advantage, especially as a means of warding off their pursuers. The only weapon that they were favored with was the steel dagger sheathed at Bantan's right hip.

While the bronzed giant had always been reluctant to slay a woman, Tama felt no qualms of conscience should he be compelled to do so. Knowing from experience how cruel and merciless the mermaids could be in their treatment of a helpless captive, he justly felt no sentiment in their regards. But now it was only a helpless shrug he could give, realizing as he did how hopeless the situation appeared.

With the passing minutes the distance spanning the canoe and the pursuing mermaids steadily decreased. The sun still was high above the western horizon. Eventual darkness would not be of much help now, for the mermaids were drawing still nearer to the slowing canoe. A scarce hundred yards intervened, and Sirena's gleaming eyes were clearly to be seen. Close behind were several of her followers, while others trailed not too far behind, as all performed magnificently in their endeavors to keep as near their queen as possible. Being the excellent swimmer that she was, was reason enough that Sirena was the leader, for no lost motion was executed in her perfect strokes.

Young Horwath was again experiencing a siege of nerves as he realized the pursuing mermaids were steadily gaining. Each time that he looked in their direction, he would again ply his paddle almost wildly with the result he was more acutely aware of his tiring arms and that his lungs ached from the air he forced into them with gasping inhalations and then expelled with moaning sighs. His heart thumped like a trip hammer and his senses were becoming giddy.

Again the calm voice of the bronzed giant cautioned him that nothing was to be gained by becoming unduly excited because of the precarious position they were in with the closer proximity of the mermaids.

"The mermaids are bound to become wearied soon, Bob," Bantan added hopefully. "Maintain steady strokes, and don't become excited. In that way you'll conserve your strength."

The young man tried to smile assuringly, and for the time being became more steady of purpose and his strokes were more effective. For a few brief minutes the canoe actually appeared to gain upon the pursuing enemy, but short indeed was their spurt of speed, for soon the canoe again slowed because of young Horwath's wearying arms to such unaccustomed exercise. To compensate for this, Bantan plied his paddle more strongly, but his herculean efforts could not overcome the seemingly tireless, well executed strokes of the flashing arms of the pursuing mermaids.

Again the distance decreased foot by foot until almost unbelievingly Bantan was aware that Sirena was almost within arms' reach. Gloatingly the mermaid queen looked up at him.

"You shall not get away this time," she called out jeeringly. Then she turned and called to her followers to hasten as the moment of capture was near.

With a triumphant laugh, her magnificent arms flashed as she cleaved the surface with perfectly executed strokes and forged her way the length of the canoe, keeping about a dozen feet from it.

As the unbelieving eyes of young Horwath looked upon the mermaid queen and he saw her finned tail thrashing the water, he forgot to paddle. Sirena looked up at the young man in silent wonder at first, but observing his awe, she laughed exultantly, revealing her perfect set of white teeth.

"Paddle, Bob," the tense voice of Bantan was heard. "Don't let your surprise get the better of your common sense."

The young man's jaw trembled. With a violent shake of his head, he removed his attention from the gloating mermaid. Once again he plied his paddle wildly, splashingly.

"Steady, Bob," the voice of the bronzed giant was to be heard. "Now is the time to be cool, calm, and collected."

Even though Bantan had every reason to be discouraged, he endeavored to keep the young man's courage at its highest pitch. Already Sirena's followers were drawing close. There were six of them, with others trailing slightly to their rear. Three swam to the right of the canoe while the other three were upon the left.

Sirena was some dozen feet ahead of the water craft

and she now turned over upon her back gracefully and swam thusly, easily keeping her distance.

"Turn back," she commanded. "We have you surrounded." She drew the trident sheathed at her right side and waved it menacingly. "Do not resist further and it will go easier for all. Return to the shore. I warn you. Resist further and we will damage your canoe so that you will have no other choice."

Tama moaned in despair, for once having been a prisoner of the mermaids, he entertained no desire to again be one.

"That I only had a spear," he muttered. "I would end Sirena's life here and now."

Bantan shrugged hopelessly.

"It's no use, Tama," he said in a low voice. "We have failed. We don't want them to damage the canoe, for it is our only hope of ultimate escape."

Looking to either side, the bronzed giant saw that all the mermaids had unsheathed their tridents and were holding them menacingly.

Young Horwath had ceased paddling and was looking about at the mermaids with their drawn weapons. Then he turned to face the bronzed giant with a shudder.

"Is this the end, Bantan?" he gasped.

A nod was his answer.

"We have failed for the time being," was the answer in a low voice. "But we are not to be without hope. It is better that we agree to paddle to the shore."

With his words he looked toward Sirena.

"We are surrendering," he announced.

A triumphant gleam appeared in the mermaid queen's eyes.

"It is well," she said. "It is better for all that you do not resist, for your punishment would be greater." Then in a more soothing tone of voice as she appraised the handsome, bronzed giant, she added: "Perhaps you will learn that I can be merciful to those who do not oppose me."

Bantan merely shrugged and his features became impassive.

CHAPTER XXIV

Sirena's Plea

THE MERMAID QUEEN then issued the command that the canoe be turned about. When this was done, Sirena sheathed her trident and swam gracefully to the aft portion where Bantan knelt. She could not keep her eyes from the bronzed giant's handsome features.

"It is more fitting that the queen be taken ashore in the canoe," she said. With her words she extended her right hand to Bantan.

Tama watched in silence with glowering eyes. Young Horwath stared in awe as the bronzed giant reached for Sirena's hand, gripping it with his. The young man fairly gulped as he saw the magnificent body of the mermaid queen be drawn within the canoe in a single movement.

Ensconcing herself comfortably in front of Bantan with no shame because of the nudity of the upper portion of her body, Sirena nodded that they were to proceed on their way.

While the canoe was paddled shoreward, the mermaids upon each side swam leisurely along keeping pace. The bronzed giant tried to avoid the queen's directness, for she unquestionably did not withhold the open admiration she experienced through her hazel eyes as she appraised his handsome features and Apollo-like body. A smile touched her thin lips and she spoke softly to him.

"And I mistook the native for you, Bantan," she said in purring tones. "How could I have been so blind?"

The bronzed giant's dark eyes met hers momentarily,

SIRENA ADMIRES BANTAN

and he merely shrugged as he removed his attention from her beautiful features. Her beauty aroused no spark of interest within him, however.

The mermaid queen was not affronted by his lack of gallantry. It only inspired her to be more bold.

"Look at me when I speak to you," she murmured in a soft command.

As his eyes met hers, a smile touched her lips and her hazel eyes became soft. Her naked breasts rose and fell to her labored breathing.

"I do not wish to feel that our relationship is of captor and captive," she purred.

No smile touched the bronzed giant's lips and his features were impassive.

"How else may I consider our position?" he demanded.

Sirena pretended coyness.

"It is because you do not understand, Bantan," she murmured. "When we reach the grotto there is much I wish to tell you—and then you will surely know."

The bronzed giant merely shrugged.

"I will have no choice but to listen since I am your captive," he answered. "But to understand—that may be something else."

The mermaid queen smiled artfully.

"I think you will understand," she answered in a purring voice.

He made no comment.

Presently a slight frown creased her forehead.

"Where did the young male who is paddling come from?" she asked.

"He was near death and found drifting," he replied. "We cared for him."

The queen merely nodded, then she suddenly recollected the huge male who had been upon the beach, shouting.

She turned her head and looked shoreward, but could see no sign of him now.

"The other who was on the shore," she added; "was he a friend of yours as well? Did you bring him hither?"

"He, too, was found near death, drifting," he answered. "He did not believe your kind of people existed. We brought him here because he insisted. He wished to remain here."

The mermaid queen uttered a purring sound, but asked no further questions on the subject. A faraway expression appeared in her eyes and she seemed to be thinking deeply of what Bantan had said. But such thoughts did not claim her attention long, for she again began studying the bronzed giant almost minutely; and though he was aware of her marked attention, he tried to avoid her directness as much as possible.

In due time the canoe was paddled to the cove. Bantan wondered at the whereabouts of Mike Decker, for no sight of him had been obtained since previous to their capture. The mermaid queen directed that they proceed within the aperture that led to the amphitheatre.

The bronzed giant had not forgotten that his dagger still was sheathed at his right hip, and why Sirena had neglected to relieve him of it he could not understand. But when the canoe passed within the aperture, and semi-gloom enveloped them, his right hand quickly slipped the weapon beneath the grass upon which he knelt. He realized it would be safer there, for surely at a later time he would be relieved of it, and it was questionable that he might recover it again. He had formed a strong attachment for the steel dagger which had been timely in usage upon many past occasions in defense of his life, and others dear to him as well.

When the canoe grounded, all disembarked. It was drawn free of the water which was at its highest. All proceeded to the end of the corridor. A group of mermaids with tridents drawn and in readiness preceded the captives, and others followed in their wake. Tama and young Horwath were followed by Bantan, and close upon his heels Sirena slithered along.

Reaching the end of the corridor, Bob's eyes widened in surprise at sight of the phosphorescent-lighted amphitheatre. Now, for the first time, he was actually able to see the mermaids slithering along the smooth, rock floor and he was amazed at the speed they moved.

One of the young mermaids, Ela by name, took an immediate fancy to young Horwath. She was quite beautiful in judging the standards of beauty among the mermaids. She was slim but well proportioned in the ways of womanhood. Her hair was dark and long. Her features were round and nicely fashioned, and her soft, gray eyes did not conceal the admiration she felt for the young man.

As Bob became aware of her proximity and looked down at her, a gentle smile touched her lips, and her even, white teeth were revealed. The young man did not know whether to smile, but the softness of her doe-like eyes resulted in a slight smile touching his lips. Emboldened by his apparent friendliness and to reveal her own feelings toward him, the mermaid gently stroked one of his hands. She spoke to him in a gentle voice, but he of course could not understand her. He shook his head and, without giving thought, spoke to her in English, which of course she could not understand either.

Sirena now spoke to her subjects.

"Look after these two," she said, indicating Tama and young Horwath. "I wish to speak with Bantan alone in my apartment."

When one suggested for her safety that a couple of mermaids act as guards, the queen smiled and shook her head. She had observed her captive wore no dagger at his right hip.

"I am capable of taking care of myself," she assured her solicitous subject.

Turning to the bronzed giant, she indicated for him to proceed. Without a word he did so and presently they were in Sirena's apartment. The queen slithered gracefully to a stone chair where she ensconced herself thereupon. She then bade the bronzed giant to seat himself before her. When he had done so, she looked down upon him with kindly eyes.

"As I have told you," she said, "I do not wish to consider you a captive." She sighed deeply as she saw protest appear in his eyes; but she raised a hand for silence on his part and not speak the words that were upon his lips. "Listen to me, please."

He nodded with impassive features.

"As you say, Sirena," he answered with a shrug.

"Our history goes far back in the annals of time in this world," the queen then said. "The tales of our forefathers and mothers have been handed down through the generations until the present time. Those early ancestors lived more in the water than on land since they were born with gills, and the water they breathed served the purpose of air. Later generations preferred living on land, and so it came to pass that gills were no longer necessary for their living existence. Children were born without them, but that did not lessen their innate desire to take to the water whenever the mood overtook them. It is strange that those earlier generations preferred the land to their native element, for they were clumsy floundering about with no legs and feet.

"I need not remind you of the ridicule and scorn to which they were subjected because they differed from normal people. The fact they were considered freaks was unjust. Though they loved the land bordering a large body of water, at last, unable to bear the insults of normal people, they were compelled to abandon their homes to search for other lands where they might live in peace and contentment with themselves.

"From land to land where they sought to settle, normal people always came, and ridicule and scorn made it necessary for our ancestors to move again. And so at long last our forebearers came to this island where they were permitted to live in peace and happiness without the ridicule and scorn of other normal people to affect their way of life.

"It also has been told that some generations ago mermaids had been seduced by normal males. In some instances perfectly normal children, taking after the father, were born. They usually were males. At a later time, when realizing how they differed from us, they would flee and never be seen again. Their mothers loved them, though they differed, and were saddened to know their children spurned them. In the instances when a female was born of such matings, the child was a mermaid, and for that reason she would not feel the necessity to desert her mother."

At this juncture in her narrative, Sirena paused and Bantan observed the troubled expression that had overcome her features. She heaved a deep sigh and then her eyes met those of the bronzed giant. A slight smile touched her lips though her eyes were anxious.

"I am not wearying you?" she asked.

"No, Sirena," he answered, slowly shaking his head. "The history of your people is not a pleasant one. It is regrettable that conditions were as they had been."

The queen's smile became brighter.

"You are beginning to understand, Bantan," she murmured. "I told you that you would understand if you listened to me."

"Please continue," he said with a nod. "I may as well hear your entire story."

With a pleased expression upon her beautiful features, the mermaid queen nodded.

"You will admit we are not to blame for being the freaks that we are considered?" she asked.

He nodded, and was sincere in his admission.

"For many, many moons our people continued to live upon this island in peace and contentment," Sirena continued her narrative. "They bothered no one, and in return were bothered by none. In due time I was born of the king and queen and, as I became older, I was told of our mermen making a pilgrimage once each thirteen moons to some other island for the purpose of honoring our sea god. As a young girl I thought it foolish; but then, religion is religion, and there is nothing that can be done about that sacred subject. Where the mermen went none of the mermaids were told. It was a secret among themselves.

"Upon the occasion of the last pligrimage, several suns following their departure a terrible storm raged. It was evident all of the mermen were caught in its fury, for not one returned to our island, excellent swimmers though they were. For many suns the females waited in vain for the return of their loved ones, but no trace of them was ever found. Even my father perished at that time. My mother was unable to bear her grief. Though I was an only child nearing adolescence, she committed suicide, as did many other mothers and sweethearts. It so happened at that particular time there were no small males left upon the island, and so it has been in the many moons that have since passed.

"We mermaids love life as does any other class of normal people. Even though we are considered freaks, when the mermen existed, we were content to propagate our own kind. But with the absence of males we are doomed to extinction. As the moons passed, we watched and waited in vain that males of a normal people might come to our island. Some came as time passed, mostly dead; but those that were barely alive we were unable to prolong their lives. At the present time our numbers which were many once upon a time have been reduced to a total of fingers upon both hands by counting them twice.

"Many of the older mermaids, losing hope that they might have a mate, committed suicide rather than live the barren life that seemed destined for them. For that reason, you may have noticed that the remnants of our tribe appear to be nearly of an equal age. We are still young, and many of us are considered beautiful except for the fact we differ from normal people by having no legs and feet. But we are women, and we want mates. We want children, whether they be as we or as normal people. It is difficult to live without the love of a male. Now, Bantan, do you understand what I have been telling you?"

The bronzed giant nodded slowly as his eyes met the anxious ones of the queen. He could read the entreaty in hers.

"You do understand our plight?" she insisted.

Again he nodded hopelessly.

Sirena's smile was seductive. She arched her back and her well-formed breasts protruded as ripe melons.

"Look at me, Bantan," she said softly. "Do you not admit that I am beautiful?"

The bronzed giant's eyes met her anxious ones and he was constrained to nod his head in acknowledgment.

"You are very beautiful," he said.

The queen's hands rested beneath her pulsating breasts and the erect nipples quivered.

"These breasts of mine have long wanted to feel the suction of a baby's lips," she added in husky tones. "Queen though I am, I am still a female, and a female wants to bear children. It is her nature. All of my subjects, being females, are similarly inclined. Is it wrong by the standards of normal people that we feel this way?"

Strangely, Bantan was not abashed nor did his finer instincts revolt at the sight of this beautiful, unashamed mermaid queen and listening to her confession.

"What you say is true, Sirena," he replied.

Before the bronzed giant could utter a further word, in the winking of an eyelid, the mermaid queen had slid from her chair and was in front of him. A tremulous sigh escaped her lips. One of her hands went about his neck while the other sought one of his and she pressed its palm upon her pulsating left breast. As though in a trance he could feel the wild pounding of her heart beneath the softness and warmth of the melon-like mound. A surging emotion coursed through his veins making him giddy as the femaleness of Sirena was inhaled. She was striving to bring his face down to hers and her lips appeared to be working feverishly.

"Kiss me, Bantan," she moaned. "Love me as I want you to love me. Ever since I knew of you, I've wanted to bear you a child. At night when I try to sleep I have imagined your arms about me as I clung to you as though you were life itself. Make me with child, please."

Beneath the steady pressure of her strong arm, the bronzed giant's face was drawn near Sirena's. And now with suddenness her other hand released his at her breast and she flung it about his neck, bringing his face in contact with hers. At once his hand left her breast and sought her shoulder. Her lips clung to his feverishly and gnawed upon them as her hot breath fanned his face. The hard tips of her nipples pressed against his naked flesh, almost hurting him. Perhaps this was what aroused him from the seeming trance that had overcome him.

With an effort, her lips clinging to his to the last, Bantan managed to draw his face from Sirena's. With both hands now pressing against her naked shoulders, he drew away from her so that her hands locked about his neck were forced to release their hold.

Panting heavily as a result of her emotional upheaval, the mermaid queen's eyes wonderingly sought his, unable to believe that the handsome male was rejecting the offering of her beauty. The well ordered dreams she had experienced recently had not been thus. There must be some mistake. Dreams and reality should be the same. Once again a seductive smile overcame her features and she closed her eyes. Though she still gasped her breath somewhat, she again spoke in a husky, trembling voice.

"Kiss me and love me, Bantan," she murmured. "Make me with child."

A tremulous sigh escaped the mermaid queen's feverish lips and her eyes opened and looked imploringly up at Bantan's for the gratification of her desires being fulfilled. Her arms lifted and sought once again to lock about his neck, but because he held her from him she was unable to do so.

"Sirena," he spoke to her gently. "Listen to me."

There was a note of authority in the bronzed giant's tones that temporarily calmed the queen's aroused passions.

"What is it, Bantan?" she whispered, her eyes searching his in silent wonder.

"You asked me to listen to you and understand," he added. "I listened and did understand. Now, I want you to listen to me and try to understand."

Sirena closed her eyes and heaved a deep sigh.

"Bantan, I should hate you," she murmured. "Quick,

tell me what you have to say; but I cannot promise I
will understand—unless what you say is favorable to me."

The bronzed giant shook his head in dismay, for the
moment nonplused as to how to phrase what he had in
mind.

"Listen, Sirena," he said in a low voice. "While you
are a mermaid queen and very beautiful—"

Sirena murmured a contented sigh at hearing this compliment and she smiled as her eyes opened to look up
at him in adoration. Her hands reached for one of his
as it rested upon her shoulder and pressed it warmly.
Then she raised her head and pressed her lips upon the
back of the same hand.

"Yes, Bantan," she murmured. "Tell me more. What
you have said pleases me very much."

He shook his head, slightly perplexed at what he must
say.

"Listen, Sirena," he again said. "Do you forget that I
have a sweetheart whom I love most dearly?"

CHAPTER XXV

Hope—And Despair

A DEATHLY SILENCE prevailed during the following moments. A tremor pulsated through the queen's body as she stiffened somewhat. The smile disappeared from her lips, and the adoration in her eyes faded to be supplanted with darkening concern. Upon the instant she recollected that Pegra and Beta with two mermaids had been dispatched to the island where Nulu and Mauria awaited the return of their lovers. A crafty light appeared in her eyes, but this she concealed by averting her head slightly so that the bronzed giant might not guess what was in her mind.

"Continue, Bantan," she said in a low, tense voice. "I am well aware that you have a sweetheart. Say what you intended."

"In love there is honor, Sirena," he resumed then. "Although you are a queen—and very beautiful and desire me—were I to fulfill that desire I would betray the love I treasure for my sweetheart. With sincere love for one woman a man of honor cannot desire another. Do I make myself clearly understood?"

A strange chill overcame the mermaid queen at hearing this solemn declaration that likewise made her realize Bantan was rejecting her. She looked up at him with an odd expression in her eyes.

"If your sweetheart were not alive," she said, "do you think you might learn to love me—even though I am a mermaid?"

A faint smile of perplexity touched his lips.

"Sirena," he declared, "as I've told you before and I will repeat." He shook his head sadly. "You are very beautiful; but in my heart I do not believe I could ever learn to love you."

The mermaid queen drew a sharp breath and her features became contorted with indescribable fury. A shrill hissing issued from her lips. In a flash she squirmed free of his hands. Before Bantan could move, she had seized her trident where it rested at the side of the stone chair. With it clutched in both hands, Sirena presented a picture of thwarted rage intent upon revenge. She fairly trembled in the throes of the seeming madness that had overcome her. Her lips had drawn back, revealing her teeth.

"I could kill you," she snarled. "You, too, consider me a freak, and unworthy of you because you are a normal male."

The bronzed giant slowly arose to his feet, his eyes intent upon the scorned queen's, for in them he would have a forewarning of any rash action that she might conceive. He shook his head slowly and appeared dismayed.

"I didn't think you would understand," was all he said.

The queen's bosom was rising and falling spasmodically because of her forced breathing. The rage in her glittering eyes had not lessened.

"Yes, I understand too well," she hissed. "I am not good enough for you. But know now if I cannot have you willingly on your part, your sweetheart will not have you either. Four mermaids have been sent to the island from which you came to capture her and Mauria. When they are brought here I shall gloat as you watch them be tortured to death as an appeasement to my wrath for having my love rejected by you. After you have seen your sweetheart die, I shall not tell you what fate awaits you, but I can assure you it will be far from pleasant. If I have never known the full meaning of hatred in my life, then now I am fully aware of it. I hate you! I hate you!"

As Sirena continued to hiss her hatred, Bantan's intent eyes were not unmindful that the points of the trident that she clutched with both hands dipped floorward. The distance between them was scarcely two yards. While he stood, shaking his head sadly, he was tensing upon his toes, preparatory to making a leap upon his tormenting captor.

And then, as Sirena uttered the phrase, "I hate you!" for the tenth time, she shook her head violently, her slightly damp, reddish hair brushing her naked shoulders, and her eyes almost closed. At the next moment, so swiftly the bronzed giant acted—lightning could not have equalled his movement—he leaped forward. His left hand seized the handle of the trident before the queen could prevent. With another instant's passing he had stepped to her left side. His right arm went about her crushingly, his fingers closing upon her arm above the elbow in a grip of steel.

So enraged the queen was, she did not think of immediately calling for help. She fought him, even trying to bite his right hand, but he jostled her rudely and prevented her teeth from fastening into his flesh. Her hold upon the trident, meanwhile, was broken as paralyzed fingers could no longer retain a grip upon the weapon. As it dropped to the stone floor, Bantan's left hand clamped upon her mouth to stifle the belated scream for assistance that would have been emitted.

A grim smile now touched the bronzed giant's lips as he looked down into the glaring, hate-filled eyes of the mermaid queen.

"Now, Sirena," he said in a low, metallic voice, "you are *my* prisoner. I do not wish to kill you, however. But

BANTAN DISARMS SIRENA

my friends and I am going free—at your command. Otherwise—"

In a flash he uncovered her mouth and released her, then snatched up the trident from the floor where it had dropped. The queen was too confused, so quickly he acted, to have screamed for aid.

"Now," he added, menacing his prisoner with her weapon, "let us go. Remember, one false move on your part and I shall not hesitate to plunge this weapon through you. It is your life against mine and my friends."

The deadly tone of the bronzed giant's voice was not to be doubted.

Sobbing in despair now, the mermaid queen appeared cowed. What regrets she now entertained that she had not taken the precaution to have guards present was smothered into extinction. With head lowered, and Bantan close behind her, she slithered to the door leading to the amphitheatre.

Cries of dismay from the mermaids were to be heard at the appearance of the two with Bantan menacing the queen with her trident. Some of them raised their weapons and their very attitude bordered upon a concerted attack. Aware of her subjects in such a state of mind, Sirena raised a hand to prevent any such hostilities on their part that unquestionably would result in her own death.

Surprise and awe appeared on the faces of both Tama and young Horwath. The native heaved a sigh of relief. Bob looked down at Ela of the doe-like eyes and he read her disappointment at the unanticipated turn of affairs.

The bronzed giant saw the mermaid queen looking toward the still surface of the pool, and he at once guessed her intentions. He quickly stepped to her left side, barring whatever plans she contemplated.

"Don't try anything rash, Sirena," he warned.

Hatred flashed through her eyes and a snarl contorted

her beautiful features. Her lips moved convulsively, but she uttered no sound.

Bantan indicated the aperture through which they had come with his left hand, then called out to Tama and young Horwath in English.

"Hurry to the canoe. I'll join you presently."

Several of the mermaids crowded about their prisoners, but a warning cry from their queen resulted in them drawing back mutteringly. Tama and Bob Horwath drew away from their erstwhile captors and lost no time heading for the aperture leading to freedom. In another minute they had reached the opening. For a moment they hesitated and looked back at the bronzed giant. He waved with his left hand. Meanwhile, he cautioned Sirena against any form of treachery as he sidled about to place himself in a closer proximity to the corridor's opening. When he felt he had reached the desired position, he looked warningly toward the mermaids who were stealthily advancing toward him, then he waved his trident at them as though intending to cast it in their midst.

"I'll leave you now, Sirena," he said to the queen.

She hissed as he turned and ran toward the aperture that led to freedom.

"After him!" Sirena shrieked to her subjects.

At the mouth of the corridor, Bantan paused for a split second to see the queen snatch a trident from the nearest of her subjects, and she was already slithering in his direction. Her fiercely contorted features of unsuppressed rage defied description.

At the next moment the bronzed giant was racing at top speed in the semi-gloom of the corridor along the smooth, rock floor. Looking ahead, he could distinguish that Tama and young Horwath had pushed the canoe into the water and were awaiting him. As he drew near, he spoke to them.

"The mermaids are following me. Let's lose no time. Darkness will favor us now."

Quickly stepping into the canoe which had been turned around, he snatched up a paddle. To his rear he could hear the swishing of the mermaids in pursuit and the sound of their tridents clattering upon the rock floor. Tama's shoulder was much better, for he had taken up a paddle and, together, paddling in unison with powerful strokes, the canoe presently emerged into the shadowed cove, for by this time the sun was near setting.

Before they reached the end of the shadowed water, Bantan turned to look backward and he had reason for both expectancy and surprise. The mermaids were appearing from the opening at the base of the cliff—and upon its summit the burly figure of Mike Decker was to be seen. He stood there with hands akimbo, looking down at the swimming creatures as they appeared and were following fleetingly in the wake of the canoe.

"Look, Tama and Bob," the bronzed giant said. "There is Mike."

And now, more surprising, Mike Decker started shouting in stentorian tones to the mermaids in the cove. As though astounded, the creatures halted in their swimming, and, turning about, treading water, they looked up from whence the loud shouting was to be heard to see the burly figure standing upon the edge of the cliff. Awed, they forgot the canoe and its occupants they had been pursuing.

Mike Decker paused in his shouting to look toward the canoe to see that all three occupants were looking in his direction. The sun's fading rays silhouetted his huge figure with a grotesque halo. He cupped his hands to his mouth after waving briefly to them and shouted distinctly.

"This is it! Good luck—and thank you!"

And while the mermaids in the cove had seemingly forgotten their quarry, the burly figure standing at the edge of the cliff poised momentarily and then executed a perfect dive. As the water cascaded upward and he disappeared beneath the surface, the mermaids swam toward the disturbance, Sirena being among the first to greet him with wondering eyes when he rose to the surface with a huge grin upon his face.

"Here I am, babes," he announced. "This is either the end of my life of misery until now—or the beginning of another more enjoyable one."

Meanwhile, Bantan and Tama resumed paddling, and while young Horwath strained his eyes against the setting sun's rays, he presently announced that the mermaids were not pursuing them. They had swum with Mike Decker through the opening at the base of the cliff.

"Poor Mike," he sighed. "I wonder if life will be happier for him from now on?" And as he spoke he was thinking of the doe-like, gray eyes of the mermaid who had undeniably been attracted to him; then, straightening his slumped shoulders, he remembered that he was an American—so that was that.

"Mike said he'd help us if he could," Tama remarked with a smile. "His timely appearance was to our benefit."

"He has my sincere wishes for a happier future than his past," was all Bantan commented. But then, recollecting what Sirena had told him, he added: "We haven't seen the last of the mermaids yet. Four of them were dispatched to take Nulu and Mauria prisoners. Let us hope we are in time to save them."

With grimness stamping their features, the bronzed giant and the native continued to paddle in earnest. At a later time young Horwath took his turn; and in this manner the progress of the canoe was unabated after darkness had enveloped them and the stars were their guide. The one who rested was kept busy preventing water from seeping through opened seams in the canoe's bottom.

✓   ✓   ✓

Meanwhile, Nulu and Mauria found time in passing long indeed after their sweethearts with young Horwath had taken Mike Decker to the mermaid island. They earnestly hoped that all would go well and, as Bantan had promised, they would return in due time. Then, on the following day, they could at long last embark upon their trip which would take them to their ultimate goal—Marja Island.

The blonde-haired girl and Mauria seated themselves upon pallets of grasses near the lean-to following their evening meal. They watched the sun sink beneath the waterline, and soon afterward darkness enveloped the far-reaching stretches of water and the island. And then the stars began to appear in the darkened canopy above. Their eyes were constantly upon the western horizon.

"I hope all is well with them," Nulu murmured for the countless time. "Had it not been for the two castaways, by this time we would probably be upon Marja."

Mauria smiled and a tremulous sigh escaped her lips.

"I'm sure everything will be all right, Nulu," she answered confidently. "It seems wherever Bantan is, no matter what goes wrong, he always manages to come through in safety. We have experienced that many times in the past."

"You have a lot of faith in him, haven't you, Mauria?" she was asked.

The native girl sighed deeply.

"I don't know what we would have done in the past without him," she answered. She reached out and clasped one of Nulu's hands in hers. "You are so very fortunate.

I hoped that I might claim him, but I'm happy that you are to be the lucky one."

"Somehow I have a feeling my good luck may come to an end," the blonde-haired girl murmured with a slight shiver coursing through her. "It seems too good to be true that Bantan and I will be mated in the near future."

"You are deserving of him if anyone is," Mauria added.

"When I think of the unfortunate ones he loved in the past," Nulu said, "I wonder that something might happen to me as well."

The native girl laughed assuringly.

"What is in the past is past," she declared. "The future is what we hope and live for."

Thereafter, they lapsed into silence, but not for a moment did they remove their eyes from the western horizon. The soft swishing of the water washing upon the beach and retreating was all that was to be heard, for the surf was unusually gentle on this early evening since there was no breeze stirring to ruffle the water needlessly.

As the long hours passed, upon a number of occasions both girls yawned until at last they began to experience an uneasiness that could not be dispelled.

"I'm becoming worried," Nulu murmured. "It seems that they should have returned by now."

Mauria attempted to conceal her anxiety by uttering a soft laugh of assurance.

"To those who wait time always seems long," she replied. "Let's take a short walk along the beach."

The blonde-haired girl arose.

"Yes, it would help lessen our fears," she agreed. "You do not deceive me that you, too, are not worried."

Mauria hugged Nulu for a moment then linked an arm with her companion's.

"Yes, I am worried," she admitted.

Side by side the two strolled along the beach for a

couple hundred yards before they returned to the landing place. Always they watched the water in the direction from which their loved ones would return. Their ears strained to hear the sound of a paddle striking the side of the canoe to apprise them of their near presence. Pausing for a long minute, but hearing no such glad tidings, Mauria suggested that they repeat their stroll in an effort to still their anxiety.

While they did so, from out beyond the gently breaking waves four pairs of eyes, long accustomed to the darkness, were aware of the two girls strolling along the beach.

Treading water, as did her three companions, Pegra spoke in a whisper.

"Sirena will not expect us to return immediately with the prisoners," she said. "We'll capture and bind them, and after we have slept the balance of the night, we'll start back with them in the morning."

The three mermaids nodded in agreement.

"Now, let's swim ashore and await their return," Pegra added.

The gently breaking surf enveloped them and within a few minutes four sleek forms were slithering up the beach to the edge of the foliage. In silence they awaited the two girls who were now returning to the immediate vicinity.

Again Nulu was murmuring plaintively her fears for the safety of their loved ones.

"Why don't they return?" she asked of her companion.

"Everything will be all right," Mauria assured her. "I'm sure it—"

And then, without warning, four slithering creatures surrounded them with drawn tridents, and the voice of Pegra spoke warningly to them.

"Do not resist and it will be better for both of you."

Both Nulu and Mauria were paralyzed momentarily by the voice they recognized as that of a mermaid. Upon the instant each realized some dire fate must have happened to their loved ones. Suddenly, then, feeling if they had been captured and doomed to death, without them they had no desire to live. At the next moment with cries of anguish both turned upon their foe with unmitigated rage.

Pegra had warned her companions beforehand that the two were not to be slain. Discarding their tridents now, they flung themselves upon the two girls who had suddenly gone berserk. They wrapped their strong arms about their legs and tripped them. With the odds in their favor, despite the fierce opposition, within a few minutes the mermaids had overcome their victims.

While Nulu and Mauria were held upon the beach helplessly, Pegra slithered to the hollowed log and within found several lengths of grass-braided rope. Returning to the captives, she divided the lengths of rope suitably, then bound the wrists and ankles of each captive. When she had finished, she turned to her companions wearily.

"Now we can be more sure our rest will not be disturbed, for I am very tired."

All four then sought the lean-to and were presently fast asleep upon the pallets of grasses.

Left alone upon the beach nearby, Nulu sobbed in helplessness and despair while Mauria, her own spirits at an exceedingly low ebb, tried to comfort her companion as best she could.

"I know something must have happened," Nulu sobbed in misery. "I should have known my happiness was too good to last."

"Hush," Mauria murmured as the handsome features of the bronzed giant appeared in mind. "Bantan will rescue us—have no fear."

MAURIA AND NULU OVERCOME BY MERMAIDS

CHAPTER XXVI

Bob's Choice

UNERRINGLY THE CANOE'S COURSE was maintained, and in due time it neared the gentle surf's outer breaking waves bordering the island which was the objective of the paddlers.

Bantan's sharp eyes had been straining to catch a glimpse of two figures on the beach, awaiting their return. He and Tama had been paddling, and at the bronzed giant's request they now idled their paddles while they stared shoreward. Young Horwath, too, strained his eyes, wondering if all was well.

"Do you suppose the mermaids who preceded us could have captured Nulu and Mauria?" Tama asked in a low voice.

"We saw nothing of them on our way, look though we did," Bantan answered. "Being excellent swimmers, they must have reached the island before us."

"Since there were four of them," the native added, "and Nulu and Mauria were not expecting them, I fear that the mermaids swam ashore and overcame the two girls and made them captives."

"I was thinking the same thing, Tama," the bronzed giant replied. "Come, we'll go ashore and be prepared for whatever nature of surprise may await us. Bob, be prepared for anything when we land."

"I will," was the young man's assurance.

"Then now, Tama," Bantan said.

With expert strokes they guided the canoe through the

gentle surf to the beach. Quickly and quietly all disembarked. The bronzed giant whispered to his companions to remain silent. His sharp eyes had caught sight of two huddled forms a few yards from the lean-to. Had they been seated, he would have known that perhaps Nulu and Mauria had fallen asleep while awaiting their return. The fact they were lying down was unusual, for had they wished to sleep they would have chosen the lean-to. He turned to his companions.

"Bob, remain with the canoe while Tama and I investigate," he said. "Tama, take a paddle for protection— just in case."

The native reached within the canoe and withdrew a paddle. With this improvised weapon he announced he was ready. Bantan then withdrew his dagger and clutched it in his right hand.

Cautiously they advanced up the beach toward the huddled forms. The sharp eyes of the bronzed giant now suspected what had happened, for he heard Nulu and Mauria comforting one another in hushed voices.

"Nulu and Mauria," he spoke in a whisper as he neared them.

A gasp was to be heard in answer, and the huddled forms moved about, managing to attain a seated position. Their features were happy and their hearts thumped wildly.

"Is it you, Bantan?" Nulu whispered in a trembling voice.

"Tama?" Mauria whispered questioningly.

At the next moment the bronzed giant and the native had reached the side of the bound girls.

"Four mermaids overcame us a short while ago," Nulu whispered. "We are bound hand and feet. The mermaids are in the lean-to, sleeping."

With his dagger Bantan cut the thongs about the

wrists and ankles of each captive. As soon as they had attained a standing position both Nulu and Mauria were enfolded in the arms of their respective lovers. Presently they drew apart.

"Are my weapons still in the hollowed log?" Bantan asked.

"We didn't touch them," Nulu answered.

"Then they must still be there," he said, turning to Tama. "I'll get them. Return to the canoe with Nulu and Mauria. We'll pass the night in the grotto. In the morning we'll give the mermaids a surprise."

While the native and the two girls went to the canoe, the bronzed giant sought the hollowed log and gathered all his weapons which had not been disturbed. Then he returned to the canoe where the others were awaiting him. He handed his weapons to them. He then told them he would procure fruit and nuts, for he was hungry and knew Tama and young Horwath must be as well. With arms loaded, in a few minutes he had returned to the canoe, then pushed it into the gentle surf. In a few minutes they were paddling beyond the breaking waves.

They experienced no difficulty locating the cove which led to the grotto. The canoe was guided through the opening and shortly, reaching the end of the water, all disembarked. The fruit and nuts were gathered by Tama and young Horwath, while Nulu and Mauria reached for the weapons. Bantan drew the canoe several yards up on the rock floor. Then all proceeded to the temple of the sea god.

While the three men ate of the fruit and nuts, Nulu and Mauria wanted to know what had happened on the mermaid island, and they were told.

"Since Sirena told me four mermaids had been sent here to capture you both," Bantan added, "after we escaped from the island our thoughts were concerned for your welfare."

"Poor Nulu was worried before and after we were captured," Mauria added. "I tried to comfort her that you would rescue us—and I was not wrong."

The bronzed giant smiled deprecatively.

"When the mermaids wake in the morning," Tama said, "they will be surprised to find their captives missing."

Bantan yawned and stretched his arms.

"That is another day," he said. "Right now I'm so tired I could close my eyes and sleep."

"And, I, too," the native added.

All made themselves as comfortable as convenient, and within minutes were sound asleep, and slept the entire night without waking once.

In the morning, Bantan was the first to wake. Yawning and stretching, he quietly arose to his feet. His first concern was that the canoe was as it had been left the night before, and an investigation revealed that it was. His keen nostrils were aware of the aroma of fruit and nuts within, and in the semi-gloom he reached within searchingly and was happy to find some had been overlooked on the previous night. Gathering what there was, he returned to the temple.

His companions had recently awakened and were wondering at his whereabouts when he appeared. They greeted him warmly, noticing the fruit and nuts he carried. With what was left over from the night before, there now was sufficient to satisfy the hunger of all five. Nulu and Mauria were anxious to know of the immediate plans.

"We'll return to the landing," Bantan said. "Should the mermaids be there, we'll drive them away and warn them to never return hither again. Armed with our bows, arrows, and spears I don't think they'll offer much resistance."

And so it was a little while later the canoe was being paddled along the south shore toward where the hollowed log rested high on the beach at the edge of the foliage near one of the lean-tos. Sharp eyes scanned the beach in that vicinity, but no sign of the mermaids was in evidence.

"It's possible they are still sleeping," Tama suggested. Bantan nodded.

"If they are," he answered, "they'll have a rude awakening. We'll beach the canoe."

As soon as they were ashore, keeping an intent watch upon the lean-to, Bantan and Tama armed themselves with spears. Nulu and Mauria took up a bow and some arrows. Young Horwath reached within the canoe for a paddle, and with a smile nodded as he caught the bronzed giant's attention.

Bantan carefully observed the sandy beach, looking for recent markings that would indicate the mermaids had been astir, but no such signs were to be seen. He nodded to his companions, and with Tama at his side, they moved in the direction of the lean-to.

As might have been surmised, all four mermaids, wearied from the long swim of the previous day, were still asleep. Their tridents were sheathed at their right side. The bronzed giant smiled and nodded, then turned to the sleeping creatures.

"Awake, all of you," he shouted.

Instantly the four sleepers were startled to wakefulness, and when they recognized the two males—the third they could only wonder at—and the two girls they had made captives the previous evening, their surprise was clearly evident. Through instinct each made a move to draw their tridents. But Bantan and Tama menaced them with their spears. Nulu and Mauria stood with drawn bow and arrows ready for release.

"Don't make a hostile move," the bronzed giant warned them. "You have failed in your mission. Come, all of you, out to the edge of the beach. You may have some fruit and nuts to eat, then be on your way from whence you came."

With impassive features the four mermaids slithered out of the lean-to while five pairs of eyes watched them carefully. From the hollowed log they were allowed to select what fruit and nuts they wished. When they had eaten to their fill, Bantan then spoke.

"When you return to your queen," he said, "tell her that I bear her and her subjects no ill will for the harm they would have done me and my friends. Before this sun has come to pass we are leaving this island never to return. You may also tell Sirena that this is the island to which the mermen came many moons ago to worship their sea god. Upon the west shore there is a grotto, and within is the temple. Tell her as well that I am sorry that conditions exist as they do upon her island, but there is nothing I can do to help matters. Now, be on your way."

Understanding had come into Pegra's dark eyes and a wistful smile touched her lips as she sighed.

"It is regrettable that there cannot be a male like you for each mermaid in our tribe, Bantan," she said. "We would all be very happy if it were so."

The bronzed giant looked toward her three companions in turn, and upon each lovely face there was a sad smile and wistfulness in their eyes. He shook his head sorrowfully as he again looked at Pegra.

"I am very sorry for each of you," he said. "You are very lovely. "But have hope—perhaps sooner than you think your individual hopes may be rewarded."

Pegra's smile was a forlorn one as she turned to her

companions and reminded them they had a long swim ahead of them. The four mermaids slithered to the edge of the water and entered the gentle surf. Within a few minutes they had reached the calmer water beyond.

Bantan and his companions remained upon the beach in silence, watching them. To their surprise, the four mermaids waved in parting, and unconsciously the five on the beach as one waved in return. Then the swimmers resumed their way.

The bronzed giant shook his head. Looking at each of his companions, he saw they were still watching the mermaids. Young Horwath's features were impassive but his eyes appeared thoughtful.

"Though we have every reason to hate the mermaids," Bantan said in a low voice, "I feel very sorry for them, understanding as I do the conditions that exist upon their island. I do hope, however, that Mike Decker realizes the happiness he seeks."

Young Horwath shook his head in an effort to dispel thought of the doe-like, gray eyes of the mermaid who had been attracted to him.

"And I, too, feel sorry for them," he declared. Almost sheepishly he added: "Do you know I almost asked them to take me along with them? As Mike said, 'What have I got to lose?' But at the last moment I remembered that I was an American and my place was back in the good old U.S.A."

Tama, Nulu, and Mauria looked at the young man in surprise.

With a smile, the bronzed giant turned about.

"If we wish to leave for Marja," he said, "we have fruit and nuts to gather. And I must patch the seams that leaked in the canoe's bottom as well."

"While you are attending to the canoe," Tama suggested, "we can gather the fruit and nuts that will be needed."

An hour later the hollowed log had been replenished with fruit and nuts. The canoe's bottom had been thoroughly patched, and a quantity of pitch remained for any possible future repair jobs. As they were now ready to take up their trip to Marja, Bantan confronted young Horwath.

"Coming with us, Bob?" he asked.

The young man smiled and shook his head.

"No, I'd rather remain here and hope to be soon picked up by some passing ship that is bound to be searching for the survivors of the wrecked ship I was on," he answered.

"You'd be perfectly welcome to come with us," the bronzed giant added.

Bob was adamant in his decision. He again shook his head.

"Suppose the mermaids return to this island?" he was asked.

Young Horwath merely smiled, but continued to shake his head.

"I'll take my chances," he replied.

Bantan reached within the canoe and withdrew a spear, a bow, and a number of arrows.

"Take these," he said. "They may come in handy."

The young man accepted the weapons with thanks.

As the bronzed giant turned about, Bob spoke up.

"Should we never meet again," he said, "there is one thing about you that I'll remember to my dying day."

Bantan paused and looked back at the young man with a curious expression in his dark eyes.

"What is that?" he asked.

"That you *are* a South Seas Tarzan," was the smiling answer.

Some ten minutes later the canoe with the hollowed log in tow were in the calmer water beyond the gentle surf. The course was set, and Bantan and Tama were paddling. They paused momentarily to wave to the lone figure upon the beach, and the wave of an arm answered.

"And now," the bronzed giant said to his companions, "let us hope this time nothing interferes until we reach Marja."

CHAPTER XXVII

Man and Mermaid

BOB HORWATH REMAINED upon the beach almost motionlessly with a choking sensation in his breast, watching the canoe containing Bantan, Tama, Nulu and Mauria until it could no longer be seen. Then with a deep sigh he shook his head and turned to face the foliage. An ineffable sense of awe pervaded him.

"I wonder if I've made the right choice?" he soliloquized. "Will I ever regret the one I've made?"

With another shake of his head he wearily walked up the sandy beach to the lean-to which he and Mike Decker had occupied. With a deep sigh he lay down upon his back, resting the back of his head in his cupped hands. Closing his eyes, he wondered how Mike was faring in his choice of going to the mermaid island. Would he be happy as Queen Sirena's consort? With a shrug, he shook his head unknowingly with the recollection how cruel Sirena could be.

And then came to his mind the gray-eyed Ela with the doe-like expression upon her comely features. At once remembering that she, too, was a mermaid, Bob shivered involuntarily. Quickly dispelling her vision, his thoughts quickly reverted to America and his home town. He visualized Clara Faulkner, the girl who had always claimed his attention from the time he had been a small boy. It was true, she had been sophisticated beyond her years, and likewise had been an outrageous flirt from the time she had been only thirteen. But young Horwath had always felt she was his ideal until that night outside a dancehall where he had seen her in a parked car with his best friend. They had been locked in such a tight embrace that one might have thought they were Siamese twins. That had been the last straw as far as she had been concerned.

In dejection the next day, but silent to his parents as to his future intentions, Bob had left home. A few days later he had signed on as a deckhand upon a ship that was destined for the South Pacific, and a new life for him had begun.

Again the young man shook his head with apparent relief from his disgust as the vision of Clara was dispelled from his mind. With eyes closed, he was now aware of the physical weariness that he felt. Thoughts of possible danger were drowned as the doe-like features of Ela again appeared in his mind. Before he was aware of the transition, he was fast asleep.

Once during the night he woke briefly to sit up with straining ears. All he could hear was the everlasting song of the surf as the water rushed up on the sandy beach and then retreated sibilantly. Not even conscious of his hunger, he stretched his arms aloft and yawned deeply. Then he lay upon his right side and within moments was again fast asleep.

The warm rays of the rising sun woke the sleeper to the full realization of the new day, and as well awareness of his gnawing hunger. The refreshing night's sleep had sloughed the physical weariness from his body. With alacrity he arose to his feet, breathing deeply of the scented air and exhaling almost with reluctance.

Without pause, the young man went to the edge of the beach and cupped handsful of water from an incoming roller. Bathing his face, neck and arms, he felt considerably refreshed. He then went to the foliage where he gathered fruit and nuts for his morning meal. Squatting at the side of the lean-to, he ate to his fill. While he did so, his sharp eyes scanned the shimmering watery surface before him as though hopefully expectant of sighting a vessel of some sort. Nothing of that nature was to be glimpsed other than several gulls flying a short distance above the surface just beyond the breaking waves.

Having eaten to his fill, the castaway arose to his feet. Again he surveyed the watery expanse hopefully, but the results were negative. Upon an impulse he started walking along the shore at the edge of the foliage, wondering what the evening tide might have stranded upon the beach.

Several hours later, the young man returned to the lean-to, his search unsuccessful. Somewhat wearied, he rested beneath the shelter. For the first time he was assailed with doubts, and remorse sought to dampen his spirits because of his choice of remaining upon the island when he might have joined Bantan and his friends. After shaking his head several times in retrospection, he squared his shoulders. His eyes strayed toward the watery expanse searchingly. Almost at once his interest was alerted.

Toward the west, in which direction beyond the horizon the mermaid island was located, some couple hundred yards from the surf he unmistakably caught sight of flashing arms that, as the minutes passed, appeared to be wearying.

Instantly young Horwath wondered if the swimmer could be a mermaid. If so, could her identity be Ela of the doe-like expression? He thought it strange that his thoughts should be of her. With a slight smile touching the corners of his lips, he arose and hurried to the edge of the beach. With intent interest he watched and awaited almost impatiently as the swimmer appeared to be experiencing increasingly greater difficulty, for the flashing arms seemed to be tiring rapidly.

When the swimmer was about fifty yards beyond the surf, the flashing arms were to be seen no more. The head appeared as a blob, breaking the otherwise still surface. And then, faintly, the watcher's keen ears could hear a wail of distress issue from the swimmer's mouth.

Although Bob realized he was no champion swimmer, he knew he was capable of rendering aid to the distressed one, for the distance was not so great as to preclude that possibility. Without a moment's further hesitation, he plunged into the surf and with strong strokes forged through the surging water to presently gain the calmer water beyond. Shaking his head to free the moisture from his hair that had a tendency of running into his eye sockets, he quickly looked about and ascertained the presence of the bobbing head.

A few minutes later he was drawing close to the weakened swimmer, and the presence of long, dark hair about the bobbing head made young Horwath realize it was a female in distress. One glimpse at the wearied features was sufficient for recognition that she was none other than Ela. Mildly he wondered if she had swum to this island in the hope of finding him.

Presently he had come to her side. Only as he slipped his right arm beneath her armpit did she become aware of the presence of another. Her gray eyes filled with fright until she recognized her savior, and then a happy smile touched her lips and the fright was dispelled from her eyes. Her left arm weakly went about him as, with a smile of assurance, he started swimming shoreward.

No words did Bob speak, for his attention was quite occupied in swimming and keeping the mermaid afloat. That she was considerably weakened, there was no question, but she did manage to assist him by moving her finned tail.

Through the tumultuous surf they were swept shoreward, and the moment young Horwath felt the sandy beach beneath him, he arose to his feet with the mermaid clasped in his arms. She was conscious, but very weak, and her eyes remained closed until the young man had borne her to the lean-to where he laid her down gently upon a pallet of grass. Then did she open her eyes and her gratefulness was clearly revealed as a weak smile touched her lips.

The rescuer realized he would be unable to communicate with her, so he wasted no time doing so. Believing she must be hungry after her grueling swim, he peeled a banana and knelt at her side, offering it to her. She opened her mouth, revealing small, even white teeth. She took a small bite and chewed it slowly before swallowing. Thereafter, with each bite that she took, her gray eyes met those of young Horwath and she would smile gratefully. A coconut was broken open and the mermaid was given some of the liquid to drink.

The young man surveyed her hopelessly.

"I know it's useless to ask you why you swam here," he said to her. "Somehow I have the feeling I know."

Ela watched him somewhat eagerly as he spoke, and thought she did not understand what he said, the sound of his voice seemed like music in her ears. The doe-like expression overcame her features and her eyes were soft as she looked up at him for long moments. Then she yawned daintily. Though she strove to keep her eyes open, wearied Nature overcame her resistance. She almost immediately succumbed to sleep.

Young Horwath looked upon the sleeping mermaid with gentleness. As his eyes trailed from her relaxed features to the hips about which a mesh encircled her mid-section, they then looked upon the tapering portion of her body where her thighs should have been and down to her finned tail where her feet should have been.

A shudder involuntarily wracked him as he turned about with head uplifted and his questioning eyes stared at the clear blue sky as though he might find the answer he sought to the problem that confronted him. Presently, with a shake of his head, he walked slowly along the beach until he came to rest beneath the shade of a puka tree. Burying his face on his arms that rested upon his knees, he remained thus for what seemed a long while.

"What can I do with her?" was the anguished cry in his heart. "I am an American and a human being. Though I dislike to admit the creature is a mermaid, she would be considered a freak in the estimation of other humans. I know she loves me—had she not, she would not have swum the miles intervening her island to this one in the hope she would find me here. What shall I do with her when she wakens?"

Raising his head, Bob again looked for long moments heavenward before again burying his face on his arms. The features of Clara Faulkner rose upon the screen of his recollection and she appeared to mock him. She pointed at her legs and feet and uttered the words:

"Legs and feet, Bob," she seemingly mocked him. "I have legs and feet, but your mermaid has none. She is a freak. She is a freak."

With a violent shake of his head, young Horwath banished the mocking vision from his mind. In a more rational state of reasoning he became calmer.

"What does it matter?" he soliloquized. "If the mermaid is sincere and honest in her feeling toward me, what more could a man ask? With her this island could be a paradise."

And yet, the recollection that he was a normal human

being and an American, of which heritage he always had been proud, claimed his immediate attention. And, too, there was the possibility of an early rescue. Supposing in the intervening period he learned to care for Ela—as a man could care for a woman—would he pass up the opportunity of a rescue and eventual return to America, leaving a grieving mermaid behind? Or, should he take her with him and be subject to the ridicule and shame that most certainly would be his lot?

Bob Horwath realized the difficult decision that would be his to make. He deeply regretted that Ela had come to this island, but the fact she had was something he could not change. He did not believe he would have minded the lonely days and nights in passing he might spend here alone, for during the daylight hours he could always find something to occupy his time. For instance, he could better his living quarters. Should the weather become inclement, he could always go to the temple of the sea god for sanctuary.

And so the young man's trend of mind during the hours that passed. Time and again the doe-like features of Ela would steal into his thoughts and, though he dispelled the vision upon a number of occasions, it would invariably return. At last with a shrug, he arose to his feet and squared his shoulders. He drew a deep breath of the scented air into his lungs and with reluctance exhaled. He would return to the lean-to and see if Ela had wakened.

As Bob walked along the sandy beach, time and again he would shake his head almost violently, as though he were repelling thoughts that were unwelcome. As he neared the lean-to, his eyes were anxiously seeking the mermaid. Almost hopefully, he wished that upon awaking, and finding him gone, Ela might realize she was not wanted, and that she would sorrowfully return to her own island.

But no, such was not the case, for the mermaid had awakened, and she was sitting upright with a most forlorn expression upon her features. At sight of the young white man approaching, a remarkable transformation overcame her. Her eyes brightened and a lovely smile radiated her features. Her lips parted and she spoke to him in greeting in a fairy-like, musical voice that of course he could not understand, but did comprehend her gladness at his return.

As young Horwath stood there before her, he could not repress the smile that touched his lips. The mermaid was so happy that he had returned that his heart could not reproach her for the misfortune that had been her lot to be born a mermaid. As he looked down at her radiant features, he inwardly compared them with the mockingly insolent ones of Clara, and he had to admit Ela did not suffer by comparison, even though she were a mermaid.

Ela shyly reached for one of his hands as it hung limply at his side nearest her. Taking it in her small ones, she pressed it to her cheek while she crooned softly in her joy. Then she kissed the back of his hand repeatedly before drawing it to the region of her heart which he could feel beating quite rapidly. A flush mounted to his cheeks because of innate modesty and he withdrew his hand from hers. He winced somewhat at sight of the sudden moisture that appeared in her eyes and the sadness that overcame her features.

Bob became determined upon the instant that he must try and communicate with her. He seated himself at her side, and he was pleased to observe that she appeared happier because he had done so. He indicated himself.

"Bob," he said. Then he repeated his name. Indicating her mouth, he again spoke his name.

The mermaid watched him intently, and sagacious

mind that she had been endowed with, she must have comprehended what was expected of her.

"Bob?" she said questioningly in her musical voice.

He nodded eagerly. Indicating himself, he again spoke his name. Then he pointed to her with a questioning look.

"Ela," she said. Indicating herself, she again uttered her name. Then pointing at him, she added: "Bob?"

Again he nodded and smiled.

"I am Bob," he said. "You are Ela."

Her smile was radiant.

"I am Ela," she answered. "You are Bob."

"Good!" he exclaimed.

"Good!" she repeated with smiling features.

Young Horwath regarded her for a long moment in amazement that she was so intelligent in understanding. For a couple of hours he spoke to Ela, bidding her repeat what he said. They were doing remarkably well when he realized his requirement of food to ease the gnawing in his stomach. He questioned the mermaid if she were hungry through the medium of the sign language. He rubbed a hand upon his stomach and moved his jaws as though chewing food, and then swallowing.

"Hungry?" he asked.

She mimicked him with a smile and eagerly nodded.

He quickly arose to his feet and indicated he would gather fruit and nuts. Ela nodded. When Bob disappeared into the foliage, she slithered down the beach to the water's edge where she bathed. Then she returned to the lean-to. Anxiously she watched and awaited the return of the young castaway.

In due time young Horwath returned with arms ladened with fruit and nuts, and with a smile deposited it near Ela. Then seating himself, he bade his companion to eat what she would. As they did so, he was amazed at the daintiness Ela conducted herself during the meal. Her manners were even superior to his, and he was ashamed upon several occasions when he tried to speak to her with his mouth partly full, and she would merely stare at him wonderingly, unable to comprehend what he was trying to say. When he managed to swallow the contents of his mouth, he would then repeat what he had said unintelligibly. Then she would smile and nod understandingly. If the occasion was necessary, she would repeat what he had said.

After their meal was eaten, Bob again indicated they would resume their lessons. During the afternoon they progressed very well. Ela could even speak short sentences quite properly with a little prompting on his part, and both teacher and pupil were delighted that this was possible.

When night came, the young man found it difficult to impress Ela that she was to occupy one lean-to while he occupied the other. He noted the sadness in her eyes as he bade her good night, and while he lie in the other one, for a long while he heard light, choking sobs issue from the mermaid's lips before at last wearied Nature overcame her grief and she was claimed by a fitful slumber.

When young Horwath awoke the following morning after a fairly sound night's sleep, he became aware that Ela had already arisen, and bathed, as her damp hair indicated, and as well she had prepared the morning meal. She appeared a trifle perplexed as he greeted her, but almost at once her perplexity vanished at his wholesome smile. He indicated the water and she nodded in understanding.

After a short swim, the young man returned to the lean-to where Ela was patiently awaiting him. With a smile and a nod both then partook of their breakfast. Occasionally Bob noticed that his companion would be regarding him speculatingly, but as her eyes met his, she lightly shook her head and smiled pleasantly.

Later, further lessons were again in progress and Ela appeared as eager to be taught as he was to teach her.

When several days had passed and the teaching lessons had continued unremittingly, it was at this time they could converse fairly well.

"Sometimes, Ela," he said, "I find you looking at me strangely. May I ask why?"

A slight flush tinged the mermaid's cheeks and she lowered her eyes for a long moment. Then, drawing a deep breath, she raised them to meet his inquiring ones.

"Why do you not ask me why I came here, Bob?" she asked in return.

He nodded.

"All right," he answered. "Why did you swim to this island?"

Ela's eyes misted and her hands clasped the vicinity of her heart. A wistful expression overcame her features.

"If words can tell," she said, "I shall tell you. From the first moment I saw you, I wanted you to want me as I wanted you. Does that answer your question?"

Now it was Bob's turn to experience flushed cheeks at the mermaid's naive reply. He lowered his head guiltily, for he had suspected Ela's answer to his question. During the past days he had stubbornly refused to consider the possibility of love dawning in his heart for this lovable mermaid. He had been successful in refusing to acknowledge any such feeling, and concentration on teaching lessons had aided him in keeping any such inclination at a respectable distance. But now, he realized, he was confronted with the inevitable question to which an answer was expected.

Ela was aware of his hesitation and, saddened though she was, she spoke dispassionately.

"It is true, Bob, that I am not like the kind of females you have known in your past life." She paused a moment before continuing: "I know I am what is called a mermaid. I have no legs and feet. But I am a female and have the capacity for love, and could make you very happy—if only you would let me. I have the feeling you have been in love before—and was hurt. But you would never have any reason to believe I would cause you any hurt."

Young Horwath studied the mermaid in silence before speaking. He made several futile efforts to do so before at last was successful.

"I do not question anything you have said, Ela," he admitted. "I am thinking of the day I might be rescued." He shrugged hopelessly. "It would be only natural that I would want to return to my own country." He shook his head sorrowfully. "There would be no place for you. Can you understand that?"

Ela nodded slowly.

"I can understand," she answered. "I would not expect you to take me there. But while we are here, why shouldn't we love one another until such a time comes? Don't you think I am worthy of being loved?"

The young man's heart almost skipped a beat at the mermaid's honest declaration.

"Ela," he protested in a weak voice, "you do not realize what you are saying."

The mermaid eased herself closer to him. A gentle smile touched her features and her gray eyes were steady as they surveyed him. One of her hands lifted from her side and sought his somewhat long, rumpled hair. With gentle fingers she pushed it back into pompadour fashion.

Although Bob fairly trembled because of the resistance he invoked against weakening resolves, he made no effort to draw away from Ela. His heart hammered strongly against the wall that engaged it, and his breath quickened and came in short pants from between tightly compressed lips.

Now the mermaid caressed the nape of his neck, and then her hand became still as it seemingly locked there. She pressed her cheek against his as her other hand sought one of his. Finding it, she lifted it unresistingly to press against the vicinity of her heart which he detected beating quite rapidly.

"Bob," she murmured, her warm breath fanning his cheek. "Do not think of me as a mermaid, but as a female from your own country. Think of me as the one who hurt you, but I promise I won't hurt you—now, or ever."

A sudden tremor wracked him at thought of Clara Faulkner. Never one who even considered revenge, for the first time in his life he considered such an expression. His eyes sought those of Ela, and the pleading in hers was the last straw to his resistance. In an instant both of his arms encircled her, and his lips covered her slightly parted ones, pressing upon them almost savagely. A soft sigh was emitted by the mermaid as both of her arms likewise went about him and strained him as close to her as was possible.

And so it was Bob Horwath closed his eyes to whatever the future might hold for him. The past was forgotten as well. It was only now that mattered—the immediate present when he held a lovable mermaid in his arms, one who had professed her love for him, and for whom he was constrained to admit he loved in return.

Epilogue

TWO DAYS AND NIGHTS passed with Nulu and Mauria taking turns at the paddles. The weather remained favorable and many miles were covered.

Upon the morning of the third day the wearied eyes of Bantan and Tama were gladdened, for slightly to their right upon the horizon they espied what resembled a blurry mass.

Passing hours and more miles covered revealed that the island mass that had been sighted appeared not to be a single island but a group of them.

Even from the distance there was a seeming familiarity about them that assured the bronzed giant that they could be none other than what they hopefully sought. A smile touched his lips as he looked at his companion paddler.

"There, Tama, are the islands we seek," he announced.

The native smiled and appeared to be relieved.

Presently Nulu and Mauria awakened, and they were informed the end of their journey was near. Both girls sighed and appeared very happy, even admitting from their first glimpse of the islands that they had fallen in love with them.

The present was a time for rejoicing for Bantan, for he would be reunited with old friends. What unhappy tidings awaited him, however, he could not know, for that is another story.

✓ ✓ ✓

AUTHOR'S NOTE:

The next book in this series will be titled:
BANTAN'S QUEST
Watch for it.

316